ENTHRALL CLIMAX

THE FINALE OF THE FORBIDDEN
BOOK EIGHT

VANESSA FEWINGS

Enthrall Climax
Copyright © 2018 Vanessa Fewings

Cover design by Buoni Amici Press
Cover photo from DepositPhoto: *Risia*
Formatted by: Champagne Book Design

Book edited by Debbie Kuhn

ISBN-13: 9780996501460
ISBN: 978-0-9965014-8-4

"Man cannot discover new oceans unless he has the courage to lose sight of the shore."
—André Gide

For those of you who fell in love with
ENTHRALL,
this story's for you.

PROLOGUE

Breaking Point

CAMERON

H E WAS DETERMINED TO LOSE ME.

Driving recklessly along the strip of road that is Highway 17, his silver BMW turned sharply, skidding toward the sheer drop.

Righting his car, preventing it from striking the rock face on the other side, he pressed on relentlessly, his speed increasing ever more dangerously. Richard Booth Sheppard was outrunning his past.

Outrunning his pain.

I'd tailed him in my Benz helicopter all the way from his home in Malibu—and no doubt his gaze kept darting to his rearview mirror to see if I was still there. I'd land on the bastard's car roof if that's what it took.

He broke away, taking a sharp turn around the curve of the mountain.

My jaw clenched as I gripped the controls and banked around it, following directly above him, chasing my best friend into the darkness, *filled with terror at his precarious situation. One slip of focus and his car was going over.*

My prediction seemed realized when the BMW spun out of control.

It flew toward the cliff, dust flying around its wheels as he braked hard, causing it to skid toward the drop-off. My throat tightened, heart pounding against my ribs as I prepared for him to disappear.

I watched the car fishtail perilously close to the edge—stopping just short as though my will alone had saved him.

Full of fury, Richard shoved his door open and stomped towards the cliff's edge. He stood there, his blond hair being tussled by the blast from the chopper's blades, unperturbed by the close call due to his ass-hole daredevil ways.

I landed the Benz.

Climbing out, ignoring the dust in my eyes and the sting of fuel burning my throat, I left those spinning blades behind and stormed towards Richard—grabbing him by the shoulders and thrusting him against the BMW's door, trying to snap him out of his death wish.

He slid down the side of the car with no fight left.

I knelt down and yelled into his ear over the noise of the engine, saying I needed him, we all did, promising that it would get easier and that he needed to trust me and let me deal with whatever was hurting him. I'd carry his pain.

His suicide would always be one moment away. Hard choices had to be made. Ethics would be flung by the wayside over an endeavor so audacious lives would be forever changed and innocence irreversibly shattered.

It was time.

She was out there. A young woman who could be trained as a sub-missive, a remarkable female who alone would soothe Richard's pain and give him a reason to live, a reason to fight back.

A reason to love.

I had to find the one woman who could enthrall him beyond all measure.

Damn the consequences.

CHAPTER ONE

MIA

WHY WAS CAMERON TELLING ME THIS NOW?
Staring across the restaurant table at his vexed expression, I sensed a rare melancholy rising. Or perhaps it was regret. I'd been the woman Cameron Cole had searched out and then given to Richard.

Returning to this subject was like setting off a bomb in our midst. Though I understood his reasons for fulfilling what he'd believed to be his only choice. Five months ago, Cameron had thrown me into the path of his best friend and I'd become Richard's lover, our relationship forged by Cole himself.

We'd all spiraled toward a perilous edge, very much like that highway Richard had been tearing down, because the worst possible outcome had happened—Cameron had fallen in love with me himself.

Maybe this was why he'd chosen the Auden Bistro and Bar at The Ritz Carlton near Central Park, so we'd not argue about the mistakes we'd made. Cole's chestnut gaze held mine with a riveting precision.

Quite simply, Cameron was mesmerizing—not only for his devastating beauty but his dazzling charisma. He was in his early thirties, but he looked younger.

Damn him for being such a catastrophic force, his ferocious will fulfilled with the ease of a master negotiator. With his tousled midnight-black hair a contrast to his clean-shaven jaw, tonight he looked even more extraordinary in his black tuxedo, seemingly molded over his well-toned form by a Savile Row tailor to perfectly fit his broad shoulders and towering height.

The same height he used to intimidate me into surrendering in every conceivable way, with his every word and action designed to lure me further under his spell.

I'd become his obsession—and he was mine.

His subtle cologne wafted over me as a sensual reminder of his mystique. The scent reminded me of his power, not only when he wielded his authority around the boardroom, although there was plenty of that, but in the privacy of our home where he ravished my body, bringing overwhelming orgasms one after the other. It was in the way he mastered me with the ultimate domination of a man who knew the art of blinding pleasure.

He arched a curious brow, proving he knew I didn't like to revisit our past. I hated going back to the time I had no control over my life. The time he'd pretended I meant nothing to him. Those endless days with him gone had seen me drowning. I'd fallen hard for Cameron, the lover I couldn't have, and my heart had cracked open leaving me vulnerable.

I'd never been meant for *him*...this man who circled the rim of his glass gracefully with the tip of a forefinger. It was a subconscious erotic prelude to what would happen later in the evening. He liked to circle my clit in the same fashion with a disciplined concentration, his dark gaze studying me while I trembled through the pleasure. The thought of it made me shiver.

My gaze roamed over the silver platter full of empty oyster shells. The taste of the ocean was still on my tongue, along with the lingering taste of doubt.

Why was he bringing up Los Angeles now?

He gave me a reassuring smile and his expression turned to one of devotion, making me melt like that first day I'd laid eyes on him. The measure of his beauty was only rivaled by the depth of his complexity—a kaleidoscope of mysteries waiting to be discovered. His profound knowledge endlessly wowed me. His friends both admired and feared him for his fierce intellect. Sparring with him was ill-advised.

I loved Cameron deeply and couldn't imagine my life without him. I respected his directness, his strength and his ability to say the right thing at the right time.

"Any thoughts?" He pushed me to react to his monologue.

"All that's forgotten."

His gaze saw the truth in my lie. He gave me a look of defeat.

Cameron liked this restaurant and I pretended to like it, too. We'd finished off a bottle of Chateau Lafite and my toes had curled at the price. Even now my past chased after my present with the rawest memories of poverty. Still, I wasn't ashamed of all of that because it ensured every rich experience was lived with an awareness of this privileged life. It made everything special.

He reached for his glass of eaux-de-vie Hennessy Ellipse, which had been delivered to our table as a complimentary liquor because he was a Cole, related to tea baron Raif Cole, though now Cameron ruled the empire hailed as one of the beverage world's major players. Everyone treated Cameron very well and even if they didn't know who he was they respected him because of the regal way he carried himself. He was a man who ruled a room as soon as he stepped into it.

Cole had plucked me out of my ordinary life working at an art supply store in West Hollywood, and as a waitress at The Cheesecake Factory every weekend. He'd employed me as a secretary at Enthrall with the salary of my dreams at his secret and very exclusive BDSM club in Pacific Palisades. He'd specifically hired me to work for Richard Sheppard, his assistant director and the man I'd inevitably fall hard for.

Richard had swept me off my feet with his remarkable Harvard intellect, his worldliness, and his dashing good looks and dreamy smile; his seemingly perfect life lived out in his vast, beachfront house in Malibu. All his feigned happiness had been a façade for decades. He'd carried guilt over his fiancée's death after his father had taken down the New York Stock Exchange and the American economy with it.

I'd done what I'd been brought in to do and relieved much of that agony. I'd apparently saved his life, but doing so had almost devastated mine.

What I could never have known was Richard's breaking point before all of that, the incident Cameron had just shared with me—the truth of what went down on that dark night along Highway 17.

Richard had been close to taking his own life that night and it had been Cameron's relentless pursuit that had saved him and inspired his devilish plan.

"This is me apologizing," Cameron said, nudging away his glass.

"You did it to save Richard. We both did."

"Everyone warned you off me. Even I did."

"What's going on with you, Cameron?"

He studied me as though gauging my reaction. "Last night..."

Oh, so this was why we'd taken a detour from our journey to the party.

"I liked it." My limbs shuddered as I recalled the way he'd taken me. My heart skipped a beat at the memory of how breathless he'd made me and how hard he'd made me come.

I watched him carefully as that uncharacteristic confusion marred his face, his irises dilated to black as though he recalled...*his unyielding strength as his virile fucking turned ferocious, our bodies covered in perspiration as we rolled around on the sheets, totally enraptured with each other.*

Our passion had turned dark.

I yearned to see his true nature set free, even though I had been warned by others of his secret proclivity, and last night I'd glimpsed a man possessed with something that went beyond the rawest passion.

My wrists bound together behind my back with his black silk tie, my face pressed into the pillow, his grip on the back of my neck shoving me into it, me catching each breath as though it were my last, his savage fucking, his feverish control over me causing my limbs to quake because even before this—before all of it—he'd unleashed his true power, revealing his gift for melding pleasure with a crazed torment that sent me hurtling into an unspeakable ecstasy.

I licked my lips to tease him. "Death by fucking."

"The last time you spoke those words I locked you away and applied three days of hard therapy. So watch yourself."

"You were giving me what I asked for." *Begged for.* "I want more..."

He glared at me. "You don't know what you're asking."

"I do."

His gaze broke from mine and he lifted his phone to read a message. "Sorry."

I cringed at the interruption to the conversation I'd been psyching myself up to have. Last night he'd relented, proving that our relationship was evolving and that our bond was strengthening. I was ready to satisfy him. Even if it meant facing off with the worst kind of pain. His penchant was legendary, but I'd endure anything for him.

His silence dragged out the tension as he sent his text off.

"Is it Shay?" I glanced at his phone.

"Yes."

Shay Gardner was his head of security and right-hand man. They were as close as brothers after they'd bonded while in Afghanistan during a dangerous mission to rescue Cole's brother Henry. Even now Cameron refused to discuss it.

"Shay's arrived." He shrugged. "He wants to know why we're not there."

I reached for my wine glass. "Me too."

This detour was making us late.

"I thought we'd explore your reason for keeping us a secret at work." He sat back and narrowed his gaze.

"Changing the subject?" I threw him a playful smile.

"That other matter is closed."

"Cameron—"

"Mia." He leaned forward. "Can I get you anything else? More water?"

To my left sat a full glass of sparkling Perrier. My shoulders slumped in disappointment.

How had Richard described Cameron? *"He loves to watch you burn."*

What Richard hadn't told me was that Cameron was the one who would light the fire and then stand back to savor your awakening. Those memories of once believing Cameron and I could never be still lived on in my nightmares. That was why going against his wishes was so damn hard. I wanted to please him.

I wanted, *no*, needed him in my life.

He'd been my light in the storm and I wasn't ready to turn my gaze away from the beacon that had saved me.

Cameron finished off his drink. "Perhaps your reluctance to tell your friends about us is related to how we met? You're concerned you'll reveal too much?"

"When I'm ready to let them know I'm dating you they won't need to know the details. I'll say we met at my last job."

And that was true…Cameron had strolled into the coffee room at Enthrall when I'd been hanging out with his dominatrixes Scarlet, Lotte, and Penny. It had been a party atmosphere, right up until he'd walked in and thrown everyone into a spin with his alpha-dominance.

"I've already explained," I said, lowering my voice. "I want a promotion at work from within my department. I'll prove I'm successful on my own merit."

"You'd be treated very well if people knew about us. Better than you are right now."

"What have you heard?"

"Merely an observation."

I imagined he was referring to his executive assistant Susan, and the way she'd taken a dislike to me after catching a flirtatious grin I'd given Cameron in the Cole Tea Shop. My boss Dana was a class-A bitch, too, though I didn't tell Cameron. It would be nice not feel Dana shooting daggers at me throughout the day, but I wasn't the only one who experienced her bullying. She was hard on everyone.

Maybe he'd picked up on my mood after those long days spent in the marketing department in my little cubicle. I'd been given a shot at the corporate world and I wanted to prove I could make it.

Cameron went quiet, as though hoping I'd puncture the silence and talk myself out of this so we could walk into the Mandarin Hotel tonight as a couple. Part of me wanted to see Dana's jaw hit the floor when she realized who I was with. Her caustic comments about my clothes grated on my nerves. Maybe I leaned a little too much toward a bohemian style with my silk blouses and flowing skirts, but it was my way of holding on to the old me.

I reached across the table and placed my hand on Cameron's, giving it a squeeze. "Why are we here?"

His brows rose. "Ms. Lauren, I am officially offering you an executive position in my department. The salary is generous. The hours favorable. I'll match your 401K." He smiled at that.

Considering he was a billionaire and we were months from tying the knot it was kind of funny.

"The perks are never-ending..." He suppressed his amusement at his insinuation. "I'll give you Fridays off to explore other interests."

"Other interests?"

"Other ambitions."

The only ambition I'd once had was becoming a fashion designer. Cameron had come across my sketches when he'd first visited my studio apartment in L.A. I'd hidden them away after that and never discussed them. Not all dreams were meant to be realized.

"I'll consider your generous offer."

He folded his arms across his chest. "You'll have your own office."

"I'm not saying no. I'm saying not right now."

"Isn't that my line?"

"I'm flattered, truly."

"Tonight will not be easy." He blew out a breath of frustration. "Henry will be there."

"I'll explain it to your big brother." I shrugged. "Or you can."

"There's another matter I need to discuss with you." He sat forward and reached out for my hand.

"Oh?"

His brow furrowed as he seemed to recognize someone across the room. "We should go." He gestured to our waiter for the check.

The bill was brought to our table and I reached for it, stuffing my credit card into the leather folder.

"Mia, don't," he said, looking abashed.

"I like doing it. I earn a good salary."

"Still..."

"It makes me happy." I placed my napkin on the table and folded it. "Thank you for understanding about my job."

"I want to make life easier for you."

"This is good for me." I lowered my gaze. "You spoil me too much."

When the check came back I signed it, all the while ignoring his disapproving stare.

Cameron pressed his phone to his ear. "Hey, Ben, we're ready to leave." He hung up and pushed himself to his feet, rounding the table. He took hold of the back of my chair and eased it out. "Wait for me in the car."

I rose to my feet and went to turn around, but he stopped me.

"No." His gesture indicated he didn't want me to look.

"Who is it?"

"Now, please." There came no touch of affection this time, merely an insistent look of concern.

I grabbed my clutch purse.

He whispered, "Accept my apology."

"No need."

"Last night was inappropriate." He looked surprised about my attitude. "You're about to become my wife. You need to be treated with decency."

"Where did my Cameron go?"

He shook his head. "He's protecting you from himself."

"From what, exactly?" How long had I yearned for that level of passion and I wasn't willing to let all that groundwork slip away. I looked him straight in the eyes. "It was like our very own Chrysalis."

"We'll discuss it in the car."

I gave his arm a squeeze to reassure him and strolled toward the door, leaving him behind. Unable to resist, I glanced back...

A rugged-looking, tanned man with a crooked nose, who seemed out of place wearing his sophisticated pinstriped suit, had approached our table and launched into a conversation with Cameron. Their friendly sparring seemed cordial enough. I wondered who he was. He'd certainly unnerved Cameron enough to send me out of the restaurant.

The stranger had a self-assured demeanor and his salt and pepper hair gave him a distinguished air. His grey eyes fixed on me, sending a chill up my spine.

Cameron followed his line of sight and threw me an insistent glare. I hurried out through the foyer, my forearms prickling with unease.

Stepping onto the sidewalk, I took in the sight of the surrounding New York City high-rises, feeling the never-ending vibrancy and aliveness, bursting with a palpable excitement. I breathed in the warm air, picking up the scent of expensive perfumes wafting from the guests who were heading into the Ritz. I missed L.A., but there was an allure to this city that was beginning to steal my heart.

My fingers traced over my Rolex and I counted the seconds until Cameron followed me out. This watch had a special meaning, and not just because it was the first gift Cameron had bought me when we'd arrived in New York. He'd admitted to placing a tracker within it. I didn't mind, not really, I had no secrets from him and it seemed to make him happy.

I sensed someone staring and turned to see Clint, my security guard, lingering beneath the Ritz's awning, tasked with following my every move. I smiled his way to show my thanks and he gave a nod back. He gestured for me to get in the waiting car.

When I settled in the back of the SUV, I gave a wide smile of greeting to Ben, our chauffeur, in appreciation for him waiting for us. He returned my warm smile in the rearview mirror and then looked away out of respect for my privacy. All the city's noise and chatter dimmed in here. I glanced through the back window, no longer seeing Clint.

Cameron soon joined me in the passenger seat, engrossed with texting, his mood even pricklier. Peering over at his phone's lit screen, I read Shay's name and could see they were discussing the man Cameron had just spoken with in the restaurant.

"Who was he?" I asked.

"Divider up, please." Cameron gestured his order to Ben and waited for the privacy glass to rise before turning to face me. "We were discussing the gala. It's time for your friends and colleagues to know about us, Mia."

I cringed inwardly, afraid that everyone would assume my new promotion was because of my relationship with this fine man and not garnered from hard work. "You didn't answer my question, Dr. Cole."

"It's Mr. Cole. At my father's behest I've left psychiatry behind indefinitely." His fingers traced along my gold-beaded hem. "That's a pretty dress. A little short, but I'm sure I'll benefit later."

His hand brushed my thighs and caused them to tremble. I literally felt weak when he turned on this level of burning intensity. I had to force myself not to visibly swoon.

"Are you cold?"

I shook my head. "Cameron, who was that man?"

"Lucas Chastain. I met him in France during my Harvard years. We didn't see eye to eye. I was surprised he came over."

"Why didn't you introduce us?"

"He runs in dangerous circles."

"What kind?"

"Changing the subject?" He stared at me intently. "We'll walk in together. I couldn't be prouder to show you off as mine, Mia."

"Soon." I reached up and cupped his face. "I promise."

He sat back and exhaled his frustration.

"He runs in dangerous circles?" I repeated softly.

"When I repeat a sentence to trigger the subconscious to respond and garner more intel, it's subtle."

"You've been at the old smoke and mirrors a lot longer."

Cameron held my gaze. "I met Lucas in Paris. I was eighteen. I was introduced to him by Danton Belfort. They were...good friends. Lucas invited us to an exclusive club. Then invited me to explore the next level. I declined."

"Danton was Scarlet's old boyfriend who died?"

A sorrowful shadow crossed his face, and I recalled a conversation we'd had of how close they'd been. Something told me they had been even closer than he'd let on, but I wasn't ready to know about all that yet. Cameron's complexity was as rich as his history. I wasn't marrying a saint, I knew that. I was marrying a man who'd once run the elite BDSM club in Los Angeles, and with that came a history of sexuality I'd only scratched the surface of.

Debauchery had been withdrawn because Cameron had a conservative reputation to uphold in the Big Apple, his liberal ways only revealed by his passion for the family's philanthropic interests.

A shiver slithered up my spine. "What's the next level?"

"You have quite an imagination."

"Don't patronize me, Cameron."

His baleful gaze held mine. "I look forward to fucking that disrespectful mouth."

"If your intention is to make me wet..." Sexily arching a brow, I held my own.

His expression turned affectionate and then solemn. "Add a touch of sinister and throw in a dash of nefarious and congratulations, your cocktail is laced with the potency that is Hillenbrand."

"That's not vague at all."

"Imagine Satan running Chrysalis."

"Everyone consents though, right?"

He caressed his jaw thoughtfully. "There are those who like to go too far. Push the boundaries of kink to an inconceivable level. Dabble in what is easily illegal. Lucas is one of those men."

My flesh chilled as his words sunk in and I recalled that handsome man's face. He had seemed distinguished despite his ruggedness; he'd resembled a worldly professor, in fact.

"He once had a fight with a warthog. So the story goes. He has the scars to prove it." Cameron's eyes widened. "I'm serious."

"What happened?"

"He killed it with his bare hands."

"What were you doing there?"

"This happened in Africa. Well before I met him."

"I mean Hillenbrand."

He tugged on a cufflink nonchalantly. "I was a member."

My jaw dropped at his confession.

"I was young. Impressionable. Seduced into what they had to offer. For the first time I explored my kinky side in a safe place. Danton was by my side every step of the way. We were bad boys." His grin revealed so much.

"Where did my wild Cameron go?"

"Not sure you would have liked me. I always got my way."

"Nothing's changed, then." I rolled my eyes playfully.

He shook his head at that. "Hillenbrand was shut down. I heard a rumor it transferred to another location. The members like what they do and don't want to stop. Becoming a member now is virtually impossible."

"Obviously not."

"Trust me, it's locked down. No getting in. No getting out. Not without some remarkable finagling."

"All very intriguing."

"That's the allure."

"What kind of things did you get up to?"

His dark gaze held mine as he reached up and played with a lock of my golden hair. "I love it when you wear your hair like this."

"You've changed from the man I met at Enthrall." I watched his reaction.

"In what way?"

He knew what I meant. The sex between us was wild but the most he'd punished me with was the palm of his hand in an erotic spanking. He'd once brought waves of pain to my body with all sorts of accoutrements, but since we'd arrived in New York he'd given up on his penchant for torture.

"I'm reinventing myself, Mia. You should try it."

I folded my arms in a huff.

He gave a long sigh. "Careful, Ms. Lauren, or I may just give you want you're asking for."

My hand reached up and scrunched his sleeve as a thrill rushed through me. I felt a tingling in my chest, a rush of blood that set my body alight.

He looked amused by my reaction.

I swallowed my doubt. "No catch, right?"

"I'll consider going darker…"

My cheeks flushed and my heart rate took off—and then his insinuation landed squarely on his blackmail…

I wasn't ready to be seen on the arm of my boss. I needed more time…needed to be respected for what I'd accomplished on my own.

He pried my grip off his sleeve and brought my hand to his lips, kissing my wrist. "Of course it would be dark by Chrysalis' standards, not Hillenbrand's."

"Is Hillenbrand where you learned to do those things?"

"Those things?" He arched a brow. "Hillenbrand is where I earned my reputation."

"Master of the dark arts," I whispered.

Cameron tipped up my chin. "Do we have an agreement?"

CHAPTER TWO

CAMERON

I'D BROUGHT A BILLION DOLLAR COMPANY BACK FROM THE BRINK of a hostile takeover after our shareholders had savaged it like the piranhas they were. Then I'd successfully rebranded our empire placing it way ahead of its competitors—an empire I now ruled fiercely.

Yet making Mia Lauren mine was still my greatest feat of all.

With a bruised ego, I stood alone at The Mandarin Oriental bar sipping mineral water. I could at least enjoy this vantage point to survey the party and pretend, unsuccessfully, not to be looking over at Mia's table. She sat with several colleagues and it was good to see her laugh—and she was decent enough to throw me the occasional kind smile.

Panoramic views of the city seen from expansive windows, and the modern plush décor, provided a great setting—and from the fun everyone seemed to be having tonight it was clear this function was a hit. We'd thrown the event to thank our staff for a remarkable first quarter.

All moments led my gaze back to Mia. It was hard to keep my

attention away from my fiancée—she was captivating.

With my brother Henry sitting beside her it gave me an excuse to glance their way without arousing too much suspicion. I wasn't the only man in the room gazing in the direction of the blonde, sassy bombshell. With her cascading golden locks, blue eyes and sweet smile, she enchanted everyone around her.

Making Mia happy was my priority, though it had been a rough few months going along with her scheme to keep us a secret. We'd managed to dodge the photographers for now, but it wouldn't be long before one of them snapped a shot of us together.

I set my glass down on the bar and strolled toward her table, recognizing some of her colleagues from the marketing department where Mia currently worked.

Her transition from secretary at Enthrall to serving as one of three marketing executive assistants here in our New York office had been exemplary. She'd wanted to start in a position that eased her into corporate life. My concern for her safety was ever present. On the top floor of the executive suite we were locked down when it came to security. Her floor was just slightly more accessible.

When I reached the round table I gave a friendly nod to Mia and her five friends who were deep in conversation. Concerned gazes rose to meet mine, revealing their feelings of unease that I might threaten their fun. Even though I had arranged this soirée and was footing the bill.

Henry's expression was filled with sympathy. "Come join us."

Even Mia looked nervous, as if afraid I'd out us.

I went with, "Who'd like to dance?"

"I would." The twenty-something with a short blue bob who sat on Mia's left shot out of her chair and rounded the table.

I gave her a warm smile. "What's your name?"

"Kelly." She beamed a smile back at me, obviously intrigued.

My gaze drifted over to reassure Mia as I led Kelly over to the dance floor. This was not how I'd imagined my invitation going.

Within twenty minutes I was again standing before Mia's table with all the boxes ticked for political correctness—this was just another chance for me to connect with an employee and take the temperature of my staff's moral.

It felt like shit.

I held my hand out. "Ms. Lauren."

She blinked at me. "And what did I do to earn such a privilege, Mr. Cole?"

I ignored Henry's amused smirk and continued to hold out my hand as I held her stare.

This round was mine to win.

Mia melted before me. "I'd love to."

She pushed to her feet and I led her across the floor, pulling her into a hug just a little too fast. We slow danced in a circle to Ed Sheeran's "How Would You Feel?"

She eased back a little to look at me. "I didn't know you could dance."

"We've danced before."

"You know what I mean. You don't dance. That's what you told me and yet you were impressing everyone with your sexy moves."

Yes, I didn't like to dance but that didn't mean I couldn't. Her enjoying more than one whirl around the floor with Henry had stirred my jealousy, even though I trusted them both with my life. I had assumed showing off my sexy moves would inspire her to join me. Instead, she'd obviously enjoyed the floorshow.

Mia's body brushed against mine, closing the torturous distance between us, her curves fitting against me perfectly. With her in my arms, the world righted on its axis, this inner warring dimming.

I squeezed her tightly. "I'll have Ed do all my talking, as I'm forbidden to express myself," I said, referring to the music.

She gave a sigh of contentment. "Thank you for understanding."

"That's one word for it."

"The party's going well, Mr. Cole."

I was done playing games. "Set a date."

She dragged her teeth over her bottom lip as she ruminated.

"One month."

"Two weeks. Then you'll tell your friends about us." I was close to kissing her soft plump lips to claim her in front of everyone.

"That's not enough time for a promotion."

"I'm the one who signs off on those."

"I hope you're not suggesting you'd obstruct my climb to power?"

"You've conquered me, Mia. What more is there?"

"How seductive."

"I can do better."

"Oh?"

"You're the most dazzling woman here and I can't take my eyes off you. It's potentially dangerous, since I'm close to looking like your stalker."

"Stalk away, Mr. Cole."

My grip tightened around her waist. "You're breathtaking." Whether she was in jeans, one of my shirts, or this mini-dress that sparkled with delicate crystal beads. "The next public event we attend you'll be wearing my collar."

"I don't think that would be a good idea." Seeing my frown, she added, "I'd end up falling to my knees and parting my lips, ready for you."

"Jesus, Mia." My cock quickened in my pants.

"It's all I can think about." She moaned softly.

I yanked her toward me. "This is what's on the table. I agree to take you to the next level and give you what you're asking for—even though you have no idea what that is."

"Last night—"

"The edge of vanilla."

Her eyes widened with wonder. "That wasn't vanilla."

"Two weeks, Ms. Lauren. Agree right now and I'll provide you with a demonstration that will have you running for cover."

"I thought we were negotiating?"

"I am."

"What does the next level involve?"

I arched a brow. "Really want to discuss this now?"

"A hint?"

I whispered, "I will push you to your limit and beyond."

She inhaled sharply. "I want that."

"An erotic nirvana?"

Her fingers tightened around my hand. "It will be good for us."

"Do we have an agreement?"

She threw a smile at someone across the room and then her gaze returned to mine. "My boss."

"I'm your boss."

"You know what I mean."

I glanced over at Dana Davenport, our director of marketing, and gave her a friendly nod of acknowledgment. From the way she glared back, she didn't approve. "She's a little scary." I pulled a face.

"I can handle her."

I couldn't have been prouder. When I'd first met Mia she'd been a wallflower, a little naïve I'll admit, but desirously innocent. I'd helped her blossom into the woman she was now and that made what we had all the more sacred. I knew her well, even to the extent of knowing she was about to beg for what she wanted in three, two, one—

"I'm ready."

I suppressed a smile. "Not sure you are."

"I am." She swallowed hard, unable to hide her nervousness.

In that moment the only thought I had was of me shoving my dick down her throat—I was going to explode if I couldn't touch her again for the rest of the night.

The music stopped and I thanked her for the dance, turning my back on her and heading for the bar, trying to act like she had no effect on me despite being aroused by her Black Opium perfume, which she'd dabbed in all the right places before leaving home.

Her begging me to go darker with her was destroying my will to breathe. Light-years ago it had been my reason to live. Fucking on that level was a goddamned ecstasy unlike any experience I'd ever had. My body was burning up as my imagination offered all the variations infused into formidable play—the fucked-up glorious kind. I had no right introducing her to what had once been my obsession. She deserved to be treated like a queen and degrading her was a hard limit for me as her master. My will to remain decent with her was flailing against my need to return to that rapturous practice.

Putting distance between us brought me down from the pinnacle of these debauched thoughts, yet my mind raged against my desires.

I gestured to get the waiter's attention and ordered another Perrier. I turned my mind to accounting. The recent software updates. The current state of the Stock Exchange. Anything to stop an erection.

Oh, hell no...

Black Opium wafted from behind me. "Cameron?"

I turned and gave Mia a cordial smile. "Hey."

She glanced around the room to see if we were being watched. "This is hard on me, too."

My brain launched into overdrive with the way she expressed the word *hard*.

Being forbidden to touch her was having an adverse effect. I went to brush a strand of hair out of her face and then reached for my water.

I quickly withdrew my hand, remembering I'd left my drink alone for fifteen minutes. If Shay caught me drinking from a potential threat he'd be on my case. I looked around for him hoping he could save me from breaking Mia's rule. I was about to wrap my hand around the back of her neck and drag her in for a kiss.

I chose instead to bite down on my lip like a literary heroine—tongue-fucking her right this second in front of everyone would have been preferable.

"I'm with you because I love you," she said softly. "Not for what you can do for me."

"I know."

She'd more than proven it when she'd stood by my side during the darkest hours for our company. Mia had been right there for me with her love and support, confirming we were everything we needed to be to make this work. She'd been my goddamned refuge.

"Hey, bro." Henry tapped my shoulder. "How's it going?"

"Great. You?"

Easily as tall as me and having kept up a military physique from his time as a SEAL, my big brother was garnering the kind of attention he rarely cared about. Henry was a dichotomy, a team player and yet a loner, a martial arts expert and yet as gentle as they come, and most of all a recovering soldier from a war that still wasn't over. Henry's capture back in Afghanistan had changed him irrevocably—though from his smart tuxedo and dashing smile he looked every bit the privileged executive.

We were both fans of "The Art of War" and had benefited from this essential reading material for businessmen who wanted an edge. We'd strived to make running a billion dollar company look easy. He'd dabbled in the family business but more recently I'd sensed a gnawing dissatisfaction.

He gave a polite smile to Mia to let her know he wanted to talk with me alone.

With a look of understanding, she headed back to our table. I watched her walk away and my gaze refused to break away from her devastating stride.

Henry watched her too. "Can't be easy, pretending to be colleagues?"

"This is important to her." Though it was soon coming to an end.

"So how's the wedding plans?"

"I'd marry her tomorrow if I could."

"Good answer." He glanced over at Mia. "She went shopping for a wedding dress yesterday with Mom. So there's no going back now."

"Escape is always possible." It came out wrong and I cringed at how it sounded. "Not with Mia though. She's…"

"Special. I agree."

Thoughts of my ex-fiancée McKenzie screamed through my brain, dragging all that carnage with it.

Henry slapped my shoulder. "Share that thought."

I waved it off. "I was thinking of someone else."

"McKenzie? That shit's history. File her away in the 'She Devil Drawer' and get on with your life." Henry patted my back. "And you say I have PTSD."

A rush of movement to my left made me step back, water spilling from my glass.

It was Shay, his eerily silent movements reminiscent of his stealth years back in the military. His black tuxedo camouflaged the bad boy image he'd once carried. He'd been one of the officers to storm into enemy territory to save Henry's life, and that selfless act had bonded them as close as brothers. He was everything a good soldier should be and so much more. When he'd left the SEALS I'd offered him the kind of salary he couldn't refuse.

More recently, Shay had stood by me when I'd sacrificed everything for Cole Tea to drag it out of its recent nosedive, and I was willing to do anything to keep him working for me. His heroism was now focused on keeping us safe in the concrete jungle of New York.

I might even go so far as to say I loved the bastard.

"Where the fuck have you been?" I asked gruffly.

"Was gonna ask you that." He waved to the barman. "Diet Coke. You guys want anything?"

"We're fine." I gave his arm an affectionate pat. "Have something stronger."

"I'm on duty." His tone turned sarcastic. "Thank you for doing my job all night, Henry." He was insinuating he'd spent a lot of time with Mia.

"Careful," warned Henry, his glare revealing his friendship with Mia was out of bounds.

An unfazed Shay returned his attention to me. "Everything good for tonight?"

With my nod I reassured him I had everything covered for yet another detour this evening. I'd planned it down to every detail and I'd been itching to see Mia's response to her surprise.

"What's going on?" asked Henry.

My glare told him it would soon be my time with Mia.

"I hear she found *the dress*." Shay woke me from my musing.

I smiled at the thought of seeing her walk down the aisle in a wedding gown. She was going to look ethereal. She'd cured me of my fear of commitment and had me looking forward to a wedding I'd never envisioned.

Henry grinned at me. "You're a lucky man, Cam. Mom is already calling Mia her daughter. I'm concerned all that happiness might be too much for our mother's black heart."

Thanks to Henry, my family had accepted my fiancée after he'd proclaimed she'd been the one to save him from his reclusive life in Big Bear. A spontaneous visit from her had soothed his depression. From the way they'd been huddled together earlier I could see they were close.

The true miracle here was that Mia had survived a day of shopping with our mom with the help of Aunt Rose, who had been there to smooth out the afternoon in a high-end store on Fifth Avenue. Those kinds of luxury stores were not a natural habitat for Mia.

"You can't go wrong with Vera Wang," said Henry.

I froze mid-sip as that designer's name screeched into my brain like a train derailing...

Shay studied me. "You okay?"

I spun around to face the bar as I replayed Henry's words. *Vera Wang.*

A horrifying memory replayed in my head, a nightmare visage of lush white tulle slashed into pieces, scattered all over my Beverly Hills bedroom.

"Finally sinking in?" Henry downed the rest of his drink. "My little brother's getting hitched."

I raised my hand toward the barman. "I'm gonna need something stronger."

CHAPTER THREE

MIA

THE PARTY AT THE MANDARIN ENDED AT MIDNIGHT AND WE all shared our sleepy, alcohol-hazed goodbyes. I held back as my friends and colleagues poured out onto the curb.

Feigning being single was not only hard because I wanted to be able to show heaps of PDA to Cameron all night, it was also flooding me with guilt for seeing how it was affecting him. Still, in a few more weeks I'd have the chance to establish myself as a legitimate employee and not be seen as a woman who had merely used her connections.

Although we had left the hotel separately, we were soon together again and snuggling in the back of the SUV as Ben drove us away. Resting my head against Cameron's chest and feeling safe with his arm wrapped around me, I drifted off.

"Mia."

His voice stirred me from sleep.

I rubbed my tired eyes, expecting to see the entrance to The Walker Tower that led to our penthouse, but I recognized nothing around us. "Where are we?"

"Detour." He peered up at the immense office building. "Chelsea."

It was really happening…

I followed his gaze toward the modern brick and glass structure, unsettled that he'd chosen such a late hour. We both had work tomorrow, but after the way I'd begged for this I shouldn't be surprised. "Will there be others?"

Will they watch us?

He removed something from his jacket pocket and opened his palm.

Staring down at the silver key, I muttered, "You're not leaving me here?"

He closed his fist and tapped the glass divider. "Ben."

Our chauffeur got out and opened the passenger door for us and I followed Cameron onto the curb.

He gave Ben a nod of thanks. "Wait for us."

That was my first clue this wouldn't take long—whatever it was. Cameron was always conscious of his driver's time, even if he was paid well.

We headed into the foyer, its modern chrome and sleek design contrasting vastly with the exterior. The place was deserted and the lights had been dimmed to fit with the late hour. We threw a wave at the night manager sitting behind the sprawling reception desk as we hurried toward the elevator.

"Is it a private party?" I held the rail, trying to shake off my sleepiness as we ascended. "Are we meeting someone?"

He shrugged out of his jacket and wrapped it around my shoulders. "No."

Warmth soaked into my bones as I snuggled into his tuxedo jacket. A waft of his cologne made a rush of excitement slither up my spine. "How did you find this place?"

"Did my research." He tucked his hands into his pockets with sophisticated style and gave me one of his affectionate smiles. That was another clue. Cameron hadn't slipped into his dominant demeanor yet so there was still time to ask questions.

A flood of pleasure surged through me, my skin tingling with aliveness, my nipples beading with anticipation and my clit throbbing in readiness. All I had to do was prepare for a greater level of pain. Was I capable of enduring the harshest of punishments? True subjugation? He'd secured me in a cage before now so I tried to comprehend how much more depraved this could get.

"What kind of things?" The words rushed from me.

"In what respect?"

"Dark by Chrysalis's standards and not Hillenbrand?"

Cameron looked thoughtful "Very often it's the thrill garnered from a scenario."

"So it's not just more pain?"

"It's about bringing your erotic fantasies to life." He reached out and curled a finger over my neckline, pulling me toward him and leaning in close, ready to kiss.

A tease I knew so well...

My insides liquefied as he towered over me with a fierce command. All I had to do was tip my chin up and his lips would be devouring mine.

My fantasies brought to life...

A sigh escaped my lips.

The doors slid open.

Cameron pulled back and smiled at his teasing refusal to kiss me. He knew he'd set me alight with passion and left me quivering with need. My solar plexus tingled with the thrill of the unknown.

He took my right hand and interlocked his fingers with mine as we stepped out into a hallway and headed down the dimly lit space. We passed door after door and they all looked the same. It would be easy to get lost.

"You've yet to reveal your fantasies, Mia." He glanced at me.

My cheeks flushed as my thoughts skimmed over the erotic imaginings I'd never shared with anyone—they were too raunchy to be brought out into the light, too decadent to be told. He was enough. He'd always be enough and fantasies were just that, a private reverie.

Cameron arched a brow. "That one's quite common."

My hand slapped to my mouth in embarrassment.

He leaned close to my ear. "How wet are you right now?"

I shuddered against him.

"Mia, I can read your thoughts. It's a rare privilege." He dragged his teeth over his bottom lip seductively.

My blushing face felt like it was on fire.

He winked. "We're here."

In a daze, I turned to face the door and a ripple of confusion ran through me when I read the sign: Marcella's Boutique Fashion House.

This wouldn't be the first time our society had used a front to camouflage the adventures within. The secret club Pendulum back in L.A. where masters and subs were left to their own devices was fronted by a fancy Italian light store. Or so I'd been told. I'd never been in there.

My gaze fell back on Cameron. "What is this?"

He slid the key into the lock, turned it, and led me inside. The white walls were covered in striking photographs of fashion models wearing a colorful array of glamorous designer dresses of every style. In the corner, mannequins were drenched in blue, red, and gold satin gowns, the material flowing off them and pooling at their base.

As we walked through into a more expansive area there were sketches strewn on a white central table...

Realization made me spin around. "Cameron?"

"What do you think?"

My heart rate took off and my mind scrambled back to reality because I'd been revved toward a completely different kind of climax.

I was not prepared for this.

"You'll be their intern on Fridays. If you like it you'll be invited to expand to fulltime. If you don't fuck it up that is." His eyes twinkled.

"Leave Cole Tea?"

"You'd be following your dream, Mia." He picked up one of the sketches. "Yours are just as good as these."

"This is too much."

He came toward me and swept me up in a hug. "If I gave you the world it wouldn't be enough."

Breathing him in, I closed my eyes to cope with this headiness. "How did you arrange this? Are you sure they'd want me?"

"Absolutely. You'll run errands, answer the phones, assist wherever necessary and learn from the ground up. They're all about nurturing new talent."

"This is incredible."

"You'll love Marcella. She's a world class designer."

I drew in a sharp breath of excitement realizing we were standing inside Marcella Rayella's studio, a renowned designer whose slogan for the more curvaceous figure, *Feel Beautiful Because You Are,* had made her a legend. So many times I'd swooned over those Vogue pages showcasing her talent for honoring the female form. Her clothes were unpretentious and flattering.

He looked toward the mannequins. "They're a little creepy."

I spun round imagining myself working here, realizing that this could be the start of something big. "Cam, how will I ever thank you?"

I'd never in a million years believed this was possible for a girl like me, even after all the possibilities that had come my way.

"I wanted you to settle into New York first." He revealed this had been on his mind for awhile.

My thoughts carried me back to Chrysalis, to the time when he'd been training me as a submissive and had thrown in those extra lessons, including math and etiquette, because he'd seen the potential in me.

"Seriously…how can I thank you?"

He arched his brow playfully and then laughed at his insinuation.

I threw my arms around his neck. "This is amazing."

He stepped back. "Maybe you could design your own wedding dress?"

"I found it already." My new gown really was beautiful and that comment threw me a little because he knew I'd gone shopping with his mom and Aunt Rose.

"You might get inspired to create something." His gaze swept the room. "Find a dress that's more…you."

"I'm happy with the one I have." He'd fall in love with my Vera Wang as soon as he saw it. I'd chosen a long, lace sheath dress detailed with flowers created from crystals. "It's so pretty. I can't wait to wear it."

"Fantastic."

"Wait, do you think Dana will let me have Fridays off?"

"Doubt it." He shrugged. "You'll have to transfer to the top floor where your new boss is more lenient."

All of this would make such a transfer worth every second because I was Cinderella and this was my dream come true.

"Make it two weeks, Mia," he said softly.

I gave a nod. "Two weeks then."

He scooped me up and sat me on the edge of the central table. "I want everyone in the world to know you're mine."

I cupped his face in my hands. "Thank you."

"Seeing you smile is why I get up in the morning." He looked around the showroom. "I think you'll have fun."

"I know I will."

"You should design something small to begin with. Underwear, maybe?" He ran his fingers over my hem. "Let's take a look at your panties to get some inspiration."

I lifted my skirt for him and widened my thighs, falling back until I was staring at the white ceiling with its white crystal chandelier…

I pointed up. "It's a sign."

He raised his brows playfully as he eased my thong to the side. "And when in Chrysalis…"

The back of my head crashed against the table, my back arching from the intense pleasure I felt as his mouth possessed me, his tongue swirling and flicking my clit with verve.

"Oh, God."

He smiled against me. "Close, but I'll accept it."

"You're a miracle worker."

"You're the miracle." He sucked harder, sending a shockwave of bliss into me.

My heart blossomed with all this happiness rushing in, bringing me boundless waves of ecstasy.

"Come for me." With his firm hands he eased apart my thighs a little more, his hair tickling my skin. He continued to circle slowly, his expert attention so precise I quickly rose into a blinding orgasm with his name on my lips, shuddering and writhing as I disappeared into the afterglow.

I whimpered as he brought me down with his soft kisses, his mouth trailing along one inner thigh and then back up the other.

This was him reclaiming me in a possessive show of ownership. Tonight's restraint had spurred him on to take me this fervidly.

"I need you inside me," I stuttered out the words.

His lips pressed to my ankle over the small hummingbird tattoo.

"Please…"

He pulled my dress down and eased me up to sit before him. "Let's save that for tomorrow."

"Why tomorrow?"

"You agreed to two weeks. Now I need to keep to my end of the bargain. Let's get you home."

"You're going to go darker with me?"

He pinched my jaw possessively. "Once we begin there's no going back." His tone held an edge of danger.

"I consent," I said, my voice trembling with expectancy. "Show it all to me."

He tipped my chin higher. "Welcome to the far side of the forbidden, Ms. Lauren."

Chapter Four

Cameron

T HE TIP OF SHAY'S ÉPÉE PRESSED INTO MY CHEST.
I stared at him through my fencing mask, holding my
position. It was unsettling to feel the pressure of his blade
against me in a defiant act of aggression. I'd invited him for a 6:00
A.M. bout so I could help shake my hangover from last night's party at
The Mandarin.

That deadly point resting two inches from my heart was a stellar
way to sober me up, but it was doing nothing to alleviate my doubts.

I stepped back and ripped off my mask.

He ripped off his. "Concentrate."

I shook my head, trying to clear this fog.

His frown deepened. "Let's call it for today."

Knowing he was right, I threw my épée down and it bounced
along the hardwood floor of the penthouse—no doubt leaving marks.
Strolling over to the window to regain my composure, I drew in a
steadying breath and stared out at the sprawling metropolis.

We'd had this room customized to accommodate my need to
improve my swordsmanship. Along with personalizing this and the

other rooms, we'd made living here bearable after the space we'd enjoyed in L.A. The Walker Tower offered a cozy Art Deco style, with its Venetian ceilings and massive windows, which provided welcoming panoramic views of the city. This was a glamorous, yet low-key, home.

Anywhere was home if Mia was there.

"Hey, Buddy. You okay?"

I threw him a reassuring glance.

Shay stepped closer and his expression morphed to one of concern. This man knew me better than anyone. We'd gotten to the point where words were no longer needed. The kind of place where only a shared history of devastation could provide such an unbreakable bond.

I'd personally witnessed this ex-navy SEAL in the heat of battle displaying only steely calmness. As soon as he was ready to hang up his Glock I'd claimed him, making sure he didn't say no to a six-figure salary.

Though I'd sealed the deal when I'd thrown in his very own submissive right out of Chrysalis. A sexy vixen so mesmerizing that his balls had made the decision for him. Agreeably manipulative on my part, but he was the best there was—and to prove his accessibility here we were sparring at dawn.

Hell, after he'd helped rescue my older brother from the clutches of terrorists in that nightmare of a desert, I'd have given him anything. Henry was home safe because of this man. So why was my gut telling me something was off with him?

This inner knowing had never failed me.

The psychiatric degree I'd nabbed at Harvard had helped refine these instincts into a razor-sharp insight. I garnered intelligence from everyone around me, every flicker of an eyelid, every revelation provided by either the dilation or constriction of a pupil, the pause in an intake of breath, the twitch of a mouth, even words not spoken delivered more for my intuition to draw from.

I see it all.

Shay had a secret.

And I didn't need this complication.

I had to remain laser-focused so I could maintain the business I'd dragged out of its freefall and prevent it from ever faltering again.

My gaze broke from Shay's. He had the kind of look that terrified the subs back in Chrysalis, the BDSM club I once owned and had to give up because…well, owning a sex club didn't exactly pair well with my meteoric rise as a business mogul, even if the place offered therapeutic benefits that equaled those of renowned Swiss psychiatrist Carl Jung himself.

I'd brought along to my new life these killer instincts that intimidated the hell out of everyone. I was done feigning I was no threat. Now more than ever this alpha status served me well.

I'd given up everything I'd once enjoyed, but on my terms. The one part of my past I refused to relinquish was Mia Lauren. My submissive was so blindingly beautiful that she messed with my head. Maybe this was about her? My brain playing tricks? Maybe this had nothing to do with Shay at all.

Fencing was meant to be fought in the present moment. Yet I couldn't get myself into the game.

I turned my back on the distracting city view.

It was rare for me to lose a bout with Shay. He'd taught me everything he knew until the student became the master. Like all areas of my life, I had excelled and then took control.

My relationship with Mia was no different, and yet her free spirit touched a part of me I was only now beginning to comprehend. Before her, action never preceded thought, timing was never left to fate, and spontaneity was the sport of fools.

She was both a blessing and a curse.

Having her work five floors down from mine at Cole Tower was pure torment, especially since she'd banned me from entering her office space. Last night she'd made the promise that she'd move to my floor in two weeks—or as I liked to call it, an eternity.

Shay joined me by the window. "Prenup bothering you?"

"Signed and sealed."

"Bachelor party? Mia's bitching about the strippers?"

"What strippers?"

"Richard didn't tell you?"

I reached for two bottles of water on the corner table and handed him one, suppressing a smile. They were my brothers-in-arms but they were also rogues.

Shay unscrewed the lid and took a drink. "Spill, boss."

"Mia's…wedding dress."

"She went for a Meringue?"

"No, apparently she chose a Vera Wang."

"Problem?"

"I'm reminiscing about *you know who*." For some reason my memory synapses processed this as all going down yesterday…a cruel trick of the mind.

"McKenzie?"

"We don't say her name."

He looked amused. "Go on."

I threw him a rueful look. "I was working late in the E.R. and had spiked a fever—"

"I remember."

Yes, he was right there to support me after I'd caught my fiancée McKenzie in the Harrington Suite being banged by more than one man. I wasn't averse to orgies, just not one where my woman held a starring role. I hadn't been able to shake the vision of her being taken like that—and her reasoning was still undefined.

Shay and Richard had helped me recover from my heartache when they'd joined me on the ultimate bender at Chrysalis, after I'd broken off my engagement with McKenzie, and then banished her. Along with the Doms who'd betrayed me.

"How's that connected with Mia?" Shay's voice pulled my attention back.

"The same night I got home to Beverly Hills after calling off our engagement, there on our bed—" I recalled the nightmare of seeing the cream tulle cut up and scattered all over the bedroom floor.

"What?"

"She'd slashed her wedding dress into hundreds of pieces."

"And…it was a Vera Wang, wasn't it?"

I let out a sigh. "Finding that dress cut up was the catalyst for our monumental weekend."

If what McKenzie had done to me seemed heinous, I'd turned a revenge fuck into a legendary counterblow. With Richard and Shay by my side, we'd stormed our way into infamy punishing and pleasuring anyone we'd deemed worthy.

Mia would never see the true monster lying dormant within me…the reason I'd been awarded the status of master of the dark arts. She didn't need to know the truth and from what I surmised, she assumed it was merely my penchant for cage play. My dangerous side was hidden within the darkest shadows and my proclivities were now dormant, never to rise again.

The risk of losing Mia was too great.

The New York skyline was proof time had slipped away. This was so different to Los Angeles's modest cityscape. I pined for Chrysalis and missed my dominatrixes who made the world a better place.

Shay slapped my back. "Tell Mia you want her to wear a different designer."

"And ruin her excitement?"

"She'd understand."

"What do I say?"

"How about this?" He gave a shrug. "'Bitch, you're not wearing that fucking dress.'"

I stared at him for the longest time and then burst out laughing, both of us cracking up. Shay was trying to talk but he was incoherent due to his guffawing; both of us struggled to breathe. I needed to lean against the wall to stop myself from falling over from our hysterical howling.

"Looks to me like I solved your problem." He scooped up his sword. "You're welcome."

I pinched the bridge of my nose in frustration over my dilemma.

I didn't want to hurt Mia's feelings.

Shay pointed his épée at me. *"En garde!"*

I stepped forward until the tip of Shay's sword dug once more into my breastplate. "When are you going to tell me, Shay?"

He slipped his mask down over his face. "Tell you what?"

"Whatever is going on with you affects *us.*"

"My job is to protect you."

"Your job is to be whatever I wish you to be."

He seemed to mull this over, though it was challenging to read him through the mesh.

"Well?" I pushed for an answer.

"Things are good." And yet he held his breath for a split second to carry the lie.

I might be a control freak, but I knew well enough to take my psychological chokehold off a man who could potentially shut down altogether. My superpower for detecting the truth made people wary of me. I needed him to relax again and let his guard down.

The business world was morphing me into the person I'd once feared I'd become: A hard-edged bastard with zero tolerance. Maybe one day I'd revel in it, but not today.

I threw down my sword and headed for the door.

Shay called after me. "Do you want me to talk with Mia about the dress?"

"No." I'd let this man into my world and minutes ago his sword had hovered an inch from my heart like a metaphor of my self-inflicted vulnerability.

"See you later then?" Doubt saturated his tone.

I'd given him the power to destroy me.

"My office, 10:00 A.M. sharp, Mr. Gardner."

I left him standing there.

CHAPTER FIVE

MIA

ALL HE HAD TO DO WAS STEP INTO MY LINE OF SIGHT AND I forgot how to breathe.

Behold, the extraordinary vision that was Cameron Cole, devastatingly handsome in that gorgeous bespoke suit, carrying that sleek briefcase through the Cole Tower foyer like he damn well owned the place.

Okay, he did own the place, but did he have to intimidate everyone in his orbit? He walked like a man who ruled the world.

It was hard to read Cameron's expression, but I guessed it was one of annoyance that I'd left home without him. I ducked behind a small crowd who'd gathered in the Cole Tea Shop, which was conveniently positioned near the elevators so employees could grab their caffeine fix before heading to their desks.

Braving a glance in his direction again, I saw that Cam's prickly demeanor was even unsettling the other employees who were striving to give him a wide berth. I'd mistimed coming down to the ground level to get a drink. It was free for employees and they had extra large cups, unlike the staff room.

I needed to be on my A-game today. Decisions had to be made—and fast—after my nightmare morning.

Last night I'd felt like a whirlwind of possibilities were opening up. The thought of working at one of the most celebrated fashion houses made my stomach flip. Visiting the Chelsea office and experiencing Cameron's private tour had to be one of the most romantic evenings we'd ever experienced. He had remembered my private sketches and gone out of his way to see my secret dream realized.

Yet all that joy had slipped away this morning after I'd been seconds from entering the gym to ask if Shay wanted to join us for breakfast, and had overheard his terse comment, "*Bitch, you're not wearing that fucking dress.*"

The same one Cameron had laid down thirty-five thousand dollars for me to wear on the day we were meant to be exchanging our vows. The same one that made me feel worthy of him because I saw no part of the old Mia in the mirror at that high-end store. My reflection had been that of a socialite good enough for the man hailed as a business genius.

Shay might as well have wedged his épée into my heart.

After hearing those words from him, and then their laughter, I'd hurried away into the bedroom in a daze. I'd quickly put on my ruffled blouse, short blue skirt and blazer, slipping my feet into a pair of Manolo Blahnik heels and then fleeing the penthouse. I'd broken protocol because I was not meant to be out of the place unaccompanied, or at least not without letting Shay know I was leaving.

Stepping into the line of customers to order a drink, my gaze roamed over the menu as though I was actually reading it.

My world had crumbled.

Last night had been about Cameron laying the groundwork to get me out of here—out of his life, perhaps.

The scent of his cologne reached me and I inhaled it in a slow steady breath.

My gaze settled on the *Corrupted Cole Coffee.* Might as well order the Grande…

Cameron had corrupted me back in L.A. when he'd tied me up in Shibari rope and hung me from the ceiling in that dimly lit dungeon—before doing things to my body that still made me swoon.

I stared down at my pretty high-heels. The black marble tile was polished so well I could see my nervous expression reflected.

An employee in front of us offered to let Cameron jump the line. He declined.

"Ms. Lauren?" His voice had a dangerous edge to it.

I turned and stared up at him. "Yes, Mr. Cole?" My solar plexus tingled like we'd only just met.

"How's the marketing department?" he asked, arching a brow.

"It's marketing away," I shot back.

He chuckled. "I'd like a preview."

"Of?"

"The staff designs for the new Cole Tea brand. Bring them to my office at ten. That way I can peruse the collection and have full exposure."

Jesus, even his voice sent me reeling, his deep tone making me frenzied.

The bubbly barista got my attention and asked, "What can I get for you?" When she realized she had interrupted Cameron, she visibly paled.

He stepped forward. "Two dark roast coffees, please."

We were served our drinks and I pretended the boss ordering mine wasn't a thing. He threw in a tip even though it was free. I walked over to the condiment station to add cream.

Cameron joined me and stood so close our arms touched. "What happened this morning?"

"I had to come in early." I stirred my drink with a stick until it turned creamy.

His gaze roamed my face for the truth. "Nothing else?"

I twisted the lid to make it fit better. "I'm late."

I hurried away, strolling into one of the four tower elevators as though a breakup with my one true love wasn't imminent. Cameron joined me with several other employees who were also heading up. If he was fazed he didn't show it. He merely removed the lid of his coffee and blew on it to cool it, all the while assessing me.

We reached the fifth floor and everyone trailed out leaving us to continue up alone. I watched them go like we'd spent months on a life raft together.

He came closer and loomed over me. "Don't do it again. Understand?"

No, I wasn't going to let his stark beauty throw me off balance. Now more than ever I needed to be strong. "I want a fair crack at the whip."

His brows shot up.

"With my project," I clarified. "I want you to consider my design and you can't do that if it looks like you're favoring me."

"Favoring you is my perk."

"I'm serious."

"This is not an invitation to misbehave." He pressed his firm chest against mine.

My gaze flitted to where I suspected the surveillance camera might be.

He tutted. "Fuck the cameras."

"What if security gossips?"

"I'll fire them."

I broke his gaze because it was easier then looking into his beautiful face, no matter how sincere he was trying to be.

"I'm serious," I said, stepping back. "I want you to consider my design."

I'd worked tirelessly on creating that stylish new packaging and it deserved to be in the running.

"Present yourself to my office...*sans* underwear," he mouthed. He rested his hand on the arch of my back and pulled me toward him. "In your desk drawer you will find a velvet box. Proceed with it to the powder room in precisely five minutes."

"What's in it?"

He stepped back and sipped his coffee.

My gaze shot to the door and I realized I'd arrived at my floor. My face was on fire as I stepped out and turned to look back at him.

His glare locked on mine. "Follow my order precisely."

The elevator door slid closed.

Weaving through the cubicles, I quickly reached mine. It was tucked away in the far west corner, and actually had a spectacular view. My desk was just how I'd left it, neat and organized, with those renderings ready in the manila folder for my presentation. Coming in early had enabled me to catch up on all my paperwork.

Peering over the top of my cubicle, I caught sight of my boss Dana walking toward her office—the ends of her short black bob hitting her sharp cheekbones, rounding out her black power suit and spiked heels. I ducked down hoping she wouldn't see me as she entered her office. I enjoyed the work that went into being one of her assistants, but I didn't exactly hit it off with her. Then again, she didn't seem to hit it off with anyone.

When the coast was clear, I removed my jacket and flung it over the back of my chair, then shook my mouse to waken my screen. I had just enough time to check Facebook.

My iPhone pinged and I looked down at the text from Cameron: *Now.*

Feeling as though Cameron were still looming over me, I rummaged for the key in my handbag and then used it to unlock my bottom drawer, only now realizing Cameron had a copy. I reached all the way back and removed the velvet box. My mind spiraled with the possibilities of what I was going to find inside.

My thoughts screeched back to Cameron's words last night. *"Welcome to the far side of the forbidden, Ms. Lauren."*

I flipped open the lid.

Oh, okay, just breathe and try not to look like you're about to fall into a conniption fit.

Three long, diamond-studded strands fell loosely between my fingers—and at the end of each were delicate clamps. With my sex tingling in anticipation, I wondered how this jewelry was meant to be worn.

A rush of movement brought my head up.

"What's that?"

I threw the strands back into the box and snapped the lid closed, forcing a smile at Dana—who stood at the entry to my cubicle.

"A gift." I acted as though it was boring and threw the box back into the drawer.

"I'd like to discuss today's meeting, Mia. Make sure we're not missing anything."

"Of course." I kicked the drawer shut.

"Ten minutes?"

"Perfect."

She headed back to her office.

My eyes snapped back to the drawer.

Sitting at my desk, I slipped off my panties as discreetly as possible and shoved them into my handbag. I retrieved the gift, holding the chains close to my chest as I dropped the box back into the drawer. Then I grabbed my phone.

Within a minute, I was hidden away in the luxury powder room stall with my skirt hiked around my waist and my fingers examining the delicate chain.

The three-stranded decoration was exquisite. I'd never seen anything like this before; the diamonds shimmied beautifully as I weaved them around my back gently so that they all met at the front near my pussy. I had to clip the three tiny prongs on either side of my labia to ease my folds apart. This was designed to reveal my sex. At the top where the strands met was a long row of more diamonds that dangled and teased my clit, sending tingles along it. This was going to distract the hell out of me and have me constantly turned on for *him*.

My head bashed back against the door as I rode the first wave of pleasure caused by teasing the catches in place. I tried to steady my rapid breaths, my heart soaring with an intimacy that made me feel like Cole was right here.

I left the stall and headed over to the basin to wash my hands. After drying them, I grabbed my phone from where I'd left it on the corner table and texted Cameron: *Master, it's on.*

My gaze rose to my reflection in the mirror. My cheeks were flushed.

Most excellent, he texted back.

Staring at my pink face and feeling the rippling below as those diamonds dangled deliciously, I exhaled through a pout and rode through this heady rush.

The door opened and I spun round to see Shay.

I tried to look nonchalant, assuming he was about to chastise me for leaving home without alerting him. I fluffed my hair in the mirror, wanting to ask him about the conversation I'd eavesdropped on this morning with Cameron, but was still too rattled by seeing him in here.

"No hello?" Shay strode in farther with the kind of masterdom I'd come to expect from a senior dominant. Today, he'd swapped out his ripped jeans for a pinstriped suit, so he must have somewhere important to be later.

He tapped on the closed stall doors to confirm we were alone.

"This is the ladies." I stated the obvious because he was making me nervous.

Shay leaned back against one of the sinks and crossed his ankles together. "Ms. Lauren, if you ever leave the penthouse without a security escort again, I will personally spank you myself. And it will be hard."

"I feel like I'm a prisoner." My response even surprised me.

He shrugged. "Listen, it's my job to keep you safe. Don't get me fired."

My shoulders slouched as guilt swallowed me whole. "I'm sorry."

"Let's do this then." He waved his hand through the air.

A slither of uneasiness shot up my spine when he reached into his jacket pocket and brought out his phone. "Up." He gestured to my hem.

"I have a meeting with Dana." I flushed wildly at his insinuation and my glare bounced over to the door. "My boss."

He gestured for me to get on with it. "We don't want you to be late."

I reached out for his phone. "I'll call him."

"Mia." He whisked it out of reach.

Back in our old life this erotic play would have been perfectly normal between doms and their slaves. Still, we weren't back at Chrysalis now where games like this were considered tame and there weren't fifty or so employees on the other side of the door.

Yet my arousal was spiking with every second of Cole's punishment.

"Obey." Shay's insistence intensified. "Let's not keep him waiting."

His disapproval felt like a blow to my reason.

My addled thoughts caught up with my dazed processing of this erotic play—I'd begged Cameron to go darker and this had to be a prelude.

Shay had been granted power over me.

"Surrender," he urged soothingly.

My fingers scrunched the hem of my skirt and froze there. This arousal was causing me to take short, sharp breaths, my nipples beading enough to show through my blouse, my eyelids becoming heavy. Swooning, I had to lean against the wall so I'd not wobble on my strappy heels.

"All you have to do is obey."

This erotic sparring was startlingly new.

"Your master is waiting," he added darkly.

Lifting my hem high above my waist, I followed his gaze to where glistening diamonds fell over my clit, my sex shiny behind bejeweled artistry.

He went down on one knee. "Is it comfortable?"

"I can feel it." I stated the obvious. "It pulls a little."

"Turns you on?"

I exhaled a shaky breath as I nodded.

"Reminds you who owns you?"

"Yes."

"Who owns you, Mia?"

"Master Cole."

"Did you forget this?"

I shook my head and squeezed my eyes shut at the humiliation of him being so close to my sex.

Yet Shay was seductive in his own way, rugged in his handsomeness with the demeanor of an ex-military man who didn't give a fuck. He raised his phone and snapped a few shots of my pussy. A slide of his fingers on his screen let me know he was sending the photos to Cameron.

"No," he berated. "Remain how you are."

My sex thrummed with an aliveness that sent pangs of pleasure right up to my erect nipples. I peered down at myself, mesmerized by this titillating scene, balling my fist to resist the urge to rub my throbbing clit ever so slowly, even with him watching.

A divine pleasure blossomed inside me.

A mewling escaped my lips.

He tucked my hem into my waistband to prevent my skirt from falling. "Good girl, Mia. Arms behind your back, please. You know better."

I snapped my wrists together at my lower spine, remaining in this pose, caught in a dreamy subspace where my master made the rules and dictated how every second played out to please him. This felt daring and dangerous, like a dark forbidden gift from a master who wanted to both shock and awe me.

My gaze flitted nervously to the door.

Shay read the text that came back.

"We have to tighten it." He gestured for me to obey.

What he was asking was impossible; any tighter and my clit would be completely protruding and though you wouldn't see this from behind my skirt the material would rub my most sensitive place. My thighs trembled in revolt.

"Mia?"

I stuttered out words to explain my reticence, but even as I did he was leaning forward and adjusting the delicate chain—tugging my labia apart farther as his fingers unclipped and refastened those delicate clamps. When his fingertip brushed over me I froze in panic. No one was allowed to touch me there.

"I'm being careful," he soothed. "I know the rules."

His firm fingers worked the delicate clamps and I hated how divine the sensation felt along my sensitized skin. My clit swelled beneath his gentle caresses as he fixed the strands more to his liking.

A few more photos later and he gave another nod of approval, then waited for

Cameron to send him a reply. "Your master approves."

"Good, thank you," I said. It was impossible to catch my breath as the tingling was now at a fever pitch. I was about to reach the point of bliss.

"Skirt down."

My body yearned for release or at least an escape from what was essentially edge play.

"Well done, Kitten." Shay used the same endearment Cameron spoke when he played with me.

I was quaking deliciously and my pussy was soaked.

"No coming," Shay demanded. "Unless given permission. Understand?"

"I'll try."

"Sir," he countered, tucking his phone away.

"Sir," I managed.

"Wipe yourself and return to your desk." He headed for the door. "See you at ten in the CEO's office."

After making myself decent down there, I followed Shay out of the powder room and saw the out-of-service sign that had protected my privacy.

A tug at my groin stopped me in my tracks as I judged whether continuing to adult in any form was even possible.

Shay reached the elevator and didn't even glance back.

Flustered, I made it back to my desk with my gaze down, hoping no one could guess I'd just experienced an erotic encounter with the CEO's head of security.

This...this was exhilarating.

A flood of adrenaline brought a thrill of delight, making me feel high. Whatever was happening down there was releasing endorphins and they were surging through my veins.

Back in my cubicle, I saw the screen of my phone light up with Cameron's number.

"Hello, sir," I whispered huskily.

"Are you wet?"

"Yes." I breathed in deeply, my body responding to his voice. "Yes, sir."

"Well, good."

Turning, I peered out the window at the sweeping view, feeling small against the dramatic backdrop of skyscrapers.

"Still there?" he asked darkly.

"Yes."

"How does your clit feel?"

I let out a protracted sigh. "Oh, well, you know."

"Say it."

"Nice." I dragged my teeth over my bottom lip. "Thank you for my punishment, sir."

"There's more."

"More?"

"This morning's behavior was unacceptable."

"I can explain."

"Don't interrupt."

I waited for his response.

"No guards this morning, Mia? No security escort? Do you have any idea of the danger you exposed yourself to?"

My eyelids closed as I realized this also served as a punishment. Only, this was a completely different kind of exposure.

He hung up.

I placed my phone down and stared at it, wondering what else he had in mind. With a clenched jaw and a tingly core I tried to inhale through the ripples. For goodness sake, I had a full day ahead of me and climaxing at my desk was most inconvenient—I had to hold back despite being edged right to the precipice with thoughts of Cole burning up my brain.

This was the mother of all punishments and again a reminder of how much pissing off Cole was a mistake.

My gaze swept over the top of my cubicle and settled on Dana's office.

Oh, God.

I was late for my meeting with her. I grabbed the file from my desk and hurried toward her office. The diamonds tugged and my clit stood erect in response. I glanced down at my skirt to make sure nothing could be seen, though my sex sensed every move.

Reassured, I knocked on her open door. "I have the file." I waved it and gave a cheery smile.

"Come in, Mia."

"Thank you." I felt as naked as hell.

"Everything okay?" Her stare roamed down to my shoes, a pair I shouldn't have been able to afford on my salary. Or maybe that frown was directed at my inked hummingbird; the one with exquisite blues and greens.

I still loved it.

"Yes," I replied confidently. "How are you?"

Her eyes snapped up to mine. "You seem a little breathless."

"I'm fine."

"I'd like you to lead the team in the meeting today," she said warmly. "Is this something you feel ready for?"

"Yes, absolutely. Thank you."

"Mia," she said, gesturing to the file in my hand, "I saw your rendition. I love the way you've incorporated Raif Cole's signature into the design so we remember our legacy, and remind the consumer it's a family business."

It felt right in every way. "I'm so glad you like it."

"It will be interesting to see how Mr. Cole feels about this suggestion." She gave me a thin smile. "Make sure he knows this is your personal take and not directly from marketing."

Which meant she was distancing herself from my design.

The chains were doing crazy things to my ability to speak. I hoped Dana didn't notice me balancing on one foot and then the other to take the pressure off. Nothing helped, not even leaning forward slightly or leaning all my weight on my right leg.

"Don't be nervous." Dana misinterpreted my body language. "You'll do great."

"Yes, I will." Even my breathing was having an effect on those chains, shooting sensations directly into my core.

"Do sit down." She gestured to the chair in front of her desk.

I'd not practiced sitting in this getup yet, but had no choice. Easing myself down as slowly as possible, I felt the tugging intensify until my sex was taut and being stimulated to the max.

"You have real potential." Dana picked up a pen and pointed it at me. "You take risks. I like that."

Risks? How was my design a risk?

I placed my file on her desk to buy time—all five seconds of this awkward repositioning as I squirmed in my chair.

Dana continued to discuss her expectations for the impending meeting.

After thirty minutes, with the time closing in on 10:00 A.M., I left her office and began the walk toward the elevator with a careful stride.

Had this been me walking the pathway to my master in a room back at Chrysalis, I'd have been ecstatic, but this place made it dark play. I had to will myself not to come while leaning against the elevator wall as I ascended, trying to think of anything but Cole.

Remembering all my orgasms belonged to him.

Chapter Six

CAMERON

The photo Shay sent was a fucking masterpiece.

Mia was drenched in diamonds that easily reflected the imagery of the sacred feminine, with the beauty of her sex highlighted by the stones known in Greek as *adamas*; the word diamond's interpretation of "unbreakable" or even untamable.

Like the woman who wore my bejeweled bondage.

I was pleasantly distracted from the slew of meetings. My sweet Mia had obeyed and in doing so I'd delivered on my promise. Flying toward the flame of temptation was a thrill from my past, and her begging me last night to tease her on the darker side hadn't gone unanswered.

Two goals had been accomplished. Firstly, I'd reminded Mia I was her master after she'd rebelled this morning and put herself in danger. Mia wouldn't know about the death threats, or that kidnapping was still a possibility, or even that men would harm her to get to me. No, Mia didn't need to know about any of that because making her feel safe was my priority.

And Shay's involvement in my erotic torture of Mia just now had its own objective. I imagined his steely guard would falter and lead to a confession of what he was keeping from me.

I was about to find out.

Shay's voice carried from outside my office as he chatted with Sue.

The door opened and he closed it behind him, strutting in like a man who'd just discovered a new country. That pinstriped suit looked great on him. His Armani shoes were overly polished, though, and this concerned me.

"Well, that was different." He came toward my desk.

I sat down behind it and leaned back in my chair. "She won't wander off again."

"I'm glad you're happy."

I could tell his adrenaline had spiked and, from a cursory glance at his pants, he was still in a state of appreciation. This was good—this was something I could work with. Shay had stepped on the landmine I'd set for him.

"You followed my orders?" I pushed myself up and rounded the desk. The inches of height I had over him gave me an unspoken advantage.

"To the letter."

I waved that off. "All that's behind us now, Shay. So savor these moments when I deem you deserve them."

He exhaled a steady breath as he fought with his inner demons. The same ones I'd just beckoned with an incantation that would make the Mayan sex gods proud.

"I'm not sure how Mia handled it," he finally said.

"Leave that to me."

"She looked shocked."

"Good."

"Might want to take this conversation to the roof." He used his thumb to point toward Sue's desk.

"Here is fine."

"I know what you're doing, Cam."

"Really?"

He spun one of the chairs around and sat in it. "You're trying to use your psychological shit on me. You know I hate it when you do this."

"I'm so transparent." I waved my hands in defeat.

"It's nothing for you to worry about."

"I'm listening."

"Arianna and I are no longer together."

I knew this as my contacts at Chrysalis had informed me of their flailing relationship. I'd been waiting for Shay to tell me. "I'm sorry to hear that." I sat in the chair opposite his. "What happened?"

"She loves the west coast and refuses to relocate."

"If you feel like your place is with her in Los Angeles, you have my full support, Shay."

"My place is here with you."

"You'd still work for me."

He blew out a sigh. "My thing with Arianna was never going anywhere. She's rebellious. I'm more pedantic. Methodical."

"She's out of your system?"

He held my gaze. "Thank you for being so cold."

"I didn't mean—"

"Obviously I still need time to process it." He shrugged. "You picked up on this. I should know I can't keep anything from you."

"Very true. You can talk to me, Shay. Anytime. You know that."

They'd been good together, but long-distance relationships were hard and Arianna had the kind of needs only a full-time master could provide. She'd been a steep learning curve for Shay but he'd excelled as her Dom and he had been great for her. She'd not touched cocaine since she met him, and he had been elevated to one of the most talented masters because he'd learned so much from her. I'd suspected they'd be temporary, but I was still moved by Shay's melancholy.

I'd called Richard two days ago and told him to watch Arianna and make sure she had everything she needed. Getting her a new Dom had been a priority. Still, I didn't want anyone making a move in that direction until Shay had made his decision, and there would be no circling back around to try and resuscitate their relationship.

"Thank you for understanding," said Shay.

There came a knock at the door.

"Come in," I called out.

The door opened and it was my assistant, Sue. "Sir, your 10:00 A.M. is here." She threw a smile over to Shay.

He threw one back as he pushed himself out of the chair. "Cole, I'm assuming you want to handle this alone?"

"Actually, Sue will be taking notes." I rose and gestured for her to enter. "Invite Ms. Lauren in."

Shay's eyes widened in surprise.

"Mia's showing me the new brand designs," I clarified.

Shay glanced over at Sue and raised his brows. "Right."

"Take the rest of the day off." I stepped forward and tapped his arm. "Let's have dinner tonight. We'll talk."

"I'm good, really." He waved it off.

I turned toward Sue when she came back into the office. "Book us a table."

Shay snapped his gaze to mine. "I'm not compromised because of this."

"I know."

His focus narrowed on me as he tried to read what I was thinking. If he thought he'd thrown me off the trail leading to the truth he was wrong.

"You work too hard." I turned to the door and watched Mia enter.

She wore a modest smile and her blue eyes sparkled. I noticed that her cheeks were flushed, presumably from the jewelry.

I turned to my assistant. "Sue, book a table for three at Remy's Steak House. 8:00 P.M. works for me." I held Shay's stare. "You?"

"Works for me, too."

"Got it, Boss." Sue flashed us a warm smile. "I'll send a car for you, Mr. Gardner."

"No need."

"The car will pick you up at 7:30." I nodded to confirm this was non-negotiable.

Shay's jaw tensed. "Okay, then."

"Who is the third person?" asked Sue.

I held Mia's gaze for a beat. "Someone very special."

"Shall I arrange a car for your other guest?" she added.

"No, just concentrate on getting us a private booth." Gesturing toward the seating area, where a leather sofa and several sumptuous chairs were strategically positioned to make that part of the room cozy, I fixed my attention on Mia as she followed Sue's lead.

Her careful steps toward the sofa proved she was still wearing her accessory. She placed her beige folder on the coffee table and eased herself down onto the leather couch.

I suppressed a smile. "Sue, take notes, please."

Shay glanced over at Mia and then looked at me. "Let me know if you need anything." He wasn't addressing me.

He knew subspace and he'd recognized it in Mia. He probably also saw she was struggling with staying present.

Shay headed out and threw her a reassuring glance. Mia's frown deepened as she realized this was going to be a formal meeting.

I sat on the arm of the leather chair close by. "What have you got for me?"

She swallowed hard and opened the file in front of her, spreading out ten designs. She made eye contact with Sue, and gave a polite smile as she discussed the merits of each one.

This pretending we didn't even know each other was asinine and my annoyance rose. I respected Mia's desire to prove her independence and be successful in this company despite me, but what would happen when it came out we were engaged? What then? When Sue recalled these interactions between us they could be construed as deceitful. Worse still, Mia could be considered a spy I'd placed to watch over my other employees. This debacle was meant to end in two weeks, but I wasn't sure I'd make it that long.

I massaged my brow to ease the tension. "Mia," I said softly, silently pleading with her to end this façade. "Anything else you'd like to share?"

"I appreciate you taking the time to see me, Mr. Cole." She held on to the lie.

I leaned over and reached for one of the designs. "Is that my father's signature?"

The packaging was sophisticated—a deep blue oblong box with *Raif Cole* curled along the side and the swirling Cole Tea logo beneath. It was classy, clean, and a perfect addition to our brand.

"It should be your signature, sir," Sue piped up.

I threw the design back with the others.

Mia's pupils dilated and her breath stuttered. This was her design. Only Mia would have known this new tea had been personally crafted by my father in the midst of a hostile takeover—right before I'd altered the course of history. Only Mia would know that such a gesture wouldn't bruise my ego.

I gave a nod. "There are a few that are an easy *no*." I let my gaze drift back to her design. "Thank you for stopping by."

"I've been asked to run the meeting," Mia said, smiling. "I mean later."

I gave her a look of indifference.

"Thank you, Ms. Lauren." Sue pushed to her feet. "I'll see you out."

Mia's gaze shot to mine. "Are there any designs that you particularly like?"

I turned my back on her and strolled over to the desk. "That will be all, Ms. Lauren."

Mia followed Sue toward the door and glanced back. Whatever she'd expected from this meeting hadn't happened. I watched her leave and began a mental estimate of how long it would take her to reach the elevator.

I dragged out my phone and swiped through the apps until I had the security camera up in the VIP subterranean parking lot. Shay climbed into a red Lamborghini. Mine. Nothing unusual there, but he usually preferred the Bentley.

My ruse had worked. Shay being tasked with directing Mia in a stunning erotic ritual, and then being summoned to my office in an aroused state had delivered the gift of a boner that kept on giving, triggering the kind of response that would bring answers.

I buzzed Sue at the desk. "Cancel the rest of my meetings."

"All of them?"

"Do I need to repeat myself every single time?"

"No, sir, I can do that," was her chirpy response.

"Have Ms. Lauren return."

"When would be a good time?"

"Now." I hung up and stared at the door.

CHAPTER SEVEN

MIA

I TREMBLED WITH NEED WHILE WAITING FOR THE DOORS TO THE executive elevator to open, ready to descend into tears, barely able to sustain this nonchalance. He knew he'd sent me spiraling. He knew what basking in his presence would do to me.

Being bound in his jewelry had me right on the edge—and he'd denied me the kind of release that would return my vitals to normal. I was so wound up even my neck burned with a soft blush.

Every last submissive back at Chrysalis had fought for their chance with him, because no alpha came close to the power he wielded or the pleasure he bestowed; the very same pleasures he was denying me now. And for goodness sake, these chains were yanking my pussy like I had a cheerleading squad down there celebrating the Super Bowl.

For months I'd wanted to keep us a secret, but right now I doubted that decision, having forced him to pretend we meant nothing to each other.

The button pinged and the doors slid open.

"Ms. Lauren?" Sue stood a few feet away.

"Yes?"

"We have a question about one of the designs." She looked triumphant.

With my throat dry, I made my way back to her. "Oh?"

"Putting his dad's name on our packaging was a bad idea. Was it yours?"

"I can explain."

She gestured toward his office. "Off you go."

My body shuddered and she must have caught it because she misinterpreted it as dread and smirked at my expense.

I paused in the office doorway.

Cameron was leaning back against his desk. "In."

I hurried forward and stopped a few feet in front of him.

He walked past me and kept going until he reached the door, calling out, "Sue, no interruptions. Hold all my calls." He shut the door and I heard the click of a lock.

I kept staring straight ahead, my nipples perked in response to his firm tone, my adrenaline surging and my entire body tingling in anticipation.

When I sensed him behind me, I shuddered.

"Do you understand your punishment?" he asked, snatching the folder out of my hand. "Have I made myself clear, Ms. Lauren?"

"Yes, sir," I replied, my voice trembling. "I'm not to leave home without letting you know."

I remembered what my best friend Bailey had once told me. "There's rich and then there's needing a bodyguard rich," she'd said, laughing.

But this was my reality. Cameron was so wealthy we couldn't go anywhere without a security detail. *I* couldn't go anywhere or do anything and it was starting to feel like a self-made prison. Shay made sure his men were discreet, but I knew they were there.

"Obey," he growled.

I straightened and struck a submissive's pose with my hands behind my back and my gaze down. "I didn't mean to offend you."

"You're referring to your presentation?" He threw the folder onto the desk.

"Um…" That, too, but all this had made me forget about my design faux pas as I stared at the offending file.

"Does it look like we are discussing this issue now?"

My gaze snapped forward again.

His fingers worked the catch at the back of my skirt's waistband and it slid over my hips and pooled at my feet, leaving me naked from the waist down. The pretty jewelry shimmered in the fluorescent light and those delicate chains exposed me entirely.

Yes, oh, please let me stay in this room forever.

Cameron reached his desk and turned to face me. Leaning back against it, he stared at me with appreciation. "Very good, Ms. Lauren."

"Thank you for my punishment, sir."

"Did you find it pleasing that it was delivered by Mr. Gardner's hand?"

"If it pleases you, sir."

"I'm asking you."

What was I to say? Should I share that having such an interaction with Shay had aroused me? Didn't this mean I was betraying our trust? It was best to remain silent.

"Play with your clit."

My eyelids closed as his words tore up my sanity, my groan revealing what his order meant—that I was at last allowed to reach down, like I was doing now, and sweep my fingertip over that sensitive swell, teasing it. A jolt of pleasure shuddered through me.

"Slower."

I obeyed as the promise of relief neared.

"Hands behind your back, Ms. Lauren."

Dragging my hand away, I assumed my pose and waited through the excruciating seconds as the ache in my core intensified. I was certain he'd see me throbbing down there.

He folded his arms across his chest and continued to study me. My nipples beaded and the ache below was like a constant pulse of need. I licked my lips to ease their dryness.

On my left was the glass-fronted liquor cabinet he kept his expensive selection of booze in, and to my right was the luxury leather furniture I'd just sat in. Behind his desk were neatly lined books on an impressive mahogany bookcase. Yes, this ordeal was easier if I didn't look at him.

"Circle your clit again," he demanded.

With the tip of my finger, I did as he commanded—though this time my pace was leisurely; I resisted letting these sensations own my pussy. But it became overwhelming, and I had to cup my breasts to ease the pang in my nipples.

With a nod from my master, I again assumed the pose with my hands clutched behind my back; the sting of my fingernails in my palms helped ease the desire I was feeling.

He was right there, standing tall and stunningly handsome, his hands shoved into his pockets in a casual but threatening pose, as though he were the ruler of the air itself.

It became too much. "Mercy, sir."

"Come here."

I stepped free of my skirt that had pooled at my feet and hurried over, leaning against his firm chest and breathing in his cologne. His heady scent of power and control demanded my surrender.

With my body crushed to his, Cameron reached around my back and grasped the chain at my lower spine. He began a rhythmic pulling of the links that were attached to either side of my labia, stretching them well enough to tug at my clit in measured pulses. Tipping my chin up, my lips opening wide, I begged him with my eyes to kiss me.

His mouth lingered dangerously close to mine, his hot breath teasing me as he leaned closer—but not close enough. I was on my tiptoes now trying to meet his lips and each time he eased his mouth away in denial. This was the cruelest punishment of all, and I mewled in frustration, rocking slightly in response to that consistent tugging.

"Don't come," he said calmly. "Don't come."

I was whimpering now as he held me on a precipice, my clit so sensitive that one word from him would make me fall.

"Have I made myself clear, Ms. Lauren?"

"Yes, sir."

He let go of the chain and pulled away. "Get dressed."

Shaken and unsated, I went over and scooped my skirt off the floor, pulled it on, and refastened the hook at the back. This felt like a punishment so fierce that I'd never find my way back from it.

With the chains tugging me and wetness dampening my thighs, I turned to face the door.

I had to ready myself for my walk of shame past Sue.

"Ms. Lauren." Cameron grabbed my attention, "At 5:00 P.M. there will be a car waiting to drive you home *with* a security detail. Do you understand?"

"Yes, sir." Swooning still, I headed toward the door.

"Well done, Ms. Lauren."

My hand froze on the knob and I turned and whispered, "Thank you for my punishment, sir. I promise to be a good girl."

"This pleases me."

A rush of adoration struck me as I studied those sharp features that made his stark beauty so intimidating. His chestnut gaze watched me intently, a ghost of a smile appearing that hinted of affection.

Hurrying back toward him, I dropped to my knees and stared up with an expression of wonderment, grateful for these last seconds I had with him. He leaned low and slid his thumb into my mouth, easing it in and out with slow steady thrusts of his hand against my chin, and I suckled, tasting him.

I hadn't quite deserved his cock yet.

When he pulled away I let out a moan of need.

"Time for your reward, Kitten." Cameron patted the desk.

I let out a sigh of happiness when he raised me off the carpet to sit on his desk, nudging me back so my butt was on the edge and my legs dangled. I spread my thighs not caring where we were or what lay on the other side of the door. All I needed was his approval, his nurturing, and his love.

Release.

He shifted to stand between my thighs. "I know what you need."

"Oh, please."

When he dragged my hem up and hoisted it above my waist I lifted my butt to help, this all-consuming passion making me shudder with anticipation.

He leaned forward and trailed his tongue over where the diamonds connected at my pubic bone, and then lowered his face toward my sex. I almost squealed as a shock of bliss possessed me. Watching him, mesmerized, I held my breath while his mouth lavished me with the oral skills of a master. After all the tautness bundled between my thighs, I exploded into a blinding orgasm too soon, arching my back, unable to wait for permission as I trembled into the center of nirvana.

The world fell away.

All I knew was Cameron's tongue furiously flicking, suckling my clit and letting it go, letting it fill with pulsing blood that sent me reeling into another freefall, capturing it again and holding it attentively before releasing that bundle of nerves.

His hand reached up and cupped my mouth as I groaned out my release, shaking violently before him, thighs twitching.

"Please," I mumbled beneath his firm hand.

"You don't get to have my cock, Mia." He stood up straight and his demeanor transformed once more into a stern master. "Not until I truly see remorse."

"I'll do anything."

"Well, we'll see. Should you prove to me you can be a good girl and do as you're told, you'll be rewarded."

No, I couldn't wait for this, couldn't stand by and let him tease me anymore.

"Are you ready?" He eased the diamond strand aside from where it had fallen over my sex.

Hooking my hands around my inner thighs, I pulled up my legs and spread my thighs wide, closing my eyes in anticipation for the imminent additive mixture of pain and pleasure he was about to deliver.

He was waiting for me to open my eyes. "Look at your pussy."

His sternness sent a thrill up my spine as I realized each slap would force those clamps into my flesh.

That firm palm came down fast.

Whack.

I jolted toward a near climax that followed the burn of my sex, leaving me swollen and heated; a scolding so intense it shot me into subspace. Then his slaps turned tender, perhaps reflecting his merciful side, or perhaps he didn't want to alert Sue what was really going on in here, but even so they stung deliciously as he delivered spank after spank over my clit.

Clenching my teeth, trying to stop myself from moaning, I flinched when he dipped two fingers deep inside me and pressed them against my G-spot, my muscles instinctively holding onto them. But he withdrew them and smeared the wetness over my clit before resuming his teasing with slow steady spanks, until I was once more shuddering on a precipice—each timed pause of his palm a welcome relief and each slap setting me toward a climax. No matter how cruel this taunting felt, it was nothing compared to wearing these chains with no hope of being let free of this arousal.

"Permission," I managed.

"Only good girls get to come again."

"I'm good."

"Am I not the judge of that?" He delivered a faster spanking and at the same time he began a leisurely two-finger fucking.

I was plummeting—an erotic drag from gravity I couldn't resist.

Nothing mattering but this moment owning me entirely, and it went on endlessly until all that was left was to yield, shaking through another orgasm, my pussy tipping up to greet his sustained spanks as his palm struck my soaking wet sex; the soft noise delicious.

This was more than physical; my soul was one with his as he reminded me once more how easy it was to give myself entirely.

Staring into his eyes, I tried to read his expression. I heard his soft sigh, or perhaps it was mine, saw his nod of approval as his mouth came down on me again obsessively exploring every crevice, his tongue darting and searching every fold, lapping and licking hungrily and dramatically sucking in adulation, his frantic exploration refusing to relent…

Minutes unfolded… revealing a chink in his armor. He had needed this too, *needed me.*

I brought my hand up to cover my mouth to prevent a scream from escaping.

He yanked me up to a sitting position and crushed his lips to mine, sharing my sweet taste, his tongue bringing that same ferociousness to my mouth as he devoured me, forcing my mouth wider, bruising my lips and sending a shiver through me. His kiss drew all the power back to him and I gave myself entirely, moaning as another orgasm gripped me, brought on merely from him claiming my mouth.

He leaned back and looked me over, as though checking on how I was doing.

"I knew you still loved me," I said wistfully.

Cameron stared at me as if he were considering my words. "That will be all, Ms. Lauren." He stepped back and gestured to the door. "Thank you for coming in." He handed me back my folder. "I believe I've been clear."

In a flurry of movement, I straightened my skirt and gave him a cursory nod of gratitude. Then I quickly headed for the door, clutching the folder to my chest as I hurried out of his office without looking back. My pussy was on fire, and I silently exalted over the burn that proved he was still mine.

I made a beeline for the elevator.

"How was it?" Sue's voice trailed behind me.

Turning on my heels, I faced her, on the verge of saying *"amazing."*

"He told you in no uncertain terms of his displeasure?" Sue looked triumphant.

I felt myself blushing. "He was articulate in every respect. I'm glad we got the chance to go over everything. He's very thorough." So thorough in fact that this buzz I felt below still lingered deliciously.

She smirked and I realized she had misconstrued my appearance as distress.

The elevator doors opened and I leaped in and waited for them to seal me inside. I leaned against the wall, riding these post-orgasmic waves courtesy of Cameron Cole.

That man was intoxicating and I had just gotten drunk off him.

Reluctantly, I tried to turn my attention away from these sensations, preparing to return to my cubicle. My eyes widened as I felt the tug of the chains and a row of diamonds falling against my clit.

Oh, no. I was meant to continue wearing this—I was being restrained at my master's pleasure.

When I arrived back at my desk, my cell phone lit up with Cameron's number. I picked it up and pressed it to my ear. "Yes, sir?"

Go on, ask him about the wedding dress...

"How's the marketing department?"

"Still marketing away?" Though this time it came out as a question.

My body was still trembling from his pleasurable assault. I only hoped no one noticed my slightly disheveled state.

"You know I love you, right?" he whispered.

The sound of those words made me feel like I'd been kissed by heaven itself.

"I love you, too."

"Take off the jewelry," he said. "Place it back on before you leave work."

"I definitely will."

"How am I doing so far, Ms. Lauren?"

My gaze swept up to the photo of him that I kept pinned to the back of my cubicle. It had been taken from behind as a silhouette so no one would guess it was him.

"I can go darker."

CHAPTER EIGHT

CAMERON

THE RED BUGATTI WAS SQUARELY PARKED IN THE subterranean structure of The Dionysus Club on One East Sixtieth Street, right next to a silver Lamborghini Veneno. I had to drag my gaze away from the roadster's sleek lines and promise of speed.

I threw my Bugatti car keys to the valet.

I'd been in one of my "fuck you" moods when I'd bought the Lamborghini, days after I'd arrived in New York—a kind of rebellion at coming to terms with leaving my beloved profession and taking on the kind of responsibilities that would keep me awake at night. Maybe I was hoping I'd transition smoothly into a man willing to take the hardest punches as well as deliver them.

What the hell was Shay doing here?

I whipped my phone out and stood behind a pillar hoping my call would go through. With only one bar I said a silent prayer to Dionysus himself, God of ritual madness and infertility, which was in-keeping with a men's club.

"Hey, you." It was Penny, my old executive assistant back at

Enthrall, a dynamic psychologist and world-class dominatrix.

"Quick question," I said, diving right in, since we'd known each other for years and she'd gotten used to my attitude of business before pleasure.

"Anything, you know that." The warmth of her enduring kindness came through.

"Password for The Dionysus Club in the Big Apple?"

"I thought that was behind you?"

"I'm here, outside, waiting to get in."

"One minute."

Since she'd put me on hold, she must not have the answer but she knew someone who did. This request could have been construed as wrong—me following my head of security to some unknown location. But I sensed he needed me, and I wasn't about to ignore that quiet inner voice that had always served me well.

"Ready?" Penny came back on the line.

"I am."

"It changes each week according to my source. Chances are you won't get inside. The Mayor's a member and some other politicians, too. Be careful."

"I need to get in."

"The password is Midas."

"As in Midas Touch?"

"Right. Good luck."

"Don't tell your source. I don't frequent places like this anymore."

"Much to our distress, Cameron."

"I'll call you later. Catch up properly," I said, softening my tone. "I miss you, Pen."

I missed them all.

"We love you. Come back and visit soon."

I hung up and headed for the elevator, punching the only button: CLUB.

When the doors parted I stepped out into a plush burgundy foyer and was greeted with a smile from a very pretty, very young receptionist who sat behind a desk.

"Welcome, sir," she said pleasantly.

Predictably, Tamaso Albinoni's *Adagio in G Minor* set the scene, as did the scents of lavender and sandalwood to help clients unwind from a day of reaping in the billions.

I soaked it in.

"Midas," I said, holding her gaze. The young lady had an oriental heritage. I admired the shiny black locks that hung straight down her back. Her blouse was open just enough to reveal a push-up bra, and as she stepped out from behind her desk to greet me, I glanced down at her short skirt, which showed off her stocking tops. Everything about her screamed risqué.

"At your service." Her tone was sweet.

I gave her a suggestive look of appreciation. I didn't want to know her name.

"Do you have an appointment?" She peered down at her ledger. "Are you here for a session or for the club?"

"I'm open for anything." My grin was all about the innuendo.

When she blushed and looked away, I leaned over the reception desk and saw the names listed in the guestbook. Even though it was upside-down, I was able to read "Gardner" and noted the letter "D" beside his name.

Shay had booked himself a session with a dominant. Since he'd arrived early, he probably would have been invited to take a dip in the sauna first.

He'd finally faced his submissive side. He'd realized fighting his desire to be dominated by a man was futile. Still, I couldn't understand why he'd not shared this with me. Membership didn't run cheap. You paid to never have been here.

The receptionist's soft, flowery scent reached me. "We're proud to deliver most requests."

I needed to find my way to the spa, and act like I knew where it was. Two hallways led off in opposite directions.

I looked at my watch. "I'm trying to work out if I have time for a stone massage."

She glanced left. "Would you like me to have a masseur meet you in the spa? We have our aural specialist in the house."

Yes, she'd just offered me a happy ending like it was a drink off a menu. This place was an illegal haven.

"I'll pass, but thank you." I headed left.

"Sir," she called after me. "You'll need this."

I came back and she dropped a key into my palm, which I assumed was for a locker.

"Any special requests?" She added brightly. "Any past favorites you'd like me to summon for your pleasure?"

I gave her a tight smile, knowing she wasn't offering a beverage. This was the kind of club you needed a mayor to be a member of to prevent it from getting raided. Immunity to the kind of debauchery even I arched an amused brow at.

"I'm good." I threw in a wink before turning on my heel and walking away. My priority was Shay.

Soft lighting enhanced the quiet atmosphere of the spa. As I stripped out of my suit and hung it in a locker, I questioned the wisdom of getting naked. Should any of my clubs have discovered a trespasser, the fucker would've been dealt with aggressively. I was not only risking my safety but also my reputation.

I paused briefly to quench my thirst with a quick drink of lemon water, and then threw the cup in the trash. Passing through another doorway, I strolled naked toward the spa. For me, this was as daring as it got these days.

Shay was alone in the enormous spa pool, leaning back against the tile with merely his head out of the water as steam rose around him. He flinched when he saw me, those dark eyes closing in exasperation.

"Nice place." I descended the blue tiled steps and waded toward him.

"You tracked the car?"

"Just like you taught me."

He opened his eyes and rolled them at me.

"Am I paying you too much, Gardner?"

"This is what a half million dollar relocation bonus looks like." He arched a brow. "Thanks for that, by the way."

Great, his bonus had been spent on this place. It had been meant for a deposit on a loft.

I settled in next to him, enjoying the warmth soaking into my bones. "Why didn't you tell me you'd become a member?"

"'Cause we don't do this."

I felt relieved that this was his secret instead of him looking for a new job, or carrying out corporate espionage. This was Shay exploring his deviant side—and he'd chosen an elite club to do it in.

"You're in good company." I arched a brow. "Damon Spellman's currently getting his dick sucked."

"And you know this how?"

"Their coding system on the guest list."

"You worked out their coding system? You're too smart for your own good."

"I wish."

"So you know why I'm here?" He tilted his head, as though waiting to see if I'd figured that out, too.

"I could have referred you, Shay. To someone I trust. Someone who'd push your limits and make you feel safe."

"Fuck." He shook his head. "Do I have no secrets?"

This morning I'd placed him right into the center of an erotic scene and it had brought him straight here. Split the truth wide open. I was glad I'd followed him. Shay looked nervous as hell, and that always brought out his arrogant side. He'd be in trouble with an unseasoned Dom who wanted to whip the petulance out of him after misinterpreting his attitude as smugness.

"How is he? Any good?"

Shay swallowed hard.

"This is your first session with a Dom?"

"Seriously?"

"How well do I know you?"

"You can't do this." He looked frustrated. "Insert yourself into my life like this."

Yet when I'd walked in I'd seen relief wash over his face. "I'm assuming you're not hard for your Dom yet?" I asked him, my tone playful.

"Jesus, Cam, back off."

"I'm flattered. Truly."

He glanced down at himself self-consciously. "I wasn't expecting to see you. Not naked, anyway."

"I get it. You didn't want to make me uncomfortable by letting me know you'd joined Dionysus. If I can't indulge then neither can you?"

"I thought that was the party line."

"What time's your appointment?"

He twisted his watch like he hadn't checked it a second ago. "In twenty minutes."

"I told you this was what you needed," I reassured him. "To explore your—"

"Don't call me gay."

"You're bi, Shay. It's perfectly acceptable. And being gay is perfectly normal. So you can shut that shit down right now."

"Really, 'cause last time I checked I'm an ex-SEAL whose brand is being a hardass?"

"Which is why I hired you."

He leaned his head back. "Fucking reception staff."

"It's me, Shay. Nothing gets past me."

His gaze held mine. "You've had access to every man in your clubs and you've never experimented."

"Was that a question?"

He rubbed his eyes. "How fucking embarrassing…but, yeah."

I let out a long sigh. "What you said isn't strictly true."

He snapped his gaze to mine. "Richard?"

"No."

"Then who?"

I raised my hand in a gesture of sincerity. "This isn't some tale of regret. This is me sharing something sacred with you."

"You were with a man?"

I turned to face him. "I was staying with him in France and he dragged me along to one of his parties."

"Danton?" He looked surprised. "The guy who died of a brain tumor?"

He knew Danton as an old lover of Scarlet Winters, Chrysalis's senior dominatrix back on the West Coast, but that was all. In fact, this was a private matter only Scarlet and Richard knew about.

"You were together?" he asked.

"He was the best...a Dom who had the talent for keeping his subs on the edge for hours. Sometimes days."

"You were a sub?"

"Not strictly, more of an equal that savored the play. I refused to surrender. He refused to relent. I was never going to kneel."

Shay looked stunned.

"Danton taught me all I knew. He was a few years older and his skills were inspiring. He liked getting inside my head and messing with it. I fell hard."

"That's kind of...romantic."

"I named Chrysalis after him. He had a thing for butterflies."

"Scarlet?" He looked surprised. "She didn't know?"

"She did. When I learned he was dying and he planned to just be alone in his old family chateau, I sent Scarlet to be with him."

That was me stretching the truth, considering I'd tricked her into thinking she'd made the decision herself to fly off to France to join the House of Hillenbrand, though when she discovered their mainstay was gangbangs, she was more than happy to be rescued by her new Dom Danton.

"You knew he was dying?" Shay's tone was respectful.

"Later, yes. We'd parted ways by that point. He didn't want any-one else to know. Told me to keep it a secret. He needed someone like Scarlet. She was vulnerable and that meant he wouldn't send her away. I knew him well enough. Danton was the ultimate hero. He did exactly as I predicted and swept her out of Hillenbrand, and took her to the coast to his very private chateau. I knew they'd help each other."

Danton had saved Scarlet's life after she'd been close to seeing her death wish come true, but Shay didn't need to know about that very private aspect of her past. Danton had turned Scarlet around and given her a reason to live.

"You were with him when he died?"

I nodded, and those feelings of grief swept over me again…*even now*. Being with Danton when he'd died was the hardest thing I'd ever done. The words "why him" had haunted me day and night for years.

Scarlet and I had formed a bond so strong it had become unbreakable. Our love for Danton, and our loyalty to him, had stretched on after his passing, and that had meant she and I could never have been lovers. She'd always belong to him. That was until Ethan Neilson had graced the scene and swept her off her feet. We'd both sensed it had been with Danton's blessing.

"Back at Enthrall, no one knew about you and Danton?" he asked.

"Richard knew."

"Why didn't you tell me?"

"It's my memory to cherish."

"How long were you lovers with Danton?"

"I'm telling you this so you can enjoy your time with your Dom."

"Have you never thought of me like that?" He seemed to hold his breath waiting for my answer.

"I'm with Mia, Shay. You know how much I value loyalty."

"Which was why this morning surprised me. You had me attach that contraption to her pussy?"

"She begged to enter the playground."

He tilted his head. "Please tell me she's not still wearing it?"

She wasn't, but he didn't need to know that. "I'm a spectrum of dangerous you don't want to know."

"You're not heartless."

"I know your weak spot and I'm currently manipulating it."

"So transparent." He looked amused. "And yet you're one of the good guys."

"I'm taking advantage. You would do anything for me."

"There is that." He reached down to adjust himself. "Great, I'll walk in there with a boner."

"I'd be flattered if I was your Dom."

His stare lingered on mine. "Cam…"

"I can't, Shay."

He rested his head back. "You owe me."

"For what?"

"Hunting me down today."

I smirked. "Are you blackmailing me so I'll join your session?"

"It's my first time."

"I'm not meant to be here."

"What if I like it?" He let out a shaky breath. "What if I become addicted to this?"

"This?"

"After what you did to me this morning? Made me play with Mia and then fucked me in your office with the tone of your voice." He shook his head. "You're acting out."

"Excuse me?"

He turned his head to look at me. "I know you want to be part of this place as much as me."

Five months. Five days. Seven hours. That had been the last time I'd stepped over the threshold of a dungeon as a dominant. Though no way was this happening. I was going to climb out, get dressed, and return to my life of restraint.

Except Shay had a persuasive argument… He'd curled his palm around my cock and was currently stroking my erection.

He raised his eyebrows. "You feel amazing."

"Though I applaud your bravery, Shay," I said sternly, "Let go of my dick."

His hand slipped off and he grinned with mischief in his eyes. "Yeah, that's my revenge for you cock-teasing me this morning."

"Notice I didn't punch you in the face?"

"Cole, I need you there."

My jaw tightened. "You'd be begging me to take it down a level."

His gaze broke from mine and his frown deepened. He looked across the spa as if mesmerized.

Following his gaze, I drew in a wary breath at the sight of the stunning—and very young—woman wading toward us in the pool. If I had to take a wild guess from her bone structure, her illuminant dark skin and striking brown eyes, I'd say she hailed from Somaliland. She was bewitching in her nakedness, moving like a mystical water-nymph, with her hair falling down her body and curling over her pert breasts. She was a walking masterpiece. I was certain that if she ever became interested in modeling, Vanity Fair would snap her up and put her on the front cover where she deserved to reign.

"Is this your doing?" Shay gave me a "let's tag-team her" smile.

My stare snapped back to her and when I saw the swirl of an "H" tattooed on her left wrist a chill ran up my spine.

"I'm your present," she said, her words echoing around us.

They'd given us their finest submissive and that meant they probably knew who we were. My racing thoughts ran through every scenario and none of them were good.

Shay was going to hate me, but even so, I still said it. "We have to leave."

He shot me a surprised look, and then his gaze fell back on the beauty standing a few feet away. She was waiting for one of us to make a move.

"How old are you?" I had to ask.

"How old do you want me to be?" She bit her lip.

"Will you excuse us, please?" I turned around and hoisted myself out of the pool. "Shay," I snapped, breaking him out of his trance.

From his look of defeat I could tell he'd realized his appointment wasn't going to happen. I glared at him, hoping he would catch on that we needed to hurry. I grabbed a towel and threw another his way.

He waded out and followed me into the men's locker room. "Is my membership threatened?"

"That's the least of our problems."

"I need to take a shower."

"Please skip it."

"But I'll smell of chlorine."

I pulled on my pants and gave him a forced smile. "Tell me you never utilized any of their other services?"

"This isn't happening."

I lowered my voice. "This is how you'll make it up to me. You'll find out that girl's name and you'll get her the fuck out of here."

"She looked eighteen."

"Let's review this through a lens of honesty."

He rubbed his brow as though the obvious answer had to be somewhere in his brain.

I mouthed, "*Not here.*"

Despite being damp, he pulled on his shirt in a hurry. "So...I fucked up?"

I grabbed his silk tie and helped him weave it neatly around his neck. "I know of someone who'd be a good fit for you. He'll kick you into submission. Curb that craving."

Shay reached into his locker and grabbed his pinstriped jacket. "I'll make it up to you."

I tapped his arm. "Dinner's on you."

We ambled along the hallway and I threw a tentative glance toward the reception desk where another young woman was stationed. At least this one looked a little older.

When the elevator doors opened we strolled in casually.

I punched the button. "Until now you've thought with your very impressionable brain." Leaning against the elevator wall, I smirked. "Once we get your penchant satisfied you'll no longer be thinking with your balls."

"And you?" He folded his arms across his chest.

"Me?"

"When are you going to return to what you do best? What you need?"

Again, I punched the button. He was right, of course. I needed my exhibition fix where no one knew me and I could slip away unseen.

Before I imploded.

I buried that sentiment. "Shay, find out who that girl is and get her out."

He was texting. "On it."

The elevator jolted to a stop before we hit the ground floor, and then began ascending once more.

Shay's gaze rose from his phone to meet mine. He moved quickly toward the door to guard me with his body from whatever came next. Instinctively, I grabbed the back of his jacket, just as protective.

When the doors opened again it was to the sight of a stunning woman with a black bob and chiseled cheekbones, dressed in a short skirt and bustier.

"Gentlemen, I am so happy I caught you." Her accent was Russian. "This way, please."

Chapter Nine

Mia

TUCKED AWAY IN MY CUBICLE, I TRIED TO GET ON WITH MY day, or at least look like I was by checking and sending emails, and answering the phone when Dana's executive assistant's line was busy. I'd made an art out of looking busy when my day lulled.

Stealing a few personal seconds for myself, I called Cameron's office.

"He's unavailable," came Sue's terse reply.

"May I leave a message?"

"He's out for the rest of the day."

I wanted to ask where he'd gone but we were on an even playing ground as far as Sue was concerned with her VIP status as the CEO's assistant. There was one way to get her to treat me nicer and I wasn't ready for that yet.

Other than the fact that Cameron burned me up inside like a fireball ready to disintegrate, I had no complaints. Despite all that had happened to me in the past...my dad leaving us back in our hometown of Charlotte when my mom's drug habit became too much, my mom dying of an overdose on our living room floor, or even those early days in L.A. when I'd worked two jobs just to afford my studio apartment.

I had since won life's lottery. I was engaged to one of the most remarkable men I'd ever met and he loved me just as fiercely. I was privileged beyond belief to live in a multimillion dollar penthouse with the best views of New York City, and I had access to the kind of funds that could buy anything one's heart desired.

Yet all I desired was him.

My secret fiancé, who had swapped out ruling one of the world's most distinguished clubs to commanding the boardroom. His new position had bought many changes to both of us, including him swapping out dominating me for the kind of sex that verged on vanilla.

Today had been his return to the way he'd once mastered me back when I was a newbie submissive. Distracted by these thoughts, I continued to feign being an asset to the workforce.

By 4:30, I'd snuck back off to the restroom and reattached the diamond chains to my sex—and this time they were easier to clip. I made sure they were a little looser this time around. They felt incredible and I had to focus on pulling my skirt down and not stealing a few minutes to pleasure myself.

With my head held high, I walked back to my cubicle, behaving as though having the CEO own my pussy wasn't setting my nerves alight.

My phone rang and I snapped up the receiver. "Hello?"

Please, be you.

"Ms. Lauren?" It was a woman's voice and she purred my name in a strong foreign accent.

"Yes?"

"Mia Lauren?" she added.

The fine hairs prickled on my nape. "How can I help you?"

"We have a special delivery to your home. We just need an address."

"Delivery?"

"Wedding cake sample."

I caressed my brow. "Chantelle is coordinating."

Our charismatic wedding planner, with her constant high caffeine levels, had promised to see to all the nerve-wracking details that arranging an extravagant society wedding could possibly entail.

"Chantelle?"

"From Platinum Events."

Kelly Granger, my coworker with the cute blue bob who was stationed in the cubicle across from mine, had buried her face in her hands, looking distraught. We'd clicked immediately on my first day and it had been reassuring to be liked for me and not my connection to the higher-ups.

I dragged my gaze away from Kelly. "Can you go through Platinum Events, please?" I asked the caller. "She's the contact."

"Very good," she rasped. "We'll get your address from Chantelle."

"Sorry, didn't catch your name?"

She'd hung up.

I slid my finger across to my contacts and stared at Shay's number, musing how stupid I was about to sound. Still, Shay had insisted that anyone's interest in us had to be brought to his attention.

I tapped Shay's number and then pressed the phone to my ear. "Hey, it's me. There's going to be a cake sample delivered to the penthouse." I was embarrassed to bother him. Though after this morning's wrangling of those diamond chains we'd bonded a little more. "She sounded Russian, I think. Can you ask Cameron to call me?"

If Cameron was going to be calling off our wedding, now would be a good time before he overspent—and tore me apart in the process. Our break-up would ruin me for the rest of my life. I couldn't bear to think of it.

I was going to have to focus on work to keep me sane until I could challenge him on the conversation I'd overheard this morning.

I got out of my chair and approached Kelly's cubicle. "Hey, are you okay?"

She looked up at me with big, soulful eyes. "I lost a file."

My gaze wandered over to her screen."Which one?"

"Design Studio." I could hear the fear in her voice. "I've tried everything. Searched everywhere. Two days of work…gone."

"What about the recycle bin or deleted files?"

"It's not there." She glanced nervously toward Dana's office.

I gave her shoulder a reassuring squeeze. "I'll call IT."

"If you put a ticket in, Dana will see it."

"She won't. We'll have IT find it remotely."

"You're sure?" She swallowed hard.

"Yes. What's the file called?"

"Cole Brand Final."

I stared at her. "You're entering?"

"Yeah, I have this great design that's going to knock out the competition. I need that bonus real bad. My rent's a month overdue."

My shoulders slumped at the thought of submitting mine now, even if it had given me a creative high.

She read my expression. "You're entering?"

"I was considering it, yes."

She flashed a worried look at her computer.

I offered her a look of sympathy. "We'll find your design. Don't worry."

"Thanks. I used Photoshop to make it three-dimensional."

I resisted closing my eyes in defeat.

"You were in early?" She swiveled in her chair to face me.

"Had some stuff to catch up on."

"I drank too much last night. Remind me not to accept the drinks 'cause they're free."

"Did you have fun?"

"Got to dance with Mr. Cole, so yes." She widened her jaw in playful shock. "You too, huh?"

"Yes." I turned away. "Well, I best get back."

I returned to my desk and called the guys in IT. They'd already rigged my computer to ensure any communication between me and Cameron would disappear into the ether. Those personal emails Cole sent couldn't be saved in the name of sentimentality. I tipped back in my chair and gave a thumbs-up to Kelly to let her know IT was on it.

The chain tugged my sex and I regretted leaning back. A harsh reminder of the way my day had gone.

My phone rang and I snapped it up.

"Mia," Dana's tone carried a condemning edge. "My office, please."

A wave of doubt caused butterflies to invade my stomach. Had she somehow discovered my private request to IT after I'd specially asked for discretion? I carried my notepad with me toward her corner space, running through all the ways I could defend Kelly and take the blame.

"Hi, Dana," I said brightly.

She rose. "So we have an interesting update."

"Oh?"

"Don't sit." She cut off my attempt to get comfortable. "Apparently you're leaving us?"

"Perhaps you have me confused with someone else?"

Dana glanced down at a memo. "It says here that you're moving to the executive level... immediately?"

"There was some talk of this, yes." *Though two weeks had been our agreement.*

"Mia, what happened when you went upstairs?" She lowered her gaze. "Were you offered a promotion?"

My face blushed at the thought of her reaction if I announced the details of my erotic pussy play.

"Did you accept the offer?" she added.

I backed toward the door. "I need to look into it."

I felt her glare on me as I hurried away.

Cameron owned me and this was his way of proving it—and every tug of these chains served as a reminder. My brain told me this was wrong in so many ways, but my body rebelled against this assault to my feminist side, raging against the men in my life who loved to dominate their woman without compromise.

My skin tingled, my sex squeezing with desire, my submissive nature rearing to tease the promise that blinding pleasure awaited.

Alone in the staff room, with my hands trembling, I tried to hold an ice-filled glass beneath the water fountain. A cold drink would help take this inner heat down. I was burning up with passion again from reminiscing about my time in Cameron's office.

If I moved upstairs, this play was going to be a daily occurrence. This promotion was not without its benefits, I mused.

Damn Cameron. He'd left me with this unquenchable thirst. I'd needed his cock inside me like I needed oxygen.

He was dragging out his demanding kinkiness by forcing me to continue wearing these chains as a reminder of what I'd missed after he'd revved me to the max. My body shuddered as those memories swept over me…every move, every step, pulled and tantalized—leading all thoughts back to *him*.

Why couldn't he have just taken me hard on his desk and put me out of my misery—he was punishing me for leaving early without him this morning.

Gulping more water to quench my thirst, I tried to think of anything but him, his touch, his kiss, his mastery, the devilish way he spanked my pussy, yet I was desperate for more.

I was ablaze, enraptured by the way his cologne lingered. Pressing my forearm to my nose, I inhaled his provocative scent. I could have told him *no*, could have insisted I get back to my desk, but he'd stood there with his hands shoved in his pockets ruling the room and wielding his authority.

I was addicted to his touch; the way his hand moved over me with the ease of a man who'd explored my curves and knew what I needed and could perfectly deliver it.

By the time I made it back to my cubicle, I had perspiration spotting my upper lip and my heart was racing from the effort of trying to subdue this terrible ache inside me.

I whipped my cell phone out of my handbag, ready to beg him to let me take off the chains. The call went to his private voicemail.

Right. Great. This is fine.

Fuck it…

With trembling hands, I fumbled trying to get Shay on the line. My call went to voicemail again.

Leaving early could get me in all sorts of trouble. Still, with just half an hour left, it was possible that no one would notice if I just slipped away...

The memory of Cameron's touch down there caused me to shiver. I was caught in the eye of a storm that was Cameron Cole. Snapping up my purse, I scurried over to the elevator and practically leaped in when the doors slid open.

Pressing my phone to my ear, I left another message. "Cameron, please call me."

Ignoring my calls was his way of proving he had power over me. That teasing in his office had been the least of his manipulation. Cole was a persuasive man, yet I still had some fight left in me.

In a daze, I walked through the foyer and headed for the exit, stepping through the revolving door. Light rain touched my skin and brought freshness to the air. Raising my face to the sky, I let the drop-lets fall on me and sprinkle my clothes.

I wanted to run through the rain. Let the freedom soak in.

The idea of making my own way home sinfully beckoned.

CHAPTER TEN

CAMERON

HYPER-VIGILANT, I WALKED BESIDE SHAY AS WE FOLLOWED the dominatrix down a sprawling hallway, my thoughts processing every possible scenario.

These places tended to have heavy hitters running them. Although I admired this high-end club for having its priorities straight by not letting just anyone in—like me, the man without the membership— it was unsettling because I'd not had time to research the place. The stakes were high if an interloper got hold of sensitive information or even snapped a photo—the risk of blackmail ever present to the elite who'd entrusted their fetishes for a steep price.

The voice of Ariana Grande replaced the classical music. That, and the modern décor, seemed specifically designed to appease a younger clientele with too much money.

I gave a sideways glance at Shay. I'd sabotaged his adventure and now he was going to have to endure my witty repartee on how I saved his ass.

Within a minute, we were standing in what looked like the director's office. Our dominatrix host folded her arms across her chest and leaned back against her impressively sized desk.

A brief scan of the room confirmed the office was possibly hers. A blue Louis Vuitton handbag lay on the seat of a leather chair and the room's décor exuded a feminine touch.

She'd haphazardly lined up her books on the left hand bookcase, avoiding a reverence. The number of books on travel told me she obviously had a thing for Europe. On the back wall, she proudly displayed her instruments of kink: bejeweled butt plugs, whips, handcuffs, chains. The sight of them, and other accoutrements, stirred my intrigue and had me feeling nostalgic.

This was her territory and I'd be wise to let her know I accepted that.

"I didn't catch your name?" I asked.

"Galina." She shot me a hard look. "But you will address me as Mistress."

So she wanted to play it that way.

Her vying for domination over us was awe-inspiring, but allowing her the upper hand wasn't going to happen. I scanned the room again as a whisper of intuition told me this wasn't her office after all. Though she'd wanted us to believe it.

My gaze landed back on her, and I tried to get a take on what we were dealing with. A flutter of her eyelashes revealed she wasn't the boss and was used to deferring. Her pouty mouth had quivered when we'd first stepped out of the elevator, and she'd glanced behind her as we'd followed. Someone else was in charge and she seemed fearful of them.

I stepped forward. "Mr. Gardner had no idea I was coming to meet with him." I threw in a smile.

Galina bit her lip, showing a further hint of sub by lowering her gaze. Then her expression settled into a serious frown. She was thinking, "What would the boss do?"

She turned that dark glare on Shay. "There's a fine."

"Of course," Shay replied, contrition in his tone.

"Five million." She delivered it with panache.

Shay's back stiffened. "No way."

"It is in your contract, Mr. Gardner. Or your membership is rescinded."

I applauded her Domme spirit. "Look, this is a misunderstanding."

"Excuse me?" she snapped.

My jaw tightened. "I am a trustworthy source. I understand this community. I won't divulge the existence of this place. You have my word."

"Had you been a member, we could have confirmed this with a background check."

"I need to speak with your director."

She ignored me. "You had an appointment, Mr. Gardner," she chastised. "We expect you to keep it."

"Is this part of the play?" He shoved his hands into his pockets. "It's kinda hot." Shay was trying humor, but it wasn't going to work.

This woman lived the lifestyle and wasn't about to cave for a new member and his interloping friend.

"Our clientele depend on our rules to protect them," she said.

"I get it," I said, moving closer to her. "I'll pay a fine. However, it's not going to be anywhere close to the sum you mentioned."

A knock at the door had us all turning to look at the Somali beauty who'd tried to seduce us in the pool spa. She bowed her head as she approached Galina and handed her a note.

We both got the chance to take another look at the young woman, who avoided our gaze and quickly scurried back to the door. She was right there within reach and it pained me to let her leave. From her appearance I could tell she was barely even close to the age of consent—though it was hard to be certain because she was playing the submissive role so well.

If I asked Galina about her and she became defensive, we could lose the chance to help her.

Galina's gaze rose from the note to meet mine. "Cameron Cole?"

Shit. There went my anonymity. Her security had researched Shay's contacts and my name and photo had obviously come up alongside his.

She pointed at me. "What if this man was with the press, Mr. Gardner, and not from Cole Tea, Inc.?" Her smirk carried a threat.

"You have a good point," Shay agreed. "I'm not comfortable with that fine though."

Her gaze narrowed. "Compromise then. You keep your appointment and reassure us this will never happen again."

Shay nodded. "Of course."

"Mr. Cole will accompany you." She looked triumphant.

I turned to face Shay to reassure him I had his back.

But Shay gave me a look of intrigue, as though he were trying to let me know he wanted more time here to suss out the place. I didn't need him to be a hero.

"We have to go now," I told Galina.

"Oh, the fine still stands." She was back in that defiant pose.

"I'll see you back at the office." Shay gave me a knowing look and then headed out without glancing back.

Stubborn bastard. This had "bad idea" written all over it.

Maybe I'd misread Shay's decision. Maybe this was him taking the hit. I ran through his expression, his body language, his quick exit from the room as I returned my focus to Galina.

With a shrug I admitted defeat and headed out into the hallway. A wave of uncertainty hit me about leaving Shay behind. This had probably been his way of getting the spotlight back on him as he took the fall.

My back stiffened when I recognized the man walking quickly toward me as Lance Merrill. He reminded me of a silver fox with his shiny grey hair and beard. His air of sophistication and his five thousand dollar suit revealed the wealth he'd garnered from his oil baron status.

This man had almost destroyed my friendship with Richard five months ago, when he'd come after Mia back at Chrysalis, having won her at an auction. He'd literally had me hiding her away in London to avoid him. He'd tracked us down and had turned obtaining Mia into a sport. It shouldn't surprise me he was a member.

Later, when the truth had spilled like that oil he was so fond of, I'd ascertained he'd believed I'd somehow threatened his daughter, when in truth it had been me who had talked her off the roof during a suicide attempt. I'd saved her life—which was probably why Lance greeted me with the warmth of an old friend. I'd have been willing to take a detour through hell today in order to avoid him.

His face brightened and he pulled me into a hug. "Cole! How's the family?"

"Fine, yours?" My back stiffened further as I remembered what he'd done to Mia. That man had almost gotten her raped in England.

His expression changed. "Helete and I are divorcing."

"Sorry to hear that."

Lance looked amused. "Thought you hated her?"

I gave him a wry smile, not wanting to get into it. After all, it had been Helete who'd led Lance to believe it was me who'd ruined their daughter after a weekend at Pendulum, and not the senator Helete had tried to protect.

"How long have you been a member?" I asked.

"This place is not what it used to be. You joined?"

"Visiting." I turned to glance at Galina, who was standing a little ways back, apparently waiting to escort me out. If she knew Lance, she was pretending she didn't, which was kind of odd, but I didn't want my brain to focus on the banal.

"Good to see you." He threw a courteous smile at Galina.

There was a crackle in the air and it wasn't coming from me.

I mirrored his friendly sentiment with a forced smile.

"My daughter is doing great. They both are. Thank you, Cameron, for all you did."

"Of course."

He leaned forward and whispered, "Don't join."

His remark proved my gut feeling about this place—it wasn't what it seemed. "It's good to see you, too, Lance," I replied flatly, feeling Galina's stare fixed on us.

One thing I'd never considered a possibility was me relating to the man walking away with a wary step in his gait.

Leaving Shay felt wrong, but I had to trust his decision. I summoned the elevator and stepped in.

Galina followed until she had me backed up against the elevator wall. "You know Mr. Merrill?"

"Old acquaintance."

"That is right. You used to run Chrysalis?"

How the hell did she know that?

"You miss it?" She closed in on me.

"How long have you worked here?"

"This is my life's calling."

"I respect that."

Her alluring perfume wafted over me. I had a sudden urge to reach out and wrap my fingers around her throat because I knew she'd like it. An interesting reaction but then again she'd dug her manicured fingernail into my chest, and if she was going for pain she'd hit her mark.

She let go and with a tilt of her head offered herself. "My office or a dungeon, Mr. Cole?"

Thoughts of Mia yanked me back from the brink. "I'm impressed with your security. Keep up the good work." It sounded obtuse but I wanted her to get the fuck out so I could descend.

"So you are the great Cameron Cole?"

"I've retired."

"Yet you are here?"

"Galina, I have to go."

"Your penchant is what we specialize in. Anything you desire."

"I'm late."

"Isn't your fetish to chase, catch, and fuck?"

A direct blow to my privacy.

Maybe her boss knew me. This was a private desire someone back at Chrysalis had leaked. A submissive perhaps, after I'd chased down willing victims and owned them for more hours then they'd deserved.

I hadn't minded it coming out back then. My badass attitude to dominate had served me well. Richard had found it amusing, mainly because he always boasted he was too lazy to hunt. He wanted them already trained. He wanted them ready to submit and his reluctance to train Mia had started me on an unpredictable path.

The thought of returning to Mia made me want to end this situation in a hurry.

"Tell me what you like?" she purred.

I'd not seen the benefit of giving away my game play. Not then. Not now.

Her palm rested on my chest. "Your pupils are dilated. You want in."

"It's a dark elevator," I replied coldly, knocking her hand away.

"I'm sure your friend is having fun."

"Good for him." I glanced at the DOWN button.

"Luckily, Mr. Gardner is a seasoned submissive, so he will be able to handle the session."

"What is that supposed to mean?"

"He booked an hour with Master Kristoff."

Galina smiled, reading my expression. She knew I'd heard that name before. Kristoff was a psycho and he'd been banned from the west coast clubs because he was into the hard play—whether his client consented or not—all in the name of ego.

This place made Chrysalis look tame.

I clenched my fists when I thought of him touching Shay. "Take me to the room he's in."

"You will have to agree to let the scene play out."

"Have you ever seen one of those exhibitions where they skin a dead body and then display the corpse?"

She stepped back. "Body Works?"

"If you don't take me to Mr. Gardner right now, that's going to be your new look." I forced a smile. "It'll go with your Louis Vuitton."

She showed no reaction, other than a nod, and spun on her heel and swaggered out. I followed her into the heart of the club, moving fast down the sprawling hallway ready to extract Shay from whatever situation he'd gotten himself into. I wasn't about to let one of my friends be subjected to a Dom with no talent or scruples.

Galina led me to the doorway of a room, and I gave her the kind of look that told her she wasn't welcome inside. She walked away unperturbed.

The lights were dimmed in the dark chamber, which had burgundy walls. The temperature felt overly chilled, perhaps to enhance the feeling of vulnerability. The kind of equipment one would expect from a high-end club was present; chrome and wood balanced to showcase a natural aura. Accoutrements decorated the far wall.

Here and there were ancient torture devices, and I fondly recalled having seen some of these replicas back at Chrysalis, though they'd been museum pieces that resembled what you'd find in a London dungeon—and they had never been used. What these devices were doing in here was baffling.

I should be horrified.

They say if you hate someone it's because you see yourself in them. It was a painful reality to bear, especially for my realization that I was envious of Kristoff. He continued to thrive in the scene with no consequences.

The view from the shadows was mesmerizing.

I missed *this*.

Shay was naked and strapped to a Saint Andrew's Cross. He'd been bound in leather restraints to hold him there. Red light shimmied off his sun-kissed torso and rock hard abs, and his erection let me know that he wasn't fighting this…yet.

Any normal man with a conscience would have stormed over to their friend and removed him without question—yet I hesitated, inexplicably taken with the setting. The compulsion to take control was so alluring. Here I was condemning Kristoff, and back in the day, I could've probably been accused of some fairly dangerous acts when I'd dabbled—though I always received consent from my carefully selected partners, intricately mastering the submissive, many of whom had traveled across continents to satisfy their need for a more immersive experience.

I was hit with a raging desire in my soul to prove life was more… so much more than boring routines and my carefully orchestrated restraint for order's sake, which felt more like suppression.

My chase, catch, and fuck addiction had first been explored in France when Danton had shown me the thrill of releasing our captives into the wilderness and then hunting them down in the private forest surrounding the Hillenbrand estate, our secret manor nestled in the countryside where I'd first explored my devilish side.

The darkest night. A raging storm. Rain drenching our clothes and me feeling concern for our sub being out in such a downpour. Danton and I splitting up during the hunt as we competed for the win with the other Doms. Dripping wet from the rain as we followed the hounds through the woodland, burning up with the thrill of searching for the submissive who had bolted from the house. After we caught her we'd bring her back to Hillenbrand and then punish her.

Then the fun would begin all over again.

With the girl's written consent, of course. They left the manor sated, with a healthy bank balance, and we left Hillenbrand fulfilled.

I'd defended myself against this chase as no woman was taken by force; it was with a mutual understanding that the hunt was the most exhilarating rush a Dom could experience. I rarely dabbled in the other events at the club. I wasn't into sharing, or orgies, or taking virgins, I wanted a woman who put up a fight because she knew her worth.

Danton had understood my dark side. Maybe looking back he'd nurtured it too freely, encouraged my need to push the subs in the dungeon to their limit. More profoundly, he'd followed my lead to use these skills to divulge our subject's deeply hidden psychological shadows and then release their pain so that by the end of her session she was reborn.

He'd honored my fantasies and welcomed me into his world with kindness and respect. Danton had introduced me to women who craved what I could give and provided a pathway to peace for all involved.

He'd shown me I belonged on the higher end of the spectrum of decadent. Satisfying these needs at Hillenbrand had enabled me to return to Harvard and complete my studies without any inner turmoil, a yearning so strong it was part of my DNA. Still, those wild years were behind me. Chrysalis was behind me. Enthrall a memory now, and I'd not stepped into a dungeon again until today.

I had Mia to watch over and the kind of responsibilities a man of my standing strove to live up to.

And yet…a familiar titillating feeling soaked into my bones.

In less than the eight minutes it had taken for me to get here, Kristoff had secured Shay to the post and was moving things along at lightning speed. He was slapping Shay's erection, and it looked painful. But from the way his victim pumped his hips, it wasn't hard enough.

There'd seemingly been no time for conversation of what was expected. No exploration of his fears or hard limits, no gentle coaxing to get Shay swooning in subspace. No time to develop trust. It wasn't so much amateur hour but a Dom's impatience to satisfy his own needs with total disregard for the sub's.

Kristoff teased Shay's chin with the handle of a bull whip and it made me flinch. We never had those in the club—they were just too damn harsh. We used a smaller, less agonizing version as befitting a foundation based on ethics. That thing he wielded was going to split Shay's flesh open if he didn't use it right.

Shay's gaze slid over to mine.

Confusion, that's what I read in him, and I knew where it was coming from. He'd always wanted to be dominated by a man and explore his bisexual side. This was meant to be a special event, enthralling even, and he'd probably noticed my disapproving stare.

So many thoughts buzzed around in my brain. Part of me didn't want to sabotage this experience, and part of me felt guilty for having stepped into this room without discussing it with Mia first.

I gestured to Kristoff to step back. He did so, looking intrigued.

I approached Shay, resting my forehead against his to connect with him, wanting to take his extraction from this place nice and slow. I needed him to see I understood what this meant to him, and that I acknowledged the bravery it took for an alpha with a tough guy persona to willingly be put in this position.

"We're leaving," I said.

He squeezed his eyes shut.

"Take a breath," I told him. "I've got this."

Shay's chin rose as if to kiss me, and I pulled back a little as though I hadn't noticed his need to be soothed.

"You can't storm in here and end my session," snapped Kristoff. "Who the fuck are you?"

Turning to look at him, I answered, "Ever had one of those nightmares you just can't wake up from?"

He threw down the whip. "Don't do anything you'll regret."

"Cole," Shay whispered.

It was the way he spoke my name that sent a chill down my spine. In that moment I knew he wanted to stay. With a shake of my head, I conveyed this wasn't an option.

The muscles of Shay's jaw tensed. "You're trespassing into my private session."

My fingers worked the straps of his left wrist, releasing it while ignoring his glare. I moved swiftly over to the other strap, and then knelt to undo the leather binds at his ankles. I stayed ready to fight off Kristoff if he tried to stop me.

Shay had a penchant for finding danger. He dabbled in reckless, having been the first soldier in to rescue my brother in Afghanistan. Still, something else was going on here. He was a great judge of character, and he should have grasped who Kristoff was upon meeting him.

When Shay was free, he immediately grabbed my shoulders, spun me around and shoved me hard against the metal cross. "You don't dictate what I do."

Pain wracked my spine. "Gardner?"

He blinked at me, looked horrified and confused. "You don't get it, do you?"

This wasn't him.

"We're leaving." I delivered the command with such authority he'd have no choice but to obey.

He stormed over to a chair, grabbed his shirt and began to dress. For the first time since I'd known him, I questioned where our friendship could go from here.

"Before you book a session with me," Kristoff snapped at Shay, "Talk to your boyfriend first."

I ignored that retort and headed for the door, sensing Shay was right behind me. He was hopping along as he slid on his overly polished shoes.

By the time we stepped into the elevator I was seething. The doors closed and the floor jolted as we began to descend.

"If you ever touch me like that again…" I let my glare say the rest.

"I'm sorry, okay?"

"What is going on with you?" I clenched my fists in frustration.

Shay covered his face with his hands, and when they slipped down I saw his barely controlled anger. "You're the one who's stalking me."

"I thought we'd ascertained this place is shady?"

"Cole, you're just jealous that the rest of us get to keep this in our lives while you've closed the doors on it."

"That's not it." Though my analytical brain was considering the truth of his accusation.

"You want to know why everyone is on a razor's edge when you're around? It's because we all have to play life by your rules."

"Something is going on. I'm worried about you."

"We've been over this."

"Enlighten me, Shay."

The elevators doors opened and he stormed out.

I followed. "You're going with the Dom I choose and that's the end of it."

He made it to the Lamborghini and spun around. "You don't get to make that decision."

"I admit to being controlling. That's nothing new, Shay." I rested my hand on his shoulder. "But I'm here for you."

He shoved my hand away.

"You want me to fire you. Is that it?"

He stood there looking back at me with pain in his gaze.

"Talk to me."

"I was right there—" He gestured to the club elevator. "And you had to interfere."

"You're making vast inroads into the frontier of assholes," I retorted. "Some might say you're the Neil Armstrong of asinine exploration."

He was staring at me with a mixture of trepidation and confusion. It was the same look he'd given me when I'd first met him.

"I know you want to fuck me, Shay. You're going to have to get over it."

"Are you getting off on taunting me?" He looked astonished. "No, wait, this is that thing you do. You push my buttons until I'm about to implode and then you get me to admit what's really wrong."

"So…what's wrong, Shay," I whispered.

"No, you don't get to manipulate me with your psych shit."

"You love my psych shit." I smiled fondly at him to break the tension.

"You had the chance to get rid of me when I asked months ago." He covered his face with his hands again. "Why do you do this?"

"Then go, Shay, if you're that unhappy." I'd always fought for our friendship, but now it seemed selfish.

"You're so smart, and yet you can't see what's right in front of you."

"Evidently, I need help here."

"I want my first session to be with you, Cam."

Because what Shay had once endured was too painful and still too raw. He wasn't ready to spill his life story.

"I'm…" He couldn't find the words.

I reached out and squeezed his shoulder. "I get it."

"If you refuse me I'm out of your life."

"Don't say that." I shook my head with a smile. "You're my fencing partner. I trust you more than anyone. What if I double your salary?"

"You like to dig the pain out of your subjects," he confessed.

"When I was a therapist, yes." I had gone to extremes and had no regrets.

"I need you to dig out mine."

"What's hurting you?"

"I'm in love with a man I can never have." He shrugged. "I'm obsessed with you Cam. There, I admit it."

"I'm desperately fond of you—"

"Ironically, the one person who's hurting me is the only one who can save me."

"Shay…" I felt like an idiot.

I already knew he'd had a mega crush on me, but these new feelings were far-reaching.

He looked annoyed. "It worked for Richard."

"Richard and I were never—"

"How do you think you got to wield all that power at Chrysalis?" Shay waved his hands in frustration. "Why do you think everyone falls at your feet?"

"I'm intimidating." I needed him to calm down. "And I have a pleasant face, apparently."

He looked like a broken man.

"Stay, please," I said softly. "No matter what."

He reached into his pocket and pulled out the keys to the Lamborghini. "My first session will be with you."

"Oh, is that right?"

"I will have your answer by tomorrow." He gave a nod. "Until then, I'm looking after Mia…unless I'm fired?" He climbed into the Lamborghini and slammed the door.

He drove away through the subterranean structure, brakes squealing—ironically fleeing me in my own damn car.

CHAPTER ELEVEN

MIA

THIS WAS THE FREEDOM I'D MISSED—AND I DIDN'T REGRET bolting from work early without telling anyone.

With my ear buds in and Harry Styles singing "Sign of the Times," I ran through the pouring rain, splashing through puddles. My clothes stuck to my body as I weaved around the pedestrians and sprinted past luxurious shop windows. The tugging between my thighs had me feeling like an orgasm was one leap away, and I laughed through the pleasure shamelessly.

Taking a shortcut, I broke another rule and hurried down an alleyway. And then my mind forced that memory back in…

I'd not be wearing my wedding dress.

Just feet away, a black SUV slammed on its brakes and sent a wave of water over me, drenching me to the skin.

Great. Just great.

Realizing this wasn't a coincidence, my heart thundered in my chest and I went to turn and run…

The driver's door opened. I saw Clint, one of our bodyguards, get out and hurry toward me. "Ms. Lauren," he called out. "Please, get in."

He closed the gap between us and gripped my upper arm, guiding me to the back door of the SUV.

Inside, a burst of freezing cold air conditioning met my wet skin. "I'm dripping on the seat." I met his gaze in the rearview mirror.

"Don't worry about that." Clint looked relieved. "I didn't get the call you were ready to leave work, Miss?"

"That's because I didn't make it." I wiped a few damp strands of hair out of my face.

"Mr. Gardner will not be happy, Ms. Lauren."

"How many times have I told you to call me Mia?"

"Thank you, Ms. Lauren." He navigated the car out of the alleyway.

I slumped back. "I could have walked."

"You can't be on your own." His voice wavered as though considering the consequences he'd have to face for having missed me.

"No one needs to know."

"I have to report daily."

Great, now Shay and Cameron would be on my case all night.

Fighting this was impossible and I had no choice but to ride the rest of the way, staring out at the city I'd had no choice but to live in.

Within minutes we were out of the car and hurrying through The Walker Tower foyer, making a beeline for the elevators.

I spun around. "I'm fine now. Go dry off."

"It's door to door, Ms. Lauren." He threw a warm smile at Mr. Jones, the concierge.

Jones threw a concerned glance at us and called the elevator. I offered an apology for dripping on the tiles.

"The weather turned quickly, Ms. Lauren," said Jones. "How was your day?"

"Fine." If you ignored the fact I looked like a drowned rat. "How about you?"

"Very good." His gaze turned toward the front door and I suspected he was looking for Cameron. "You have a delivery, Ms. Lauren."

"Oh?"

"Yes, a young lady went up to leave a package for you." He glanced over at Clint and added, "She's with Platinum Events."

"Oh, right," I recalled the phone call earlier as I scurried into the elevator. "Stay warm, Mr. Jones."

Clint stepped in behind me and we shot up to the top floor.

I wanted to get inside, strip off, unclip this thing from between my thighs, and climb into a hot bubble bath. I couldn't wait for the heat to soak into my bones.

The doors opened to the foyer that led to our vast place. Just this area alone was the size of my apartment back in L.A. I really was living a privileged life.

When I was halfway down the hall, I noticed a brunette sitting in a chair holding a box on her lap.

"Hello," I greeted her brightly.

She sprung up. "I'm glad I got here before it began raining. It's your wedding cake sample."

I took it from her. "Thank you so much."

"Just let us know what you think, okay?" She walked past me and into the waiting elevator.

I hugged the box to my chest and turned to Clint. "We're kind of keeping it a secret from work."

He glanced at the box. "I've been briefed."

"Good. Well, thank you." I gestured to the door. "I'll be fine from here."

Clint nodded and headed back down the hallway, pausing briefly to watch me rummage around in my handbag for the key. I entered the penthouse, grateful to be home. With a wave of thanks I shut the door behind me and headed down the hallway that led to the kitchen.

I placed the box on the marble island. This would be a good excuse to start a conversation with Cameron about what was going on in his head at the moment.

Caressing my chest, I reassured myself that after today's hot session in his office we were where we needed to be—a perfect symbiotic relationship, perfectly compatible.

A knock at the door ended my daydreaming.

Hurrying back, I hoped it was Cameron, who couldn't be bothered to find his key. He was the only one who could soothe my doubt. Staring at the wall camera, I felt disappointment when I saw a fair-haired man outside. He was holding a box.

"Hello?" I called through the intercom.

"Sorry to bother you," he said, with an English accent. "I have a delivery. Marbella gave you the wrong box. Sorry for any confusion. This is the right one."

"Oh, okay." I let go of the buzzer.

I hesitated, remembering that no one was supposed to enter the place without Shay or Cameron's permission…and they meant *no one*.

I pushed the button again. "Can you leave it by the door, please?"

"I have to pick up the other one. Switch it out. It's for a party that begins in an hour."

I cringed through this hard decision and opened the door.

"Here you go." He handed me the box, which had a white envelope balancing on top. "I need the other one."

"Be right back." I carried the box into the kitchen and placed it on the counter. Picking up the other one, I turned…

He was standing in the kitchen doorway and his smile didn't reach his eyes. "I really appreciate this."

The hairs prickled on my forearms as I handed it to him. "Here it is."

He took the box and I hurriedly stepped back.

"Thank you." His demeanor changed subtlety. "So you live here?"

"I think we're all good." I pointed to the box.

His gaze held mine for a long beat. "Enjoy your cake." He turned on his heel and left.

When the door clicked shut I scurried down the hallway and locked it, a shiver slithering up my spine as I made my way back into the kitchen.

That had to go down as the stupidest thing I'd done all week, though it had a lot of contenders. I wondered if I'd ever be as worldly as Cam.

The envelope probably contained the receipt, I mused. I'd taste the cake later when Cameron got home. It might actually be fun. I lifted the envelope, ripped open the seal and slid out a sheet of paper.

My throat constricted as I stared down at the photo of a dark dungeon with Shay strapped to a Saint Andrew's Cross. Cameron was right in front of him, resting his forehead against Shay's. The photo was time-stamped 12:07, today's date—though I didn't need that clue, as Cameron was wearing the exact same suit and tie from this morning.

It was the way they held each other's gaze...

In a daze, I found myself standing in the bathroom, having no memory of walking the distance from the kitchen to here. I turned and locked the door behind me and slipped down the wall, landing on the cold tile.

With trembling hands, I raised the photo of Cameron and Shay again, studying it closely. Their passion for each other was obvious.

Tears stung my eyes.

Had this envelope even been meant for me?

Chapter Twelve

CAMERON

I POURED MYSELF A GLASS OF CABERNET SAUVIGNON AND WENT looking for Mia.

She'd certainly had an interesting, if not exquisite, day at work and I imagined she'd be looking forward to more of the same.

The bathroom door was locked. "Hey, sweetheart. You in there?"

Water swooshed in the tub, giving away her presence. Pleasant images of her naked and surrounded by bubbles aroused me—a seductive distraction from Shay derailing my day.

"Why is the door locked?"

"Is it?" She called back.

"We're going out for dinner, remember?"

"I remember."

"I poured you a glass of wine." She could have mine.

She didn't answer and a wave of doubt hit me. Perhaps our office scene had been too intense. Or maybe it was Shay prepping her pussy. Either way, talking to her through the door was problematic. I needed to observe her body language and read her expressions.

"I'll have this one then."

Making my way back to the kitchen, I took a sip of wine and was impressed by the delicious, full-bodied flavor. I made a mental note to order a crate.

I set my glass on the central island and pulled the box toward me. After prying open the lid, I stared at the plainly iced cake. I dipped a finger into the frosting and it sunk through the sponge. I brought my creamed finger to my lips.

"Don't!"

With my fingertip a millimeter from my mouth, I frowned at Mia and then lowered my hand, reaching for a napkin. "What's wrong with it?"

She was wrapped in a plush towel and her damp hair tumbled over her shoulders. Her make-up was smudged with that bad girl chic and her eyes were red. My stare moved down to her left ankle and that delicate blue and green hummingbird tattoo I adored.

Mia yanked open her towel to reveal her stunning nakedness and her irresistibly bejeweled pussy, with those chains dangling over her hips. She looked like Mata Hari and that was the point.

She sniffed, breaking the spell.

A wrench of pain hit me at seeing her distraught. Running through all I'd done today, I settled on her finding out I'd ordered her transfer to my floor.

Still unsure, I went with, "You could have taken it off. You know that, right?"

"I like it." She looked down at herself. "It reminds me who I belong to."

Delving into the female brain was not without its risks; she may or may not reveal what was bothering her anytime soon and along the way she'd lay a few distractions like landmines waiting to be stepped on. I usually loved exploring these complex machinations, but not when Mia was hurting.

I took a sip of wine. "Are you angry about moving to my department?"

"Dana knows already."

"I was hoping to discuss it tonight. Go over the details."

"Don't I get a say?"

"I thought we'd already decided on this?"

"She made it sound imminent and not the two weeks we'd agreed upon."

I questioned what was safe to share after the time I'd spent at The Dionysus Club.

"You're not going with my design are you?" she added.

"When it comes out that you and I are romantically involved there will be accusations of favoritism."

"When were you going to tell me you don't like it?"

"I love it."

She looked like she didn't believe me. "I'm always out of the loop."

"Come here." I opened my arms to her.

She didn't move.

"Let's talk about this on the way to Amelie. You love that place."

"Can I say *no*?"

"To dinner?"

"The move to your floor?"

With all the extra security, transferring her was the best decision. I had to make the executive order even if she hated me for a few days. At least she'd be safe.

Her gaze slid over to the cake.

I gave her a warm smile. "That looks nice."

"Didn't buy it."

My intuition screamed that something else was bothering her. "Want to talk about it?"

A loud knock was followed by the sound of a key turning in the lock. Mia pulled up her towel to cover herself.

I turned to see Shay stroll in.

He glared at Mia. "You did it again?"

She glared back. "Maybe."

"Why?" he snapped.

She shrugged.

"Cole," he continued, "may I speak with you privately?"

"Talk to him here," countered Mia.

Shay ignored her.

I gave a shrug as though I didn't care that they were going at it. "What happened?"

"She walked home." Shay tilted his head with the delivery. "Alone."

I stared at Mia, who looked back at us with defiance.

"No, you didn't," I said, though I knew she had.

She looked defeated and for a split second I thought she might burst into tears. My brain cut back to her mood before Shay had stormed in and I remembered something was worrying her. "We'll talk, sweetheart, okay?"

Shay looked astonished. "Mia, that message you left me—"

"The one where I asked you to call me?" She shrugged.

Shay's gaze fell on the cake. "Tell me you didn't have any?"

"What is going on?" I threw my hands up with annoyance.

"I double checked with your wedding planner," said Shay. "This didn't come from them."

"Okay." I forced a smile. "Was there a card?"

"A man delivered it," Mia piped up. "I let him in because he told me his colleague had delivered the wrong one. He wanted to switch it out."

"And you let him in!" yelled Shay.

"Let's keep this civil." I moved over to the island, searching for any sign Mia had tasted the cake. *Hell*, I'd been seconds from tasting it myself.

Mia hurried off down the hallway.

"Hey," I called after her.

Shay came over and studied the box. To the right of the cake was an envelope.

I reached for it and peeked inside. It was empty. My gaze rose to where Mia had stood seconds ago. "I'll talk with her."

"I'll check the security footage." Shay picked up the box. "Maybe it was from your mom?"

"For what occasion?" I turned to look back at him. "Am I paranoid?"

"I encourage you to be."

"Still."

"Look, I want to apologize for today."

"We'll discuss it later," I assured him.

"Have you given it any thought?"

"You asked for the answer tomorrow. Tomorrow it is."

"I appreciate that." He sighed. "Cameron, I need to talk to you about what Mia mentioned in her voice message."

"Later, okay." She was my priority right now and seeing her unhappy was a blow to my heart. I threw a wave at Shay and followed Mia's damp footprints.

She was in our bedroom sitting on the end of the bed, dragging a comb through her tangled locks.

"Go without me to dinner." She watched my reaction. "Shay's better company."

I sat beside her and took the comb, gently easing it through her golden hair. "I'm not angry that you let a stranger in. But I am concerned."

She threw me a sideways glance. "I messed up."

"Anyone else would have done the same."

"You wouldn't." She wiped a stray hair out of her face. "He told me there was another party he had to get to. I didn't want someone to go without their cake."

"You could have left it outside. Told him to stand back."

"Wouldn't that look weird?"

"It's a better look than dead." I waved off my morbid statement. "Dangerous people can be very convincing." I cringed at the thought of making her paranoid. She already had a hard time making friends.

"I assumed it was from Chantelle's wedding company." She eased the comb out of my hand. "Because of that phone call."

"What call?"

"The one I got letting me know a cake sample was on its way.

Some Russian lady—"

"Russian?"

Shay appeared in the doorway. "Sorry to interrupt, but I think this is connected with what happened today. The place we visited."

Yes, buddy. I'm already steps ahead of your annoying ass.

My visit to The Dionysus Club hadn't gone unpunished.

Mia glared at Shay. "This is our private space."

"Hey," I chastised her. "Apologize."

"It's fine," said Shay.

I reached over and lifted Mia's chin. "What was in the envelope?"

She pulled away from me and leapt up. I rose and moved fast to block her from running out.

"Please, let me go," she whispered.

"Leave us." I shot Shay a look to let him know I meant it.

He held my stare for a beat too long and then turned and left. I'd deal with him later. Shay was uneasy from having shared his secret, though the fact I was in a committed relationship should have been enough for him to know the chances of anything happening were slim. Still, this issue was ailing him and if I didn't get to it soon it would become a liability.

I went over and closed the door. "Mia, did someone say something to you about me?"

"Forget it."

"No," I said firmly, "you don't get to change the conversation. Not after that outburst, madam."

"You don't get to talk to me like you are all high and mighty after what you did today."

"I am high and mighty."

It made her chuckle, but then she turned serious again.

"What did I do?"

"Time to confess."

"Mia." My voice carried enough authority to rein her in.

She trembled and fell against me. I peered down at her realizing this was fear and pushing her for more could result in her shutting down. Letting her open up naturally was essential no matter how much I needed answers. There was always another way with her and all paths led to domination.

"I need to remind you…" I said darkly.

Slowly, her gaze rose to mine.

"I'm in charge here." I gestured to the bed. "In here I rule."

Her stare fell away.

I lifted her chin again. "It pleases me that you're still wearing my bondage."

A soft blush covered her chest.

"Good girls get their reward. You know that."

"We're going to be late."

"Yes, we are." I left her standing there and strolled over to a drawer, removing red strips of silk. I threw them onto the bed and held my hand out for her towel. "From the way you're holding yourself I can see you didn't come without me?"

"I obeyed."

"Good girl."

She slipped into subspace as she tugged off her towel and handed it over to me revealing her nakedness, her nipples beaded, her hips decked in glistening diamonds that fell over her sex, the chains revealing her clit like a flower in full bloom.

She fell to her knees and bowed her head.

Ignoring her, I walked over to the chair and unbuttoned my shirt, pulling it off. Then I kicked off my shoes and removed my pants. I kept going until I, too, was naked.

Standing before her again, I gave her a nod of permission that she may take me in her mouth.

She moaned as she drew me all the way to the back of her throat, and my cock hardened further at the lashing of her tongue. I stared up at the frescoed ceiling, considering all the ways I was going to make her obey.

Inside that envelope was something that had frightened her. Mia had never shown jealousy before, but that emotion was what she'd directed at Shay.

A bead of cum appeared on my tip and she lapped at it, smiling up at me, radiating an innocence that I would guard with my life. Returning once more to suckling, she worshipped me with her tongue, running it along my shaft and around my frenulum until I was tensing my jaw.

Who the hell threatened my girl?

I was going to destroy the person who'd instigated this incident with what looked like a harmless gift, and then add The Dionysus Club to the many properties owned by the franchise Chrysalis, Inc. It would belong to Richard by the end of the week.

I peered down at her. "Good girl, Kitten."

Widening her eyes, she held my gaze.

I reached down and ran a thumb over her lips. "That jewelry is on you for a reason. Want to find out what that is?"

She gave an uneasy nod.

"First your punishment." I stepped closer. "Do you need to pee?"

She shook her head no.

Since she'd disobeyed me yet again by leaving work unannounced, I was going to have to use a punishment to get through to her. I used the silk ties to secure her arms, binding them above her head and tying them to the headboard, then using the ones on each of her ankles to spread her legs.

I admired my handiwork and took a minute or two just to survey the beauty who lay naked and vulnerable before me. All this serenity could be gone if I didn't get through to her.

It was time to whip some sense into my submissive...

I strolled over to the dresser, pulled open a drawer and took out my whip. Carrying it back to her I loomed over her naked body and raised it above my head, ready to bring it down on her thigh. I'd start there and work from limb to limb, before focusing between her legs. I'd tease her with it until she was soaking wet.

Though Mia was writhing like a sex-starved siren, a wave of doubt seeped in. All I had to do was bring it down and snap her flesh and she'd be marked with a welt. The pain would solidify this moment and it would send a jolt of warmth through her. A delicious sting. A lesson to obey.

And yet...

Mia was an affliction as well as its cure, she was light personified, a breeze on a hot summer's day, an English garden in spring where rare flowers bloomed, coloring the landscape with their astounding beauty. She was the *only* way to nirvana for me, sharing a love so boundless that a wise man would know well enough to honor her...

I lifted my hand, the whip poised high, frozen in place like a statue. From Mia's furrowed brow she'd caught my hesitation.

Blinking at her, my face held an intense expression as I processed what was happening to me.

Her...that's what had happened.

Never had I loved any woman as much as Mia. It was an inexplicable feeling in many ways. I'd always loved her, perhaps before we'd ever met, but as I explored these emotions they felt like I was descending into madness. She'd quite simply sent me reeling over the edge.

Delirious.

She was ethereal, exquisite in her grace and maddeningly sweet, with her flawless skin and curvaceous figure, the kindest spirit reflecting from her soulful eyes.

Right.

Think fast.

I threw down the whip.

Strolling away to hide my expression of confusion, I went for the tall mahogany framed full-length mirror and dragged it across the carpet so that it faced the bed.

"Time to reveal the meaning of the jewelry."

She worked through that thought and nodded that she was ready.

"The benefit of keeping it on long enough for your master to see it on you is experiencing its significance."

"Are you okay?" she whispered.

"Why wouldn't I be?"

"I'm ready for whatever you think I deserve."

"Good."

Her gaze slid toward the mirror. "What are you going to do?"

I quickly untied her. "Stand here."

I sat on the end of the bed and pulled her down so she was sitting with her back to me on my lap. Her thighs hung over mine, her toes off the floor. This was the position I'd first taken her in back in my Beverly Hills home, and she'd surrendered then too, softening against me and giving me all the control, which had begun the spiral to having her become mine.

"Take me inside you," I ordered.

She let out the softest sigh as she rose a little and positioned my tip to her vagina, then sank all the way down onto me. It felt so damn good and I centered myself so I could pull off this tantric method which would result in her pleasure only.

My needs, my desires, would be delayed because subconsciously she had to see this was all about her.

This is what my lover deserved—not pain but a blinding pleasure that would endure well into the evening, and at the same time allow me to trance out providing the time to process. Pain had always been my thing and yet this epiphany rocked my world—all my emotional pain was gone.

Mia was my remedy.

And I was hers.

Looking at our reflection, I admired the way her pussy shimmered and the beauty of me being buried deep inside her; her wetness glistening to enhance the erotic display. Fulfilling this ancient ritual was imperative if I was going to get her into a deep trance.

"Slow your breathing." I reached around her and, using the mirror to guide my hands, I unhooked one of the chains that was clipped to her labia and proceeded to wrap it around the base of my cock. Then I re-clipped the fine diamond studded chain back to her labia. I did the same with the other diamond links, appreciating the dexterity of having bound us together with an erotic knot. She wasn't going anywhere.

We were enslaved by each other.

"This is not so much a fucking as it is a binding ceremony."

Her muscles clenched around my shaft; though it was challenging to know whether it was trepidation or exultation.

She held my stare in the mirror. "I like it."

She'd prefer this to the sting of a whip. Pure ecstasy would help Mia expose her truth.

I gave a nod. "We will remain like this until the optimal goal is achieved."

"Goal?"

"You will master the art of sensual meditation."

She exhaled in a rush, her nervousness rising.

"Let's begin with the basic Chakra." I tapped her clit and she shuddered with arousal. "I need you to relax. We will remain bound together with me inside you. This will continue well into the night. So relax and give yourself over entirely."

Her eyes met mine in the mirror. "Can I come?"

"As many times as you like, but you must follow the rule."

She waited for me to share it.

"Mia, only I say when the session is over."

Chapter Thirteen

Mia

V AGUELY, I RECALLED CAMERON TELLING ME ABOUT THE seven Chakras.

Something about wheels of energy in the body, something about the first one being called Muladhara, and it was meant to make me feel safe. The next one inspired creativity, though I couldn't recall its name—I'd already drifted into nothingness.

Cameron had explained Number Seven, which was something about enlightenment, and I'd whimpered through my third orgasm wondering how I was going to endure any more. His cock was so hard and deep inside me I felt like I'd been impaled by a sex God. I suppose I had in many ways.

Glancing at our reflection, I could see that I'd soaked him right down to his balls. His eyes were shut and he looked like he was out of it. He reached around my waist and began stroking my clit with very slow circles and I wanted to tell him this wasn't fair. In rebellion, I reached low to massage his balls.

"Hands behind your back, Mia."

I obeyed and my thighs shuddered in rebellion. I tried rhythm squeezing around his cock to hurry him along. It made no difference other than sending me over the edge again, and I whimpered through another climax.

Our reflection could have been considered a modern master-piece—the kind you see in those foreign galleries where people aren't ashamed of their own bodies. The twinkling gems and the way the chains dangled over us both cast an erotic scene. Maybe that was why Cameron had kept his eyelids closed, and me being a newbie, I had stared at my pussy like an amateur.

After what felt like well over an hour had melted away, I was so gone and slightly sore from the multiples, I burst out, "It was a photo."

He opened his eyes. "Of?"

"You and Shay."

"Where?"

"In a dungeon. I think it was taken this morning."

He gave a nod.

Even though I suspected it was true, seeing him acknowledge it hurt.

Cameron wrapped his arms around my shoulders and groaned, his hips pumping as he came hard, shuddering against me, yelling his pleasure and shooting his heat inside me.

Afterwards, he held me for a minute and then worked to release the catches that bound us, lifting me off him. My legs buckled when I tried to stand and he caught me and laid me on the bed.

I curled up onto my side, spent and sated. "What happens now?"

"We sleep."

Snuggling against his warm body, I let out a sigh of happiness. He pulled up a fur throw to cover us, and the dreamy warmth had me drifting off.

Stirring awake, I realized I'd not moved from this position for what must have been hours. I wanted to stay like this forever and savor every second, with my head resting on his chest as it rose and fell, his scent filling my senses. My sex throbbed with a delicious ache from having him inside for such a long time. How he'd lasted so long

I didn't know.

His fingers played with my hair, making my scalp tingle. He opened an eye to look down at me, smiling with contentment. Our love burned brightly, and I knew it would endure for a lifetime if we trusted in each other.

"What do you want for your birthday?" he said, finally breaking the silence.

"I have everything I need."

"That's a trap. I'm not falling for it."

I raised my head off his chest. "Surprise me, then."

"Okay, I'll buy you one of everything."

"Silly."

"We should go somewhere." He inhaled a thoughtful breath. "Paris, maybe? Or Italy?"

"I would love that."

"We could always sneak into *Il Segreto Casa*."

"What is that?"

"A private club, much like Chrysalis, but it's in Milan. You and I have an open invitation. Scarlet's a member."

"Sounds wonderful."

"It's very much like the Carnival of Venice. The masquerade masks are exquisite and the parties are legendary."

"Have you ever been?"

"That's a very personal question."

I tickled him and he squirmed beside me, grabbing my hands and holding them together at the wrists.

"You have." I tried to pull free.

"I might have popped in for a Prosecco." Seeing my confusion, he added, "A glass of wine."

"Do people fuck in front of each other there?"

"Can't remember." He laughed when I slapped his arm. "Hey, that's spousal abuse."

"We're not married yet."

"It won't be long now, and then you'll have to get used to walking with a ball and chain around your ankle."

This was good…he was still talking about us being married, and it gave me the hope I needed.

He played with a lock of my hair. "You've already chained my heart, Mia."

"I love you so much." I broke my gaze from his because his dark stare was too much to bear. "Sometimes it scares me."

"What scares you about it?"

"It's all so perfect."

"Well, as long as you're not scared of me."

Dragging my teeth over my bottom lip, I gave him a look that hinted I still felt some wariness. There was more to Cameron than he'd shown me. I knew this from the tales Scarlet and Richard had shared. Or that rumor that had reached me of his infamous time at Chrysalis with Richard and Shay in tow. That legendary night when he'd revenge-fucked those pretty subs to get over McKenzie's betrayal in the Harrington Suite.

He tipped up my chin. "I scare you?"

"You're unpredictable."

"How so?"

"That thing we just did." I bravely held his gaze. "Being able to hold off for as long as you do. You know so much about everything."

"How did you feel when Shay dressed you in my jewelry?"

"Aroused."

"You begged me to take it darker."

I nodded and rested my head on his chest. "I was aroused for hours."

His hand slid between my thighs and he cupped my sex, his fingers caressing me there, sending ripples of pleasure throughout my body. "I'm a very generous master, Mia. Nothing gives me more pleasure than knowing you're wet because of me."

"That was mild compared to what you really do, right?"

"Small steps." He grabbed my chin with a flash of power and a shudder of arousal flooded through me.

"Go stand in the corner."

I pushed myself up so I was sitting on my knees. "Why?"

"Do it."

Shoving myself off the bed, I padded over to the corner and faced it, my humiliation growing, and yet what followed was a stark arousal I couldn't ignore.

"Hands behind your back, Mia." The sound of his voice revealed he was coming closer.

He reached around and placed the tip of his finger on my clit, caressing it in a circular motion, causing me to lose my balance. I brought my hands around and rested my palms on the wall.

"Your cunt is always wet for me," he whispered in my ear.

"Yes." His circles were agonizingly slow, a cruel tease that would bring me to orgasm and have me standing here riding through it for ages.

How my sex was even ready to go again I couldn't fathom, after our marathon session a few hours ago. Maybe this was why he'd insisted we sleep.

His breath brushed my ear. "The photo of me and Shay showed nothing. Because nothing happened."

"Why am I punished for it?"

"You thrive under punishment." His hand slid down my back. "Stick your ass out for me."

I obeyed, sensing that he'd stepped back from me a little.

He spanked my cheek but it only stung a little. "You're being punished for not showing me the photo the second I walked in."

"Why were you in that dungeon?"

"To get Shay out." He gave an exasperated sigh. "He joined The Dionysus Club."

"Someone is going to try and blackmail you?" I glanced back at him to see if he was going to spank me again.

Instead, his palm caressed my butt with affection. "Go get the photo." He delivered another spank.

I ran over to the dresser and opened the top drawer, rummaging through my underwear until I was able to fish out the picture. I brought it back to him.

He stared down at it with a frown.

"What if they publish it?" I wrapped my arms around his waist.

"That won't happen. They know I could cause a lot of mayhem."

"So why did they give it to me?"

"They want to tear us apart, Mia." He gave a shrug. "They know you're my weak spot."

"That's why we have to trust each other."

"Exactly, and if you ever get something like this again," he said, tapping the photo, "you show it to me."

"I'm sorry."

"I'm sorry it hurt you." He gave me an affectionate smile. "Hungry? I need to feed you. Tame the monster."

My chin crashed onto his bicep. "Starving."

"I've booked us a table at Casa Cole." Seeing my puzzled frown, he added, "I'll cook, okay? Let's stay in."

"Thank you for understanding."

"Forgive and reset. That's the only way we're going to make it, Mia." He reached into the closet and grabbed a T-shirt off a hanger, pulled it on and then grabbed his boxer shorts. "Put your PJs on."

He scooped me into his arms, causing me to squeal with laughter, and then flung me back onto the bed.

I bounced on the mattress. "How do you do that?"

"Do what?"

"Make everything okay?" A few hours ago my world was falling apart and now I was swooning.

"Turn around," his voice rasped.

I rolled onto all fours and raised my butt in the air.

His palm came down hard on it. "I'm half tempted to eat you for dinner."

My solar plexus tingled. "I want you to."

"Hold that thought. I have to make a call."

I pushed myself up and questioned him with a wary stare.

"My mom." He rolled his eyes. "We need to find out who the cake came from. I suspect it was from The Dionysus Club, but I have to be certain."

Quickly, I rummaged around in the dresser and found my silk PJs.

Padding into the bathroom, I washed myself and then tackled my knotted hair. Sex with Cole played havoc on my locks.

"Mia!" Cameron called from the kitchen.

I found him at the central island mixing ingredients in a bowl. "I'm making crêpes," he said. "I'm craving sweets. Sound okay?"

"Sounds perfect." I reached for the bunch of bananas and peeled two off, then found a chopping board and a knife.

The cake was gone.

"What did your mom say?" I sliced into a banana.

"Didn't come from her." He shrugged. "Not really her style. She's more of a cupcake kind of gal." He grinned.

This was him trying to make me feel better, because whoever had sent the cake had meant it as a threat. Perhaps they'd just wanted to prove they could get inside our home.

"Do you think it's poisoned?" I held my breath waiting for his answer.

Cameron poured us two glasses of wine. "Which would make it no different than your cooking." He winked.

"Hey."

It sounded like Shay had taken it off to be tested. Maybe they'd be able to pull fingerprints, too, I mused.

"Grab the cream, please." He stirred the batter in a white marble bowl.

I brought it over to him. "Do you trust me?"

He turned to face me, putting the spatula down. His gaze flitted over to the can of cream in my hand. "This is getting interesting."

"Close your eyes." My gaze narrowed. "Keep them closed."

He squeezed his eyelids shut and smirked. "Okay."

"Put your hands behind your back."

"Like a submissive?"

"Kinda."

"Fuck, no."

"It'll be more fun."

"How about this?" He stretched out his arms along the central island and leaned back a little.

Kneeling before him, I sensed he knew what I was about to do, but either way this was too fun a game not to play. I pulled out the waistband of his boxers and squirted cream down and around his groin.

Then I fell back onto the floor, laughing wildly.

Cameron was staring at his cock with amusement. "Mia," his tone was seductive.

Kneeling before him, I stared into his gorgeous chestnut eyes. "Yes, sir?" My hand reached for his waistband.

He slapped it away.

"I'm going to…you know."

"You'll have to be more specific." His expression was unreadable.

"I'm going to lick it off."

"You'll need permission."

I ran the tip of my tongue along my top lip suggestively. "I can never have enough of you," I said breathlessly.

"How can I refuse? I'm all yours."

I moved in to savor him, mouth wide as my lips wrapped around his formidable shaft, tasting the delicious mixture of cream and Cole and me. *He still tasted of me.*

Chapter Fourteen

Cameron

They say right before an earthquake nature becomes unsettled—detecting the imminent devastation that was to come from invisible ripples. Yet during those quiet seconds before the chaos begins everything feels perfect.

Which was why I was wary of this happiness.

Work was fantastic, my shares were skyrocketing, Mia seemed content again, and I was getting in some big brother time with Henry that'd we'd desperately needed—and for a change I was winning this Sunday afternoon squash match. He had booked a court at the Greenwich Country Club and this time we'd both been able to make it.

Another squash ball came flying at me, though this one struck my chest. I stepped back and drew in a sharp breath. *That hurt.*

If my brother needed any evidence that my skills had gotten rusty this was it, though he didn't laugh. I preferred tennis, but this was Henry's thing and so I'd caved. Spending time with him was worth the assault.

His racket fell to his side. "Why did you stop?"

Because I was hit by a ball going one hundred miles per hour, ass-hole. "Need a second."

"You're getting old, Cole."

"Trying to keep up with you."

He grinned. "Let's take a break."

"Sure." I leaned against the wall and gently rubbed my chest.

"There's something I want to talk with you about." Henry had turned serious.

My gesture told him I was open to it.

"I've always known I have a kinky brother." He smirked. "I saw those books at Uni you didn't bother to hide."

"I admit to a penchant for the extraordinary."

His smile faded. "Tell me you never held Mia captive in a dungeon?"

Those words sliced through the air with a deadly tone. I hesitated and ran through what was safe to share. That sounded more like an accusation of wrongdoing than an inquiry.

"Cam, tell me you didn't."

It was best not to answer the potentially explosive question.

He came at me fast and shoved me back against the wall, pinning me there. "Tell me."

"Henry!"

"Did you keep her locked up at Chrysalis?"

"What brought this on?" I broke free and stepped away from him. "This is not what you think."

"What is it then?"

"Who have you been speaking with?" I ran through all the possible friends who could have betrayed me; so few knew.

"That sounds like a *yes* to me."

"Has Shay been whispering in your ear?"

"I'm protecting my source. I thought you were going to damn well deny it." He closed his eyes and then opened them again to glare at me. "If Richard was dating Mia, how come you ended up with her?"

From his tone I could tell he already knew the answer, so lying would be a bad move. "I trained her as a submissive for him."

"Are you shitting me?"

"I've pulled back on this lifestyle," I said, throwing my racket down.

The match was over.

"Cameron, help me out here. I need to get my head around this."

"Ask me anything you want."

"I'm not even sure if I want that stuff in my head." He pointed at me. "You don't deserve her. If you treat Mia like that ever again you will answer to me."

Running my fingers through my hair, I worked through how best to respond. A week ago I'd stood at the foot of the bed and felt a drastic change come over me. My BDSM days were potentially over, so us having this conversation now felt like old news.

"What kind of psychological damage have you done?"

"Henry, please." I stepped toward him. "Tell me who's been saying these things to you."

He stormed off without looking back.

"We need to talk about this," I called after him.

He paused in the doorway. "I don't know you at all."

I watched him go.

Henry wouldn't know, couldn't know, that I'd saved Richard's life with these techniques. *Hell*, I'd never performed any session without consent.

Other than the one with Mia, but she'd come out of that dungeon a changed woman, free from her past and already blossoming into the remarkable woman she was today. Mia had once believed she'd been the cause of her mother's death, those tainted memories haunting her since she was fourteen.

It had taken hours of study of her childhood in Charlotte, and the kind of precision analysis that Freud himself had utilized, to reveal those subconscious myths. Mia had suppressed the cruelest memories and twisted them into another reality, then shoved what really happened so deep not even she could recall it.

This work was an exact science. What I had done was break her down in order to explore her shadow complex, using her authenticity as a mirror, setting her soul free from the pain that bound her to the past. The sessions had been intense…even cruel. But I'd balanced them with blinding pleasure to ease her through them. Her reward for enduring her captivity was a well-lived life.

She'd willingly stepped into that dungeon. The promise of breaking out of her chrysalis was too tempting an offer; though she'd had no reasonable grasp of the method, I admit to that.

This was my truth, my reality.

Doubt crept in where it had never been before, and watching Henry storm away with disgust, I'd never felt more like a monster than I did now.

Yeah, fucking great, here was that earthquake I'd subconsciously predicted. With my head bowed I made my way out and changed back into my jeans and sweater. I didn't want to stay here one more second.

Maybe I'd even talk to Mia about all this.

Halfway to my Ducati motorbike, my phone rang and Shay's number came up. I froze, staring at the screen hoping he wasn't the one whispering crap about me. No doubt he was holding a grudge after I'd told him I needed more time to decide whether or not to hold a session with him. This last hour had tainted my mood. What had almost become a *yes* to a session had since clicked over to a *fuck, no*.

I answered my phone. "Cole."

"Got the results on the cake," Shay's voice faded in and out. "It wasn't poisoned, but the order did track back to The Dionysus Club."

"Who sent it?"

"We go back to the club together, okay? If that's your plan."

I rolled my eyes. "Who the fuck is messing with me?"

The call dropped and I glared at the screen.

CHAPTER FIFTEEN

MIA

S EE BEYOND THE ORDINARY.
Read the omens. Examine the clues. This is what Cameron had taught me and this is what had brought me to The Chatwal Hotel in the heart of Manhattan's Theatre District.

She was here…McKenzie Carlton, my fiancé's ex-girlfriend, who had inflicted more damage to his psyche than Cameron cared to admit. She'd swept into his life and devastated it.

"Your intuition will direct you," Cameron had once told me. *"You won't always understand at first what it's communicating, but follow it, follow your intuition. Trust that feeling."*

Cameron was spending precious time with Henry, and I couldn't have been happier knowing they were having fun playing squash and letting their hair down. They both needed more times like these.

"Accidently" bumping into McKenzie felt a little intimidating, but it was necessary—and despite Cameron's advice about following my gut, he was going to be greatly displeased when he found out.

If he found out.

Especially when he discovered how I had misappropriated Shay's connections in the investigations department. I'd managed to track down the enemy and had learned she was having lunch here in The Lambs Club. Apparently, Zie lunched here every Sunday with the gallery owner, who displayed Zie's art, selling it from the midtown showroom.

Zie had been hailed as a talented artist by *The Huffington Post*, an article I might have come across when scouring the Internet for gossip on her.

The biggest hurdle had been shaking off Clint, who'd been tasked with tracking my every move. I'd told him I was visiting the hotel to meet a friend and had asked him to wait outside.

With the dress code being sophisticated casual, I'd worn an elegant Ralph Lauren dress and black boots. I'd styled my hair so that it flowed gracefully over my shoulders, with my make-up natural to highlight my youth, therefore giving her a seeming advantage.

Her gaze met mine from across the room, and it seemed to reflect hate. I needed to know why that wedding dress was such an issue for Cam, and something told me I'd find answers here. If Cameron was having second thoughts it could be related to her.

A hunk wearing a tailored dark suit stepped into my line of sight.

I bit the inside of my cheek—Shay looked as sexy as hell, and he was glaring with the same frown he reserved especially for me.

I kept my voice low. "What are you doing here?"

"That's my line, Missy." He turned to glance back at Zie.

Her intrigued stare was on us both now.

"I'm here for lunch." I tried to sound chirpy.

"Right. What are you up to?"

"Nothing."

So Clint wasn't enough now. They'd sent in their big guns—this dangerous alpha to trail me, too. The indignity I felt at being followed by him caused my stomach to churn nervously.

"Firstly," he began, "your bodyguard has been lied to. You're not meeting a friend here because you don't have any."

"That's unfair."

"Secondly, this place isn't on your itinerary."

All I had to do was share what had driven me here, but then Shay could possibly avoid the question altogether and I'd be left with no answers. "I need five minutes with her."

His eyebrows rose. "You arranged to meet?"

"She doesn't know it yet."

"Well, this is a stupid idea."

"I have a right to do whatever I want, whenever I want."

"That's a nice fantasy. Look, you can't keep secrets from me, Mia." Shay reached out and took hold of my arm. "If you use my people I'm going to find out."

His grip was so strong I had no choice but to walk with him out of the restaurant and along the hallway. Feigning I wasn't being manhandled, I smiled at the friendly looking staff.

I finally yanked my arm out of his grip. "This is a private matter." I knew what was coming next, though…some lecture that if it's connected to Cole it has everything to do with Shay.

He pulled me toward a quiet corner. "Spill, Missy."

I huffed out my frustration. "I overheard you."

"What are you talking about?"

"'Bitch, you're not wearing that fucking dress,'" I repeated his words verbatim.

Shay's eyes widened in horror. "You were eavesdropping?"

"I was about to knock, Shay. Invite you to have breakfast with us."

"I'm not that brave, Mia."

I didn't laugh at his joke at the expense of my cooking.

"Why didn't you discuss this with Cole?" he asked.

"I think he's having second thoughts about me." My voice wavered.

He looked amused as he glanced toward the restaurant door. "Sometimes you can be quite intuitive, and yet infuriating."

"What does that mean?"

"You're here. About to face off with the reason those words were spoken—" He grimaced. "Here comes Cruella Deville herself. Act natural. Better yet, play dead." He winked.

"Mia?" Zie's perfume hit me first.

I turned to face her and inhaled sharply. The stunning brunette was arrogant enough to wear ripped skinny jeans and a pink Chanel jacket to a restaurant with a strict dress code. This woman oozed the kind of class that put her in the same league as Cameron.

"Such a sweet face." She reached out and brushed a lock of hair behind my shoulder, her cold fingers caressing my skin. "Such innocence…naïveté, even."

Shay gave her a convincing smile. "How are you, Zie?"

"Just perfect. Would you like to join us?" She gestured back to The Lambs Club. "I'm lunching with a friend. She won't mind."

Shay held his grin. "We were just leaving."

"How's Cam?" She purred his name.

Shay sidled up next to me. "Great, thank you."

"And Chrysalis?" She arched a perfect brow. "I do miss it. Those days were fun, weren't they, Shay? We were all fucking like rabbits back then. Particularly Cameron. That man's appetite for debauchery is insatiable."

"Really?" Shay stared at her with disapproval. "You're actually going there?"

"Well, Mia knows, right? It's not like her man's past is a secret."

"Don't take this the wrong way," he whispered, "but you can be a cunt sometimes."

Her lips twitched. "I can see why Cole likes having you around, Gardner. You can't compete with him."

"That's not true," I said.

She ignored me. "That night where you all swept through the club was legendary. Which I found strange, because you all got up to what I was accused of."

"He was single by then," I snapped in Cam's defense.

I was questioning why I'd thought this meeting was a good idea. Zie's persuasiveness made me realize this was one hell of a mistake.

She smirked. "But does she *know* Cameron's secret?"

"Come on, Mia." Shay grasped my arm.

"Well, that's insightful." She looked triumphant. "His little woman has no idea."

"Know what?" I couldn't leave without hearing it.

"They call *him* a Master of the Dark Arts."

I forced a smile. "I know."

She feigned shock. "So he's shown you his true nature?"

"I've experienced his cage." *Boom, you stupid bitch.*

Her smile turned sinister. "You have no idea do you?"

"This has been nice." Shay pulled me away from her. "But we have to be somewhere."

"Your marriage won't last, Mia. Cameron needs a submissive who can tolerate his fucked-up kink. A woman willing to submit entirely."

"I have," I snapped, walking away.

She laughed mockingly. "His reputation, Mia, have you never questioned it?"

I turned to look back at her.

She lifted her chin. "Ask him about Hillenbrand."

Shay's grip tightened around my arm. "Stop talking to her."

I dug my heels in and continued to face off, calling back, "We're perfect for each other and you can't stand that."

"Ask him about his time with Danton Belfort, Mia," her voice trailed behind us. "Ask him about *that* relationship."

Shay led me through the foyer and out into the cool air.

He opened the passenger door of the SUV idling on the curb. "Get in, please."

I dipped my head as I got in and flopped onto the leather seat, drawing in a sharp breath.

"What is she talking about?"

Of course I knew about Danton. Cameron had taken care of his friend when he'd been dying and Scarlet had been there, too. They'd named Chrysalis in memory of him.

"Back to the penthouse," Shay barked the order to Clint and then gestured that he wanted the glass divider up. "Don't play with a Scorpion and be surprised when it stings you."

"Did he take Zie to Hillenbrand?"

"No. It was way before her. Look, we're not discussing any of this without Cameron present." Shay rested his head back and stared out of the window. His jaw ticked with tension.

"I've seen Cameron's dark side."

He cringed. "Right."

"Don't tell him I went to The Chatwal."

"What were you thinking?"

"Why doesn't he want me to wear a wedding dress?"

"This is why you shouldn't listen in on other people's private conversations."

A wave of depression flooded over me.

Shay held my stare. "How much do you love that dress?"

"It's pretty."

"McKenzie's wedding dress was by the same designer as the one you chose."

"Same dress?"

"No. But it was a Vera Wang. She cut the dress up and scattered it all over his bedroom."

Oh, God.

It all made sense now as I recalled Cameron nudging me to wear something else when we'd visited Marcella's fashion house. He couldn't tell me the reason because he didn't want me to be disappointed after I'd thanked him profusely for the most beautiful dress I'd ever seen.

Relief settled in. "I can find another dress."

Shay's expression turned sympathetic and he pulled out his phone, scrolling through it and then punching a number.

He handed it to me.

I listened to the ringtone and assumed it was Cameron's. "I won't do it again."

Shay chuckled. "I should think not."

With the phone still held to my ear, I swallowed my discomfort.

Shay shrugged. "Maybe you'll get to see Cole's darkest side after all."

Chapter Sixteen

Cameron

WITHIN THE HOUR, I HAD CHANGED OUT OF MY SUIT AND tie and into jeans, a sweater, and a leather jacket, the perfect clothes for speeding down 34th Street on my Ducati.

Weaving around the other vehicles with Shay right behind me, I sped toward The Dionysus Club. This was not how I'd imagined my Monday.

We left our bikes and helmets in the subterranean parking structure and headed up in the elevator. Within a minute, we'd entered the club's main foyer and I was standing before the reception desk facing off with their young employee, the same one who'd tried to seduce us in the pool. She really was stunning and I imagined this was why she was being showcased so much.

"Hello again." She gave me a big smile.

"What's your name?"

"Nadine."

"And you're real name?" She held my stare without answering. "What are they paying you?" I leaned on the desk.

"I'm not at liberty to say."

"Come work for me and I'll double it." Shay hadn't come up with a plan to rescue her so it was down to me. "Ever thought of joining the corporate world? Chance of a lifetime."

Shay was staring at me in astonishment.

"Great decision," I threw in. "Mr. Gardner here will get you situated."

She bulked at my forwardness. "I didn't say yes."

"So providing deep throat blowjobs is your long-term career plan? Do they throw in healthcare?"

She looked stunned.

"Didn't think so." I turned to Shay. "Give her your card."

"Seriously?"

"Yes." I gave him a matter-of-fact smile.

"Shouldn't we interview her?" He was currently conducting a background check but she didn't need to know that.

Her gaze jumped to Shay and then back to me. "Are you serious?"

"Totally."

"Mr. Cole?" It was Galina, and from her expression she didn't look happy about us being back.

"I'm here to talk with your boss," I told her. "Helete Merrill."

The owner of this place and the one person I'd pushed from my consciousness so I could clear it from the debris she'd brought to my world. A once member of Chrysalis and purveyor of anarchy.

I glared at Galina and she relented. "Come this way."

I didn't move. "I'm not here for more bullshit."

"Just to steal our staff?"

"Only the illegal ones. Look, I'm all out of fucks. Tell Helete I want to see her."

She stared past me at Nadine. "Go visit our VIP. See if he needs anything. Make sure his visit is extra special today."

"You're kidding?" I snapped.

She ignored me and threw a smile at the girl. "Now, please."

Nadine hurried off and when she glanced back, her gaze was filled with hope. I threw her a reassuring smile to let her know I was sincere about my offer. Turning back to Galina, I closed the gap between us until her back was pressed to the wall. "Tell me where Helete is or I will make your life a living hell."

"I happen to be a fan of hell, Mr. Cole."

"Don't, not with me." I rested my fisted hand on the wall near her head. "I know it was you who sent that cake to my home. I imagine Helete put you up to it?"

"It was merely to suggest that you keep quiet about our practices." She raised her chin defiantly. "And our employees. They are all of legal age, I can assure you."

"I'm not. Reassured that is."

"Perhaps you should take it up with our legal team?"

"Trust me, I will."

"Get out."

"You know what I'm capable of, Galina."

"Your reputation precedes you, Mr. Cole."

"You're sleeping with Helete's husband. She and Lance are not divorced yet. Your affair could be considered discourteous."

She began to protest, giving herself away and proving my hunch. When I'd bumped into Lance over a week ago, right here where we were standing now, I'd noticed the way he'd glanced at her for a little too long. He'd admitted he was no longer a member of the place and it now made sense why he'd be visiting. He'd always had a thing for Europeans, though he'd obviously grown weary of Helete's fuckery.

Galina's beaded nipples gave her away. Evidently, she liked to be dominated by men who didn't succumb.

"Where's Helete?"

She weakened. "Do not tell her, please."

"You have my word."

"The Belgravia Club. She is giving a talk at a luncheon. You won't get in."

"I'll get in." I headed for the elevator.

"Who told you about us?"

After a push of the DOWN button, I glanced back over at her. "You acted as though you didn't know each other. I hope you're more creative when around Helete?"

"Please." She came toward me. "Helete's dangerous."

"True. And she doesn't mind Lance cheating. She just wants to be there when it happens. She likes watching him fuck other women. You broke her rule. The consequences are going to be dire."

"I am sorry about sending that package." She sounded sincere. "I hope the cake did not upset Ms. Lauren?"

"She doesn't do vanilla." I gave a thin smile. "Lucky for you."

Galina spun around and stormed off.

Shay followed me into the elevator and waited for the doors to close. "Did you really just hire Nadine?"

"Find out her real name."

"What department do you have in mind?"

"Ask about her skill-set and go from there." I made my point with a raised hand. "Typing speed, that kind of thing. Just so we're clear." I withdrew from the elevator and quickly made the distance to my Ducati. I pulled on my helmet and threw a leg over the bike. "One down. One to go."

Shay donned his helmet and lifted the visor. "Your ability to see what's really going on kind of creeps me out."

"I thought that's what you admired about me?" I revved my bike when he went to reply and stared his way.

"What?"

"You didn't tell Henry about Mia's treatment did you? Back at Chrysalis." So few people knew about it, or so I'd believed.

"No, why?"

"He knows."

Shay shrugged. "I'll look into it."

"No, just forget about it."

"Okay. Look, about my session...?"

"You mean the one where I have you pass out with pleasure?"

"Jesus," he mouthed. "Yes, that one."

"Careful what you ask for."

"I'm ready."

I revved the throttle and grinned. "Can't hear you."

He broke into a smile and mouthed, "Fuck you."

I slid my visor down and sped out of there.

The Belgravia Club sat regally on Park Avenue.

Shay and I parked our bikes and then took a few minutes to strategize as we assessed our entry point. We used Google to garner more details that might come in useful.

It was the kind of place you couldn't buy yourself into. Becoming a member was by recommendation only by an established member.

Scanning through the photos showing the crisp clean décor of white and gold amidst airy spaces, I gathered you'd also need a healthy salary to enjoy the amenities. The restaurant boasted New York's finest chefs, a luxury spa, and a walled garden where the ladies could enjoy exclusive presentations and then mingle afterward while sipping champagne.

We were buzzed through the club's front door.

I approached the reception desk. "We're tech support, here for the garden lecture. Apparently, you're having issues with the visual effects? We'll sort it out and be out of your hair in no time."

The pretty brunette studied her ledger like she had the authority to decide on the guests' comings and goings. She pointed to a map to indicate where Helete was. I tried not to blink in surprise.

We strode down a long, well-lit hallway that had spacious windows and a tall ceiling. The scent of lavender filled the air, and under different circumstances I might have enjoyed my visit to a place so architecturally pleasing.

The Dionysus Club had been firmly placed in my rearview and if Helete hadn't sent that threat I wouldn't have come here.

"I'll stand guard," said Shay.

I gave a nod of agreement and left him just outside.

A lattice ceiling covered the garden and at the end stood a podium at which Helete was regaling an audience of at least sixty well-dressed women. She'd dressed for the event in an elegant red pant suit and her Tiffany necklace shimmered brightly. Her French accent was disarmingly beautiful and her lovely sharp features were nature's way of throwing off her victims. She was the equivalent of a praying mantis that bit off her mate's head right after sex. No apology, just doing what came naturally. She reminded me of Zie.

I caught the drift of her presentation—it was about sexual freedom and in no way required any technical additions to her monologue on feminist rights. The receptionist wouldn't know this and had swallowed my lie.

I rarely twisted the truth like this. I was a man of my word and had integrity, but getting into an only woman's club was, as Galina had pointed out, rather impossible.

My specialty.

Shay had uncovered Helete and Zie's friendship and discovered they were hanging out a lot together. I focused my attention on Helete and our impending conversation. I remained at the back of the garden and folded my arms, waiting.

Watching.

Seething.

With a fixed expression that didn't reveal whether or not I'd rattled her, Helete offered an apology to her audience and then excused herself. She walked toward me with the swagger of a woman who'd tasted power. Not just off Lance's senatorial cock but in her own right. She owned those members of Dionysus, knowing enough of their secrets to burn each and every man's life to the ground.

I turned and made my way to the far corner.

She emanated iciness as she approached. "How did you get in?"

"I was about to ask you the same," I retorted.

"Did you enjoy your visit to my club?"

"Most enlightening."

"I heard a rumor that Shay fucked you in the ass in the pool spa."

"I think that's your fantasy." I glanced behind me to check how much time I had. "Or Zie's." I wanted her to know I knew they were close.

"Did you enjoy the cake?"

"What was the meaning behind that?"

"You trespassed into my club. I reciprocated by invading the very center of your home. You should chat with Mia about security. She let my man right in."

"It's so hard to get through to someone who is so damn pure."

"How are the wedding plans?"

"Fine."

She gave me a thin smile. "Apparently, Mia's wedding dress is by Vera Wang? Wasn't Zie going to wear the same designer? How sweet. When Mia's walking up the aisle on your wedding day, your mind will be filled with memories of Zie."

This woman had spies everywhere.

I shrugged, not caring to reveal Mia was considering another designer. Or maybe, just maybe, she'd wear her Vera Wang because she loved it so much.

"You're making a big mistake." She glanced behind her. "You still have time to win her back."

"Are you referring to Zie?"

"Of course."

"Or I could just slice through my wrists with the closest sharp object and bleed out, which would be a lot more fun."

"Do you want me to put in a good word for you?"

"Instead of the cake I had Mia for dessert. Now that was worth waiting for."

"If someone seems too good to be true—"

"If you ever again come within fifty miles of me, or Mia, or anyone I care about, I'll—"

"Threatening me?"

"I'm putting you in your place, Helete."

"What were you doing at my club?"

"I was there for Shay," I answered, exasperated. "I had no idea you were connected to the place."

"We have more members then you ever did at Chrysalis."

"Fantastic." I went with sarcasm because the other option was to look like I gave a shit. "Listen," I glanced back the way I'd come, "can we please settle our differences?"

She gave me a look of mistrust.

"Shay's considering remaining a member of your club," I added. "He seems to like it." And he would see his wish fulfilled to return to her club over my dead body.

"We'd love to have him back." She smirked.

"You're going through a lot, Helete. I bumped into Lance and he told me about your divorce. I'm sorry, I really am."

"Where did you see him?"

Okay, this was getting into the give-the-bastard's-affair-away territory, if I wasn't careful. I waved it off. "This is hard on both of you."

"He's just concerned his political career will take a hit."

"I didn't get that from him."

Her expression softened. "Can I tell you what my greatest joy is?"

"Sure."

"Of all your enemies, I'm the most dangerous."

A slither of dread ran up my spine because we both knew she was threatening Mia.

Shay hurried toward us with a look that warned me their security had been alerted.

Helete looked triumphant. "Your boyfriend is here."

I gave a nod to let Shay know I was ready to leave. "Just remember, Helete, I'm the man who's willing to burn down the house around me."

"After what you gave up to make Cole Tea relevant again? I doubt it." She flashed me a wicked smile. "I know exactly how to bring you to your knees."

"I don't kneel to anyone."

"None of us can understand what you see in such a classless girl. No breeding. No education to speak of—"

"Mia is everything you could never be."

"She won't hold your attention."

"Why do you even try, Helete?"

"We know what you're really like, Cameron. Deep down you need your dark fix. A sweet, innocent girl is fun for cleansing the palate, but you'll be drawn back to who you are."

"Trust me." I leaned in to whisper. "You have no idea how dark I go."

Leaving Helete standing there, I walked out of the garden and made my way back down the hallway.

When Shay and I left the building we were met with a downpour. I raised my face to the sky and let the rain droplets cleanse me.

CHAPTER SEVENTEEN

MIA

I'D BECOME FOND OF MY LITTLE CUBICAL IN A WAY. HAVING MADE it a fun space to hang out in, some part of me would miss working in marketing. One thing was for sure, I wasn't going to miss Dana.

My favorite Elie Tahari black dress and boots were perfect attire for today. I was going to get to see what would become my new office, and I wanted to prove to Sue I belonged there.

At least my worry over the wedding dress was over. Cameron had arranged for my best friend Bailey to fly out from L.A. so we could shop for another one. He'd given me a long weekend off and had promised to make it amazing, having booked us tickets to see *Hamilton*, and also arranging for us to have a few golf lessons at the Sagamore Resort. Cole was going to fly her out on a private plane. Bailey had freaked out when I'd called to tell her.

There'd been no more mention of any threats, which helped me relax again. I was due to begin my internship at Marcella's in a week.

"They found my file." Kelly leaned on the side of my cubicle. "I made it just in time to submit it."

I swiveled in my chair to face her. "That's great news."

"Thank you for helping me retrieve it."

"Of course." I was now out of the running to win. I couldn't submit my design knowing she needed the money.

She perked up. "When do you think we'll hear about the winner?"

"Not sure."

Kelly looked at the box in the corner, ready for next week. "I'll come visit you."

"I'd like that."

"I'm so happy you got your promotion."

I was trying to think of the best response when her expression changed.

Her gaze was following someone. "Is that Henry Cole?"

I shot up and peered over the top. Sure enough, it was Cameron's gorgeous older brother and he was sporting a five o'clock shadow, looking cute in jeans and a blue blazer.

Ducking down again, I wondered if I had time to text him.

"Hey, Mia!" He peered over the top of my cubicle with the biggest smile, throwing a wave to Kelly who'd scurried off back to her desk.

Kelly cupped her hand over her mouth in surprised awe.

I tried to ignore her cute reaction and widened my eyes as a warning signal to Henry.

"Hey, there, Mr. Cole. How are you?"

"Since when have you called me that?"

"I'm keeping things on the down low," I whispered.

"Okay, then. Got a minute?"

"Pretend you don't know me as well as you do," I added quickly.

He looked amused. "I'll be in the coffee room."

After thirty seconds I headed after him.

Inside the deserted coffee room, Henry was pouring two cups of Cole tea. This was a cozy room with a plush seating area, a walled TV, and a ton of free snacks.

"No sugar, right?" He turned to glance at me.

"Yes, thank you." I hurried over to him and wrapped my arms around his back, resting my forehead against him. "It's so good to see you. We're still keeping it a secret that I know the Cole brothers."

He turned and held me tighter, and I saw something reflected in his eyes that looked like sympathy. "Whose idea was this?"

"Mine." I took a mug from him and made my way over to the comfy couch.

"I'm sorry to pull you from your desk, Mia."

"It's fine."

"How are the wedding arrangements coming?"

"We have a planner so she's helping with all the big decisions. And I'm getting a new dress."

"What was wrong with the other one?"

"It didn't work out."

"Why?"

I chewed my lip. "It's nothing."

He sipped his tea. "Any doubts?"

"About Cameron? No, of course not."

"How did you two meet again?"

"I was Richard's secretary."

"Cameron hired you?"

"Yes."

"What happened with you and Richard? I mean, he's a great guy. Any girl would have considered him a catch."

"He's wonderful." I took a gulp and it burned my throat. I tried to smile despite the discomfort. "Things didn't work out."

"You don't mind me asking?"

"Of course not." After all, it was Henry.

With his vet status he had superhero written all over him, and it was thanks to Henry his parents even approved of me. During one turbulent dinner with his mom and dad, Henry had announced to everyone at the table that he owed me for helping him leave behind his reclusive life in Big Bear.

I couldn't be prouder to see him content, spending time with his family and friends and not hidden away in the forest. I loved the fact Cameron had his brother back in his life.

"How are things with Cam?" he asked.

"Wonderful. He's busy, but happy."

"How's the transition from L.A. been?"

"Cameron's doing great—"

"I meant you, Mia."

"I miss L.A. a little."

"Can I be frank?" He waited on my nod and then added, "You're still very young. You've not even turned twenty-two."

"It's my birthday soon."

He took a sip of tea. "Is he good to you?"

"Very kind. And generous."

"Has he seemed different lately?"

"Yes," I answered in a rush. "At first, I was worried it was something to do with me or Shay—"

"Shay?"

"Yes, Shay's been missing things…" I left it at that, not wanting to spill the *kind* of things.

Cameron had shared with me that Shay wanted a session and he'd not decided if this was even possible. I got it. Cameron had changed my life with his remarkable insight and I would never be so selfish as to prevent another person from having that experience.

"Has Cam treated you differently lately?" Henry scratched his head.

"Can you be specific?"

"He has a penchant for pain, as well dishing it out. This concerns me." He took my hand. "You don't mind me asking?"

"I'm glad we can talk about it."

"Has he ever…" He seemed to mull over his next words. "Upset you?"

Cole was mercurial but that didn't mean I had to tell Henry. Anyway, as his brother he knew him well. "We're both passionate about…you know."

"Does he ever strike you?"

I leaned back a little. "Not in the way you think."

Henry was digging into the most private details of our relationship. I missed our lifestyle and considering how fulfilling that aspect of our sex life was, this abstention from all things S&M made me miss it more.

"When did you first discover Cole was into BDSM?"

I hated where this conversation was going but I sensed Henry needed reassurance and shutting this questioning down would worsen his doubts. "Richard told me."

"I'm just trying to understand." His expression was one of concern.

"Henry, I like it."

"Right, of course."

"Cameron's pulled back a little…"

He covered his face with his palms. "He made you believe this is normal."

"It is."

"Mia, were you into the scene before you met him?"

I hesitated as I realized where he was going with this.

"Is it true you were *given* to Richard?" he added.

"I met him at work."

"The truth, please, Mia."

"It seems strange on the surface, but it really was part of a therapeutic process."

He looked horrified.

"I'm very happy, Henry."

"This is not easy for me to say."

I gave him the kindest smile. "Go on."

"Mia, I don't think you're the right one for my brother."

My tea whooshed in the cup, spilling onto my hand, and Henry pulled a tissue from a box resting on the table. He mopped the tea off my fingers.

A young man burst through the door and stopped when he saw us. "Bad time?"

Henry threw him a polite smile. "Give us five minutes, please."

Vaguely, I was aware of my coworker turning around and leaving. My heart was beating too fast and my mind was a swirl of confusing thoughts. Why was Henry saying these things?

Henry's focus snapped back to me. "One more question."

Dread made my spine feel like it had been wrapped in ice.

"Mia, did Cameron lock you in a dungeon back at Chrysalis and refuse to let you leave?"

I didn't reply, but that was as good as admitting this was true.

"*Jesus,*" he muttered under his breath.

"He helped me."

Henry shot to his feet. "It's a good thing he's no longer practicing medicine."

"But…he really helps people."

"I believe you have Stockholm Syndrome." He loomed close.

I arched my neck to look up at his towering height. "No. Cameron—"

"I want you to know we'll take good care of you. Give you anything you need. We would of course ask you to sign a confidentially agreement. You must promise not to reveal this trait of Cameron's. Not to the press, or your friends, and not even to your family."

My flesh chilled. "Cameron's my family."

He reached into his jacket pocket and removed an envelope. "Here's some cash. This way Cameron won't be able to track your credit card. I've booked you into The Manhattan at Times Square Hotel."

I set my mug on the table. "Henry, I'm happy. Cameron is my one true love."

"He knew exactly what he was doing. I doubt he ever meant for things to go this far."

"This far?"

"Having to marry you."

This isn't happening.

He was way off. Henry was accusing me of having developed a psychological alliance with Cameron as a survival strategy during my captivity.

Captivity…

I tried to see through the fog of these accusations.

He gestured to my wristwatch. "Take it off."

Telling him about the GPS in my Rolex had been a terrible mistake. It had been a private moment shared between us at The Mandarin, during the staff gala. I'd laughed, raising my expensive watch to show him my gift and sharing how endearing I found Cameron's unconventional way of protecting me. "I won't."

"Don't make me, Mia." His eyes told me he was ready to carry out the threat.

I unclipped the wristband and drew in a sharp breath of fear as I placed it on the coffee table. This was my lifeline.

"Well done. A car is waiting for you." Henry held out his hand for me. "Cameron won't be told where you are. This is for the best."

"I need to call him." I needed to get back to my desk so I could.

"Security is waiting to escort you out." He glanced toward the door.

"I have to get my handbag." Reaching for a magazine I hugged it to my chest as though that alone could protect me. This clue might be my one chance to let Cameron know what had happened here. I let the *Time Magazine* slip from my grip and fall by my feet. I kicked it beneath the table.

Henry didn't see what I'd done because he was too busy texting. "I'll have your handbag delivered to your room."

"You don't think I'm good enough is that it?" I spat the words. "Is that what this is?"

"I've always been your advocate. You know that. Yes, this family has been through a lot. We nearly lost this company. And yes, one more scandal and it will be over for Cole Tea. But this is not our problem, it's yours."

"Cameron loves me."

"Then why are you in a cubicle hidden away with no one knowing who you are?"

"I wanted it this way."

"He made you believe that."

"No, he didn't. Anyway, I'm moving to his floor." I pointed in the direction of my cubicle. "Did you see the box?"

He gave me a sympathetic smile. "So he could manipulate you even more?

"Everything I've done has been for your family. For Cole Tea."

"It's my time to protect *you*. Do what's right for you. Truth is Mia, you're just too damn nice for people like us."

"But my birthday's next week." I swallowed hard. "We're going to Italy."

"No, you're not."

"Please, Henry. I don't want to go."

"A birthday is a good time to start anew." He gestured to the door. "Let's make this as painless as possible."

Chapter Eighteen

CAMERON

THAT MEETING WITH HELETE A WEEK AGO AT THE BELGRAVIA Club had fast-forwarded my plan to blow Mia's cover. Still, my reasoning was sound—should anyone threaten her here our employees would sound the alarm. I'd have my entire staff aware of her VIP status.

She'd get over it.

I strolled out of my office and approached Sue's desk. "I want to order a bouquet of roses. Twenty-four. Make them red."

"I love red roses."

"Make that pink. To be delivered to marketing."

"Sure." Sue reached for a post-it note. "Who shall I send them to?"

"Ms. Mia Lauren."

Her gaze rose to meet mine.

"Write this, 'I'm excited about your move to my department. I'll make it as fun and interesting as possible. There'll be perks.'"

"Sir, that might be construed as…" She raised her hand. "Not that it's my place to say."

"It's not. Add 'I love you, sweetheart.'"

Her face went pale and I assumed she was running over all her interactions with Mia.

"Right away, please."

The lift pinged and Shay stepped out. He was carrying an envelope.

He threw a smile at Sue and followed me back into the office. "How's it going?"

"It's going good. How's your day?"

"Busy." He shut the door behind him and came over to lay the envelope on my desk. "Is Mia up here?" He looked back toward where her new office was going to be situated, a corner space that was almost as grand as mine.

"She's probably at her cubicle." I gestured for him to sit. "Why?"

He gave a shrug and shot off a message to her. "She was in a meeting this morning and didn't check in with me afterwards."

"You have her checking in with you?"

"Every hour."

I ran that through my bastard brain and liked it.

Shay took the seat in front of my desk. "Here's that report you asked for on The Dionysus Club." He read my confusion. "Nadine."

"Oh, good." I was distracted by the thought of Sue ordering the correct flowers after she'd looked dazed. When my attention returned to Shay he was back on his phone.

"Locate her," Shay snapped the order to one of his men and shoved his phone away.

I rounded my desk and sat on the edge. "What did you find on Nadine?"

"It's all in there."

I opened the file he'd brought in and stared at the photo of the girl with the perfect complexion. She'd been photographed coming out of the club. "Can you summarize?"

"Her name's not Nadine. I'll start there. It's Omani. She's eighteen. I know, I know, she looks younger. You were right to be concerned."

"Eighteen is still very young for a club like that."

"She was born in Somalia and emigrated here on a work visa. Her parents are dead. No previous work history. Her passport is stamped with frequent visits to Paris. Helete's from there, so that's no surprise."

"How did you look at her passport?"

"I have a friend in Immigration." He shrugged. "So, no boyfriend. Seems loyal to Helete." He sat forward. "The guy who delivered the cake is Helete's chauffeur."

"She didn't hide that very well." I let out a frustrated sigh. "I want to stop this before it gets out of hand. A cake is one thing. A photo of you and me in a compromising situation is completely different."

"Well, she doesn't need the money. So it's not blackmail."

"True."

Shay leaned forward. "What rattled her about my visit? It doesn't make any sense."

I picked up a pen and played with it, letting my subconscious handle this one. "Omani."

"Pretty name."

"This all started with her."

"She is a looker." He shrugged. "I mean, supermodel material. Maybe Helete's in love with her."

"I think you might be right."

"Are we still going to offer her a job?"

"Go back to the club. Book a massage. Not the happy ending kind." I smirked at him. "Find out what Omani wants." I threw the pen down. "Let's hear it from her without the pressure of her dominatrixes bearing down on her."

"I'm going to have Helete followed. I need to find out what kind of hold she has on Omani."

A knock at the door broke our focus.

"Not now." I turned back to Shay.

Henry burst in through the door. My gaze held his and my spine flinched with the memory of him shoving me hard against that squash court wall.

What the hell did he want now?

Shay's gaze was fixed on me in disbelief.

I gestured to Sue, who was standing at the doorway having followed him in. "A tray of tea, please. Oh, and Sue, why don't you take off early today. Say, around three."

"Really?" She blushed with happiness and hurried out before I could change my mind.

Henry made himself comfortable on the couch. "What a perfect boss."

Shay's voice softened, "I'll track down Mia."

"Try not to alarm her."

"Of course." Shay headed for the door.

I pushed up from my seat and walked over to join Henry. "How are you?"

He stared at me and then his attention fell on Shay as he left. "Alarm Mia?"

After Henry's attack, I refused to fill him in on the details. "It's nothing."

"Didn't look like nothing. Shay and I go way back. Don't take advantage of his commitment to this family."

I sat on the arm of a chair. "Never. So, how are you?"

"I'm okay."

"It's nice to get a visit from you," I lied. I couldn't forget about the bruises he'd left on me.

My evil side wished he'd stayed in Big Bear.

His stare held mine. "I'm ready to come back. Maybe take this office." His gaze roamed the room. "You once told me this would be waiting for me."

I had promised him that Dad's corner office on the highest floor of this high-rise could be his. But that was before I'd sacrificed everything to turn this company around and ensure a smooth transition when Dad left—and way before I'd given myself completely to this place for months, being the catalyst that caused the business to skyrocket to success.

My back stiffened. "Why now?"

He narrowed his gaze on me and it looked like an accusation. "Why not?"

I slid down onto the chair and rested my feet on the coffee table. "In what capacity?"

"CEO, of course."

CHAPTER NINETEEN

MIA

I'D ARRIVED AT THE MANHATTAN AT TIMES SQUARE HOTEL, WITH two bodyguards accompanying me.

My stomach twisted from the stress of it all and I had to concentrate on not throwing up in front of the other guests who passed us with a cursory glance. This place was a maze. So many turns this way and that until I had lost all sense of direction.

From the way I was led through the sprawling hallways, I knew this had been pre-planned by Henry. They had a keycard all ready for Room 617.

"I need you to call my boyfriend," I pleaded.

"Keep your voice down," snapped the one who'd introduced himself as Barret, his Cockney accent causing my arms to prickle.

Inside the room, I spun around to get my bearings. There was a plush couch I'd never sit on and a corner writing desk I'd never use. The windows overlooked Times Square. Down there, people were having fun. Down there, people were free to come and go.

"Help yourself to the mini-bar." Barret pointed to a cupboard. "If you want anything, just ask."

"I want to go home."

"Okay, sure," he said, following his friend to the door. "Once this is all sorted out." He closed the door behind him.

I knew Henry had my best interests at heart. On the surface my relationship looked complicated, but it was everything I'd been afraid to dream of having. Cameron was all I wanted, all I needed. I could hardly breathe knowing how panicked he'd be.

Peering through the peephole in the door, I saw Barret standing guard.

I hurried over to the phone on the writing desk, my adrenaline spiking as I picked up the receiver.

There was no dial tone. They'd disconnected it. Though I didn't care about ordering room service, I needed to get a message to Cameron or Shay to let them know what was going on.

I pulled open the door. "Can you please call someone for me?"

He gave me a sympathetic smile. "There's to be no calls, Miss."

"People will worry. You don't want the police involved do you? It will be better for you in the long run."

He crooked his neck. "Go back in the room."

Several hours later, cabin fever had set in and I couldn't stand to watch one more second of TV. I'd paced back and forth so many times I knew there were snacks in the other room, a coffeemaker that looked like you needed a PhD to use it, and enough alcohol to help the hours pass if I gave up.

I got the bright idea of convincing my prison keepers to buy me a bathing suit from one of the hotel stores so I could go for a swim. But they'd chosen the wrong size. My bathing suit pinched around my thighs a little, but I didn't care. I'd studied the hotel brochure and read they had a bar at the pool. That meant they had a phone.

All I had to do was wait for one of them to be distracted.

The area had a welcoming vibe, with a large swimming pool and a bar tucked away in the corner. Guests were grabbing drinks and relaxing on colorful loungers positioned all around the pool. Barret sat on one of them and watched me like a hawk with no shame.

The water felt warm and refreshing. After completing three laps, I went for it—lifting myself out at the deep end and trotting over to the bar with the kind of nonchalance I hoped wouldn't draw attention.

"What can I get you?" The spiked-haired bartender asked me.

"I need to use your phone, please?"

"Sure." He glanced over my shoulder and I turned to see Barret making headway toward me.

I looked back at the bartender, my expression tense. "I'm in a huge hurry," I said.

"Sure."

He pushed the phone within reach and I grabbed the receiver, dialing quickly.

"Cole." Cameron's voice sent a shiver of hope through me.

I drew in a breath to speak, and a hand grabbed the receiver and slammed it down, ending the call. I turned to see Barret glaring at me with disapproval.

"I'll order food for you," he said, plainly for the barman's sake.

"Hey, I can do that." The barman smiled at us both. "You go relax. I'll come over with the menus."

Barret's fingers wrapped around my arm and he led me away. Of course, I could have made a scene, screamed that I was being held against my will, but what kind of trouble would Henry be in if that came out? It would be a potential scandal and I knew Cameron would want me to remain calm.

All those times I had evaded his security, I really had been naïve. But never had I suspected the threat would come from inside the Cole family. Although Henry had suffered from PTSD, he'd never displayed any symptoms of mental illness before and I chose to believe he was merely trying to protect me.

Then I saw her…

Walking in with several other well-dressed women was Helete Merrill, the stunning French brunette whose husband had been the catalyst for both me and Cameron fleeing the States. She wasn't dressed for lounging, though, so I had to grab my chance.

"I'm going to swim again," I told Barret.

He held my gaze. "If you speak to anyone you're going to be staying in that room indefinitely." He leaned forward to make his point.

I rested my hands on my hips. "I know."

His smile didn't reach his eyes. "I'll be watching."

It was hard to hate Henry, but right now I wanted to kick him in the balls. I rounded the pool and then made a beeline toward the corner.

"Helete!"

I caught her attention, as well as the other two elegant-looking women with her. They all looked my way.

"It's me, Mia."

"Oh, hello." She smiled. "This is Annette White and Terri Banfield. I'm considering buying this hotel. What do you think?" She didn't wait for me to answer. "This is Mia Lauren, Cameron Cole's fiancée."

From their impressed reactions I knew that they'd heard of him.

Arms came around my waist and gripped me tightly. I didn't need to look to see it was Barret. "Tell Cameron I'm here."

Helete's frown deepened as she watched Barret leading me out of the pool area. Surely she could see how upset I was?

Glancing back, my heart skipped a beat when I saw Helete raising her phone to her ear. She was calling Cameron. I just knew it.

Chapter Twenty

Cameron

Stealing some private time in the Cole Tower gym, which was tucked away in the basement, I pounded the treadmill, staring at my fixed expression in the mirror. I had Oasis blaring from my ear buds, singing "Don't Look Back in Anger," and I briefly mused over what a shame it was that those two feuding Gallagher brothers couldn't give us another album.

Brothers…such a special bond and one I had never taken for granted, even as a child. It had been Henry who had watched over me when I'd turned up at our private boarding school with nothing but a suitcase and a head full of fear. Even at five years old I'd had a sense of how cruel this world could be. Those moments when I'd pass Henry in the hallway or searched him out in the library, I was assured of his caring nature, his patience and his wisdom. We'd always been close, so close that when he'd been captured in Afghanistan I'd flown around the world to help rescue him.

Those days would haunt me, mainly for the fact I'd spent hours trying to extract intelligence from him after his rescue—the kind of Intel needed to sway an attack on American soil. It had been Henry's recent recovery that had soothed my guilt and given me the courage to reconnect on an emotional level.

Yet someone had fractured that bond. It pained me that it had become fragile again.

It had been Mia who had coaxed Henry out of hiding and now he was ready to take on the world. Our desire to serve had been developed at a young age.

I punched a button on the panel and the belt sped up. I sprinted to refocus.

Mia was my light in the darkness. Every moment away from her felt like an assault on my senses, but I was consoled by the knowledge that she would soon be moving closer.

Five months ago, I'd run a successful psychiatric clinic in Beverly Hills while secretly managing my renowned empire, Chrysalis. At the time, I couldn't have imagined any other kind of life. But I'd made *this* work. I'd accomplished everything I had set out to do and I still had big plans for Cole Tea. A strategy was evolving to open offices in Seattle and Florida, as well as England. We were going global.

And I was the man to take us there.

Remaining stone-faced, I'd listened as Henry had delivered his monologue, explaining why he felt ready for this role. Dad would be ecstatic about Henry taking on more responsibility at the company and Mom would revel in the idea of her oldest thriving in the business he'd been destined for. I wasn't opposed to Henry coming back full-time; I just needed to work out where he would be an asset.

With both adrenaline and uncertainty surging through my veins, I slowed the treadmill into "cool down" mode. I needed time to think carefully about his request and work out what was best for everyone.

My ego was going to have to take a hit; I could feel fate's fist flying toward me.

After a hot shower, I redressed in my Brioni suit and dragged a comb through my hair. When I opened the gym door to leave, Sue was standing there.

She was holding her scheduler and exhaled in a rush of excitement saying, "The New York Times wants to send over John Mayberry. He's going to write a piece on you. I told them Friday, around ten?"

No. I'd be in Italy then with Mia. Sue didn't need to know that.

"Let me think about it." Having my personal life investigated by some ambitious journalist wasn't the most appealing idea.

"You have a 2:00 P.M. with the head of marketing. Dana wants to discuss personnel. Alex from accounting had to reschedule. His dog needs to go to the vet—"

"What kind of dog?"

"I don't know."

"Can you ask?"

"Why?"

I threw her a questioning glance. I liked Sue, but she leaned toward psychopathic, which was why I'd hired her in the first place. It helped having the human equivalent of a Rottweiler guarding my office.

I was only half-listening to her because Shay was standing at the end of the hallway, and his fraught expression shot a wave of concern through me.

I headed toward him. "What's wrong?"

"Give us a minute," Shay told Sue. He waited until she was out of earshot before speaking to me. "Mia is not at her desk in marketing."

A chill ran up my spine. "Maybe she went to get a coffee?"

"We're checking the cameras."

I reached into my pocket and brought out my phone to call her. The ringtone immediately sent me to voicemail. "Mia, call me right now. This is urgent."

"I left her a voicemail, too."

"We're idiots." I shook my head at the ridiculousness of our panic. "Her GPS?"

"What GPS?"

"The one I forgot to tell you about." I brought up the app on my phone. "She's in the staff coffee room." I breathed a sigh of relief as I flipped my phone around to let Shay see the blip.

"My people checked the coffee room."

"Well, this says she's in there." I needed to get out of this suffocating basement and to Mia's floor. I needed to see she was safe. "Check the cameras anyway."

"On it." Shay followed me into the elevator.

We quickly arrived in marketing and I stormed toward the break room.

It was empty.

This made no sense.

There, on the coffee table, was Mia's Rolex.

A shiver of dread owned my body as I picked it up and clutched it in my palm. This was definitely hers. My gaze searched the room for any sign of a struggle or anything that might stand out. Nothing was out of place...though there was a magazine on the floor.

I picked it up and turned it over. It was a copy of *Time Magazine*, the cover featuring Lt. Colonel Warren who was being hailed as a war hero after his tour of duty in Afghanistan. There was an entire exposé on him and I made a mental note to tell Henry; he'd probably like to read it.

For now, I threw it back onto the stack and turned to face Shay. "This is her watch."

"Let's stay calm."

I tucked her watch into my pocket.

"Cole—"

"Why would she take it off?"

"Maybe this is her rebelling again?" He shrugged. "She's moving to your department soon."

I focused on reducing the cortisol levels surging in my brain, stress hormones that were ruining my ability to let clarity guide me. I ran over Mia's mood this morning. She was excited about the move.

"Something's wrong."

"You know what she's like," Shay countered.

I pressed my hand to my chest to sense her.

"She's done this before, ran off without her security detail."

"Whoever took her knew she was being tracked through her watch."

"Let's not go there yet."

I hurried out and weaved my way around the staff cubicles. The other employees hardly gave us a passing glance.

I walked into Mia's cubicle and wondered how she'd tolerated this small space. My sweet Mia had sacrificed comfort for the sake of making her own way. A chill washed over me when I saw her handbag resting in the bottom of the desk drawer. I knelt to rummage through it, looking for anything that might give away her location.

Inside I found her wallet with her credit card—she only needed one because it had no limit—and some cash. So the chance of her having left the building was unlikely. Maybe she'd absentmindedly removed her watch?

That's bullshit and you know it.

I glanced over at the opposite cubicle, at the young woman staring at us. Her expression reflected recognition and I recalled where we'd met. This was Mia's friend, who I had asked to dance. Kelly, I think?

She was probably wondering why her boss was inside her colleague's workspace going through her things.

Shay lingered near the cubicle. "We'll find her."

"Contact the authorities," I snapped.

"I'll make the call." Shay's eyes widened as he read something off his phone.

"What?"

He raised his hand as though trying to get me to remain calm.

Despite his fuckup and the agonizing fact Mia was in danger, I held back on my rage.

"Speak to me, Shay."

"She went out the back via the stairs. She was escorted by two men."

"Tell me they work for you?"

Shay gave a wary shake of his head. "She got into a Mercedes-Benz SUV."

We stormed toward the emergency staircase and took them two at a time, retracing her steps and searching the ground in case Mia had dropped a clue. Behind me, Shay was ordering his men to run the number plate caught on the CCTV.

When we finally reached the bottom, I approached the middle-aged guard at the rear door and breathlessly asked, "Did you see a young blonde woman leave here with two men?"

He shook his head. "Just started my shift."

I processed the convenience of such a fact and wondered if the men had waited for the staff to change.

Outside on the pavement, I stared left and right hoping to see a trace of some sort.

Shay caught up with me, also out of breath. "From the footage, Mia's not struggling. She doesn't seem distressed."

"Witnesses?"

"Just the security footage."

"How did they get in without being seen? How did they get access?"

"I'm trying to figure that out."

"Have their faces run through your recognition software."

His phone pinged and he stared at the screen. "Okay, we have something. Lance Merrill owns a Mercedes-Benz SUV. Not sure if he actually owns the one on the camera, though."

"Where does he live?"

"I'm on it."

I inhaled a calming breath and centered myself. Mia needed me at my best.

"Get me a car."

Shay nodded. "I can do that."

"Find out Helete's address, too." I stared down at the number that appeared on my phone and answered, "Cole."

The line went dead.

I swiped my ID badge to get back into Cole Tower and redialed that number.

"Welcome to The Manhattan," answered a chirpy male. "Pool bar."

I stopped halfway down the hall so the call wouldn't drop. "Did you just see a blonde woman in her early twenties at the bar? Her name's Mia." I played my hunch.

"This is the pool bar."

"You wouldn't miss her."

"I'm afraid there are a lot of women here who match that description, sir." He sounded terse. "If you give me a room number I'll put you through."

"Someone just called me from your bar," I said, through clenched teeth. "They used your phone. They could be in trouble." Saying any more could endanger her more.

"I'm not at liberty to reveal the names of guests."

The fucker hung up on me.

"Find out if Mia's at The Manhattan at Times Square," I barked at Shay. Then I sprinted toward the elevator.

We made it back to her floor and returned to Mia's desk, searching for anything that might help…a business card, a contact in her notebook, a name on her scheduler.

"Get IT to crack her code." I pointed to her desktop.

We were again being watched by Kelly, and with her cubicle being just opposite she might have caught some unusual behavior or even noticed the appearance of a stranger.

I left Mia's cubicle and approached her. "How are you?" I softened my tone so as not to alarm her.

"I had fun the other night." She smiled coyly. "We danced."

"That's right." I ignored the stares from her colleagues. "Did Mia Lauren say where she was going?"

She glanced past me. "She won't be long. She's a hard worker."

"She's not in any trouble." I forced a friendly smile to reassure her. "Have you seen any strangers around here?"

"No."

"I have Lance's address." Shay grabbed my attention. "I have a car waiting."

"One second." I thanked Kelly and returned to the staff break room.

I reached for the *Time Magazine* issue again, resting where I'd left it on the coffee table. Anyone considerate enough to take a break and sit on that couch would have picked it up before, surely? The room was just too organized and neat for any of my employees not to have taken a second to deal with such a small detail. Or maybe I was over-thinking it?

There was a knock.

I turned my gaze toward the door and saw Kelly. "Hey, everything okay?"

"It's probably nothing."

She looked nervous, so I gestured for her to come in farther.

"Mr. Cole stopped off to say hello to Mia." She glanced at Shay. "I think they met at the charity ball."

Of course, Kelly would think that's when Mia and Henry had first met.

"My brother?"

She gave a nod. "I think Mia followed him toward the coffee room. She never came back."

Processing my brother's motivation and the fact it was Henry, I should have been willing to consider this possibility…

My thoughts circled back around as I realized Henry could very well have known about the tracker in Mia's wristwatch, as she would have entrusted him enough to share this possessive foible of mine. She'd have made it a joke and Henry would have probably hidden his disapproval.

Only Henry could have gotten men into the building without raising suspicion. My gaze returned to the *Time Magazine* and the man on the cover wearing combat gear. Had Henry warned her she was leaving with him at that very moment with no chance of returning to her desk, and her quick thinking had left us this vague clue? Did Henry suspect I was having a negative influence over Mia?

This all verged on irrationality.

Then again, this was my *thing;* seeing beyond the ordinary, peering into the looking-glass and acknowledging even the rawest truth, not falling victim to the obvious. My bruised back, along with my ego, was proof that Henry was pissed off at me.

Shay thanked Kelly and waited for her to leave before turning back to face me. "Henry is the last person who would do something like this."

My gaze rose from the magazine as my thoughts swirled with the idea that Henry was involved. His violence during our squash match revealed how vexed he was about my lifestyle. His recent desire to take over Cole Tea now left a bitter taste in my mouth.

Shay looked adamant. "What's his motive?"

"Call The Manhattan. Find out if there's a reservation in Henry's name."

"I know you're stressed. I feel like crap, too. That's why we need to be methodical."

"If they refuse to answer, send one of your men. Tell him to visit the pool. Tell him to book a room in the hotel, if necessary, so he gets access. Better still, get him into the security hub and have him scan the footage for today."

Shay's stare held mine and he gave a nod of resignation. "I'll call Henry."

"Let me talk with him. Just find out where he is."

"Okay."

"Someone got to him," I whispered.

CHAPTER TWENTY-ONE

MIA

BACK IN ROOM 617, MY HEART RACED AS I REPLAYED HELETE'S reaction to what I'd told her. She'd reached for her phone so there was a real chance she'd called Cameron. She knew how to contact him so it wasn't such a stretch to believe.

Barret was in the kitchen, talking on the phone to someone about the wisdom of moving me somewhere new. This time I was going to make a scene. Damn the consequences.

What was Henry's grand plan in all this? Did he really believe he'd make me fall out of love with Cameron?

There was a bottle of wine chilling in a silver cooler on the coffee table and beside it rested a plate of chocolate-covered strawberries. A welcoming treat for the guests who had just checked in and actually wanted to be here.

No doubt poor Shay was taking the flak for me being gone. Too many hours had passed and I never went this long without messaging either of them. I now respected their reasoning for keeping tabs on me.

From outside the room a woman's voice rose and, hearing her

French accent, I knew it was Helete. I jumped to my feet realizing she'd found me. Of all my heroes she was the last person I'd have guessed would come save me. There was a loud knock.

Barret flew out of the kitchen and hurried over to the door. "Sit," he snapped.

I remained standing and watched him open the door, keeping it ajar.

He peered out. "Mia's taking a nap."

"I'm awake now," I blurted out, earning his annoyed glare.

Helete wasn't put off by his gruff attitude. "Let me in then."

I breathed a sigh of relief when Helete shoved open the door and stepped inside.

She threw Barret a wary look and then smiled my way. "Mia, how are you?"

I tried to ignore the threat of that man behind her. "Fine."

She surveyed the room. "Is Cameron here?"

I wanted to ask if she'd called him, but the way Barret was looming, I refused to put her in danger.

"Aren't you going to offer me a drink?" She smirked.

"Of course." I reached for the bottle in the cooler.

"I'm sorry," said Barret. "We're on our way out. Mia will call you later, okay?"

Helete studied him and then turned back to face me as though summing us both up. The tension crackled and I tried to force a smile to protect her from Barret. With my wide-eyed stare, I did my best to convey he was dangerous without compromising her.

"Later will be fine." Helete reached into her handbag. "I totally understand. Let me give you my new number."

"Thank you." I went with her decision.

Helete's gaze held mine and she offered a knowing smile. "We'll do lunch."

"I'd like that, Mrs. Merrill."

Helete spun around and pressed a black device against Barret's arm. He froze and then began shaking and wailing as he slumped to his knees. When he fell forward with his face crushed against the carpet, I gawked in horror at the unconscious man.

She slipped the taser back into her Louis Vuitton. "Come on." Helete grabbed my wrist and pulled me toward the door and we stepped over Barret as we hurried out.

The door slammed behind us.

We navigated a maze of hallways until we found the elevator. Both of us glancing back to see if Barret had awoken and was following us.

When we made it to the foyer, I almost cried with relief.

Helete guided me toward a long black limousine and we leaped into the back. She slammed the door behind us and I collapsed on the seat. The scent of expensive leather and rich perfume drenched the air. If I ever smelled this combination again I'd slip into a panic. It was absorbed into my consciousness.

That was going down as one of the scariest things I'd ever experienced.

"Thank you, Helete." I squeezed back tears.

We'd joined another woman in the back, her striking high cheekbones and bobbed haircut reminiscent of an Eastern European style; she looked chic and sophisticated.

I glanced over at Helete waiting for her to introduce us.

"I tasered the bastard," she told her friend. "Well, that was a bit of excitement, wasn't it?" Helete pulled on her seatbelt and twisted to address her chauffeur. "Our next destination. Quick as you can."

I turned around in my seat toward him. "Can you drop me off at Cole Tower, please?"

Helete unscrewed the cap to a bottle of water. "Here you go." She handed it to me.

"Thank you." I quenched my thirst. "Do you think he's okay?"

Helete shrugged. "What was all that about, Mia? He looked dangerous."

"It's a huge misunderstanding." I wiped a trickle of water from my mouth. "I'm so relieved to be out of there."

"Of course you are." Helete looked horrified. "Cameron must be worried."

"Did you call him?"

She thinned her lips. "For all I knew, Mia, you were having an affair."

"Of course I wasn't. I asked you to call him."

"Still," she said, sounding terse, "it was lucky I was there. You interrupted my meeting."

Sorry for interrupting you with my kidnapping, I mused darkly.

It really had been a coincidence she was there, though. I let that thought settle and rested my head back, staring out at the passing scenery. "I'm glad I'm out of that room."

"What is going on?" she asked.

"I was checked in by a well-meaning person."

"Against your will?"

As my gaze met Helete's, my concern for Henry's reputation grew. I only hoped all this didn't cause a real problem between him and Cameron. They'd made such great progress mending their rift.

"Terrible state of affairs." Helete shook her head, frowning.

The woman beside me seemed to be taking all this in with no reaction to the fact her friend had just rescued me and tasered a man. We'd left him laying on the floor out cold and even though I hated Barret, I hoped he was okay. They both seemed unfazed that we'd just fled a kidnapping.

I offered her my hand. "I'm Mia."

She looked down at it but didn't shake it. "I know."

To hide my embarrassment, I went to take another gulp of water—holding the bottle suspended at my mouth as I recalled where I'd heard her voice—she sounded exactly like the woman who'd phoned about that cake.

My vision blurred as I tried to focus on the door. "I need to get out."

"He might be following us." Helete swapped a wary glance with her friend.

The hairs on my forearms prickled. "Please, can you let me out?"

Helete turned to her friend. "Everything set?"

The Russian gave a nod and refocused her gaze at the passing traffic.

"Can I borrow your phone?" I reached out for it, insistent.

"Mia, you're safe now." I think those words came from Helete…

Resting back, I tried to think how I was going to explain this without implicating Henry, as a wave of vertigo swept over me. The adrenaline rush was wearing off and tiredness was soaking into my bones. My gaze fell onto the bottle as it slipped from my grasp, and I tried to apologize for spilling the water, but I couldn't form the words…

Dizziness.

Lying down on the seat with my face squished against the cold leather, I brought up my legs with a heavy breath, vaguely recalling the last time I'd seen Helete had been in England at that exclusive men's club, Oberon Grove.

Richard had taken me there, and we'd been separated because those were the rules. Haunting memories caused a swell of panic to rise inside me as I remembered that Richard had been sedated after someone had drugged his drink.

A stark realization chilled my flesh.

It had been the woman sitting opposite me, who was staring at her phone as though I wasn't slipping into unconscious.

"Cameron," his name left my lips.

Chapter Twenty-Two

Cameron

The stale scent of coffee caught in my throat and brought a wave of nausea as I read the text on my phone.

Shay peered over my shoulder. "Henry?"

"He's in my office." I shoved my cell in my pocket and stormed out of the coffee room, heading for the elevator.

The ride to the top floor was a blur.

Sue was on the phone behind her desk—she met my gaze and I gestured that whatever she wanted could wait.

"Your brother's in there—" She warned.

I stopped just shy of the door before entering and drew in a steadying breath to calm my growing rage, this rising hurt. I couldn't shake the feeling that it was him.

My own brother.

My fists tightened as I resisted the urge to storm on in and grab Henry and shake the truth out of him. Any violence on my part would prove his point and would escalate this—I needed to find out as quickly as possible where she was.

If indeed it was Henry.

"Cam," Shay whispered, as he clutched the back of my jacket. "Do you think he's having some kind of breakdown?"

"No." I met Shay's gaze. "Someone misled him about what we do at Chrysalis."

"Who?"

I hesitated to answer because I still wasn't sure; though I had a good idea.

To the uninitiated it could even seem barbaric. I knew this but what followed those intense sessions that I lorded over were lives changed irrevocably for the better, the pain of their pasts extinguished and the creation of a fissure in the blackness that allowed light to seep in. Keeping the process a secret had been essential to protect those exclusive clients I'd chosen for such a controversial therapy; as well as protecting myself.

"Talk to me." Shay's grip tightened.

I shrugged off his hand. "There's no time."

Henry was sitting on the leather couch, leaning back with one leg casually resting on a knee, a glass of liquor in his hand. With a quick glance over at my drinks cabinet I could see the cork was out of the brandy. He'd poured me one and set it on the table…the drink of choice to calm the nerves.

Was it for me or him?

"Can you give us some privacy, please?" Henry stared past me.

Shay had followed me in. I gave a nod to reassure him I could handle Henry. Shay hesitated and then turned and headed out.

I heard the door shut behind me as I approached Henry. "Thank you." I picked up the glass and sat in the leather chair opposite. Casually, I stretched my legs out on the coffee table and crossed my feet at the ankles.

He arched a brow of disapproval at my casual posture.

The brandy burned my throat as I swallowed the heat. "Good choice."

"How are you?" he asked softly.

"It's been an interesting day."

"In what way?"

"Each is different. You'll see."

"So you're in agreement to me coming on as CEO?"

My stare fell on the book of Rorschach tests and Henry followed my gaze. Setting his drink down, he picked up the book and opened it, looking intrigued.

"Mom bought it for me."

"Maybe she thought it would help you transition away from psychiatry?" He grinned at the banality of that statement.

I watched the way he stared down at one of the inkblots designed to measure thought disorder. It wasn't used for therapy now. Mom wouldn't know that.

Henry turned the book around and showed me an inkblot. "What do you see?"

"You."

"Really?"

"Yes. What do you see?"

He glanced at it. "Nothing."

"Well, that's good."

"But not for you? What do you really see, then?"

My gaze rose to meet his. "Someone who thinks he is doing the right thing but in reality is causing more harm than good...a misguided man."

Henry smiled. "Impressive."

"Why, Henry?"

He studied me carefully, perhaps considering how I'd worked it out so quickly. "You know why," came his terse reply.

This man had fought the most sinister of enemies. His moral compass was flawless, but striving for perfection had been his downfall. He'd never forgiven himself for being captured, as he'd cared more about his men than himself. Their lives had been risked when they'd gone in on that rescue mission. He rarely talked about what the enemy had done to him during his imprisonment in that godforsaken desert. This was him looking out for Mia now...and as much as I hated what he'd done, I could never hate him.

I pulled my legs off the table and leaned forward, my elbows on my knees. "Talk to me."

"Mia's safe."

"She'll be scared. Do you want that?"

"She's in good hands."

"There are only two kinds of people who'd be willing to assist you with this reckless endeavor. Professionals qualified to issue a 5150 to restrain a patient or trained mercenaries. You went with the latter."

"They're old friends. They respect my predicament."

"And now more people are dragged into our private business."

"They don't know the specifics."

"I'm your brother."

He threw the book onto the table. "Mia's young and easily influenced. You took advantage."

"I protect her." Though right now that reasoning was skewed.

"You locked her up in a dungeon?" He looked horrified as he tried to grasp the concept.

Such a method would appear barbaric to the uninitiated. Those few selected clients would have ended their lives otherwise because their mental pain was too great to bear. And then there was my dearest friend, who I'd almost lost to suicide; with him gone my life would have been unbearable.

Richard's car spinning out of control, dust flying around its wheels as he braked hard, causing it to skid toward the cliff's edge.

Fishtailing...

"Have some." Henry pointed to my glass.

"I've had enough."

"How can I get through to you?"

"Was it Zie who got to you?" I swallowed hard at the agonizing sensation of time standing still, each second an unbearable eternity. "It was Zie." I exhaled sharply. "You know how much she hates me."

He reached for his drink and took a gulp. "Once Mia receives a professional psychological assessment—"

"You're violating her rights." I leaned back. "She would have called me by now. Something doesn't add up."

"We need to make sure this is what she wants."

The stab of betrayal went straight to my heart. "You mean me?"

"You sat before the Board of Psychiatry and lied—"

"No, I didn't, Henry."

"That's right…you had Mia lie for you."

"No, I would never—"

"I was there, Cam."

It would have appeared that way. Mia had come up with a scheme to reassure the medical board she was in a relationship with me and, therefore, any intimacy would be considered normal. She'd saved me that day. My reputation. My career. My life in so many ways. All the while Richard had watched on as his girlfriend had testified that she was mine, and I wondered if he'd known then he was losing her to me. The mess I'd left behind was burning a hole in my happiness.

"Henry, you know me. I would never hurt her."

"I thought I did. Chrysalis is worse than I ever imagined."

"Don't listen to Zie."

"She didn't hold back."

"You believe her?"

"You were in a position of authority. You abused it."

"McKenzie wants to ruin things between us, Henry. Surely you see this?" I gave him a frustrated look. "She wants to bring down the company and pull me down with it. Helete probably put her up to it."

"What goes on in that place?"

"Everyone at that club wants to be there."

"And Richard?" Henry took another sip. "What did you do to him?"

"Any further discussion would be a breach of privacy."

"You have double standards."

"What do you know, Henry? Tell me what you think this is?"

"Mia had a psychological block that was compromising her life." He waved his hand. "I know her conventional therapy failed so you took it upon yourself—"

"She was in deep psychological pain. She believed she was the cause of her mom's death." And who the hell had leaked this detail to Zie? A Dom? A Sub? I was going to find out and have them banned from the damn planet.

"So…a reasonable excuse to fuck her, then?"

I drew in an exasperated breath. "I know you care for Mia."

"Someone needs to watch out for her."

"So what's the plan?"

"Once we establish she's not influenced by—"

"What was her life before me, Henry?" My back tensed. "I'm good to her. I spoil her. You see that. I love her."

"She had a good life in L.A. Friends who cared about her. A good job before you lured her away."

"She worked two jobs with only one day off a week. She had dreams that would never be realized—"

"You don't know that."

"I know this world. I know my brother has betrayed me."

"What happened in that dungeon? What did you do to her?"

"The environment was controlled. Yes, it was intense but she failed other forms of therapy. I explored her shadow complex, found the root cause of her pain. I discovered the truth and had her experience a personal revelation so she'd recall what happened and use this knowledge to heal. I gave her the potential to find freedom and live a full and happy life. I set her free."

"Free?"

"She's free, Henry."

Or she was, until you locked her up.

He flinched. "All that from time spent in a dungeon with you."

"What brought this on?" I glared at him. "I mean, really?"

He held my gaze. "This has nothing to do with Afghanistan."

"I believe you."

"I don't want to hurt you, Cam. You must see it from my perspective."

"You have one hour."

"For what?"

"Bring her home." I leaned forward again to give him a pleading look. "She's my fiancée. I love her. I will protect her at any cost."

"Even bringing down the business?"

"You're the one who has put us in jeopardy."

Henry pushed himself to his feet. "This will be over by tonight. Mia will be given the chance to make up her own mind without pressure. What I'm doing is a good thing."

I rose to meet his height. "One hour."

"We both want the same thing. The best for her."

A knock at the door dragged my attention away and I answered gruffly, "What is it?"

Shay stepped in. "I have a car waiting for that other place." He'd found Mia.

I turned to face Henry again. "This is about you getting what you want—"

I barely dodged a blow to my jaw as he struck out at me.

"This isn't about that and you know it," he yelled.

"The Manhattan?" I watched his expression change to one of confusion as he wondered how I could possibly know.

In this traffic, I could be there in twenty minutes or less.

With that one accusation I'd weakened his resolve and gotten the answer. I headed for the door and left Henry standing there, possibly regretting his decision to implement his radical plan.

The cruelest thought tore through my brain that he had a point.

Maybe Mia did deserve a better man.

Before I made it to the door, I spun around—Henry could make a call to have his men move Mia.

"You're coming with us," I told him.

CHAPTER TWENTY-THREE

MIA

AWAKING TO A LOW THRUM THAT SOUNDED FAMILIAR, feeling an unnatural warmth that made my limbs heavy, I opened my eyes and tried to focus.

I was still wearing my Elie Tahari dress, but it was creased. Someone had removed my boots. Kicking off the sheet, I strained to remember how I'd gotten into this small, bare room. I reached out for the glass of water on the side table, and then yanked my hand back. Drinking anything else was a bad idea. There came a jolt of weight-lessness—or maybe it was just my head.

I pulled myself up and sat on the edge of the bed, running through what I remembered while caressing my temples to ease the ache.

Helete had rescued me from The Manhattan, and there'd been an-other woman with her. Her accent had been familiar. I needed these foggy thoughts to clear. Fighting through waves of dizziness, I reached for my boots and pulled them on.

I staggered over to the window and pulled up the blind, staring out in horror at the puffs of white clouds below.

How long had I been out?

Where the hell was I going?

I looked back at the glass of water. It reminded me of when Cameron had flown me to London on his private jet. He'd left a glass of water beside me then, and also when we'd flown from L.A. to New York, proving his consideration. It was something he did. He knew I'd wake up thirsty.

And I was so, so thirsty.

Comforted that this was his plane, I opened the door and peered out at the row of empty cream leather seats. Stepping out of the cabin, a wave of nausea hit me when I recognized the Russian. She was sitting alone.

My gaze swept toward the cockpit and I wondered if Helete was in there. When I looked back at the Russian her stare was fixed on me.

Needing to pee, I turned and shoved open the door to the small restroom. I hated going to the bathroom on planes—my fear of turbulence was even worse. I balanced as best I could, as my thoughts drifted to the fact I was meant to be at work.

I was meant to be anywhere but here.

After relieving the pain in my bladder, I faced my reflection in the mirror, seeing my eyes filled with fright, my smudged mascara and messy hair.

A fist slammed the door. "You have ten seconds to get out of there." The Russian slipped into her native tongue.

Gripped by fear, I couldn't move.

Chapter Twenty-Four

CAMERON

"WHAT DO YOU MEAN?" SNAPPED HENRY. "WHERE IS she?"

We'd made it to The Manhattan in record time and despite Henry's man telling us she wasn't here, I scoured each room anyway. I was on a knife's edge as I tried to read the truth from everyone around me. My concern for Mia was eating me alive.

After I rejoined Shay, Henry, and one of his men in the sitting room, Shay threw me a look and a gesture indicating I should remain calm. He knew I had a thin veil of restraint left and needed answers fast.

Henry's man sat on the couch with an icepack against his forehead and a useless explanation.

"Barret, what the hell is going on?" Henry sat beside him on the couch and his voice cracked with frustration. "Where's Mia?"

Barret refused to look at him. "I hit my head when I fell."

"Did she attack you?" asked Shay with an eerie calmness. He knew tempers were close to flaring.

"We saw this woman by the pool," Barret explained. "Mia

approached her and spoke with her for a few seconds. I couldn't stop it. She asked her to call you—" He looked straight at me.

"She needed my help." I let that sink in for Henry.

"That woman followed us back." Barret glared at each one of us. "The bitch tasered me. How are those things even legal?"

"What did she look like?" snapped Henry.

"I don't know," said Barret. "She sounded French."

I scrolled through Google images on my phone until I found a photo of Helete at a fundraiser and then showed it to him. "This her?"

"Yeah."

I glanced at Shay. "Helete."

"So Mia's fine, right?" asked Barret. "The woman thought she was doing her a favor?"

"Let's hope she was," seethed Shay. He was staring at me in horror.

"Well, that's good," said Henry. "At least you know her."

Dragging my hands over my face, I tried to think of where Helete would take her. Our last exchange hadn't been cordial, and though Lance had proven he was dangerous, I wasn't sure how far Helete would want to push me. *Punish me.* Mia hadn't run from her, which was probably due to the relief she must have felt after being saved from a thug.

"Find Helete," I ordered.

Henry pushed to his feet. "She sounds like a well-meaning friend."

Shay turned to Henry. "Why didn't you let Mia keep her phone?"

"Because she needed time to decompress." Henry replied briskly. "Who is this Helete?"

I scowled at him. "What were you thinking?"

He moved closer. "Call your friend and ask her where they are."

I closed my eyes in frustration.

He turned to Shay. "What?"

Shay swapped a wary glance with me. "The Dionysus Club?"

"What club?" Henry frowned my way.

"Not now, Henry." I glared back.

Shay gestured for us to leave. "I'm sure it's fine." Though he was saying that for Henry's sake.

I pointed to Barret. "See a doctor. Get an EKG."

He looked surprised. "Why?"

"You were hit by 50,000 volts."

"Is that bad?"

"Well, it's not good." I headed out of there.

Helete had been willing to bring him down with a street weapon and it made me wonder what she'd be willing to do to incapacitate Mia.

We left Barret to lick his wounds. The more distance between him and us the safer it was for him. These hired men had dubious reputations, but I'd deal with them later. I'd also deal with Henry for hiring them.

Our car pulled back into traffic.

I felt conflicted when it came to Henry. He was vulnerable to high levels of stress and something like this could trigger his PTSD. I leaned forward with my elbows on my knees and locked my gaze with his. "Let us handle it from here."

He stared out at the cityscape and then turned his angry glare on me. "Why are you not okay that Mia is with this woman?"

I sat back and Shay and I exchanged looks.

Helete knew what Mia meant to me. The fact she was at the hotel at the same time was suspicious. We'd been tailing her and it sounded like she'd returned the favor. Her men had to have witnessed Mia leaving Cole Tower, and then followed her. Instead of alerting me, Helete had grabbed this opportunity.

If this was about money, a solution would be within reach. But it never was with people like her—it was about power. I checked my phone again for any sign of a text or call from her.

"I need Mia home safe," I said. "Helete and I have had our differences."

Henry's stare moved from me to Shay and then back to me. "What the fuck does that mean?"

"It means we proceed with caution." Shay made a slicing motion across his neck to warn Henry to draw back on the inquisition.

We drove the rest of the way in strained silence, taking less than thirty minutes to reach the suburban parking structure of The Dionysus Club.

Neither Lance nor Helete had answered their phones and by the time I stepped out of the elevator I was finding it hard not to storm in and make the kind of scene I'd regret.

A slim, redheaded receptionist greeted us with a smile.

"Helete Merrill?" I rounded the desk to get closer.

"She's not here," she replied. "Can I take a message, sir?"

"Galina?"

"They're both out." Her smile became forced. "I can arrange for a VIP tour if you like?"

"Where will I find Helete?" I held back my anger. "This is important."

Henry lurched toward her. "Where the fuck is she?"

Shay grabbed the back of Henry's shirt to restrain him.

The redhead scrambled for the phone and I assumed it was to call for help.

I pressed a finger down on the receiver. "Where is she?"

"I think maybe The Belgravia Club?" she blurted out.

"Think or know?" asked Shay.

She threw me a nervous glance. "She's meeting a friend for dinner."

"We appreciate this." I leaned closer. "Don't warn Helete that we're looking for her. Do you understand?"

"Yes."

I held her stare. "We just want to speak with her."

The receptionist nodded, but there was no way to know if she'd keep her promise. We returned to the elevator and headed down to the car.

"What kind of place is that?" asked Henry, as he settled into the back.

I gave him a thin smile to let him know I wasn't in the mood for any further criticism.

"It's a health spa." Shay's frown hinted at a lie, but Henry didn't catch it.

Henry looked relieved. "Sounds like Helete took Mia for dinner."

Leaning back against the leather seat, I checked my phone again to see if Mia had called. With a shake of his head, Shay indicated that he hadn't received a call either.

The last time Shay and I had trespassed into The Belgravia Club, we'd been chased down and escorted out. This time would be no exception, though they'd probably be on high alert now. All I needed was five minutes. All I needed was to see Mia safe.

"Stay with Shay," I warned Henry, and left the two of them arguing in the foyer.

I stormed down the hallway, following the sign I'd seen last time that led to the dining room.

Around me bold colors battled with the natural light from above, the scent of freshener and rich textured perfumes permeated the air, along with the scent of money and fine food. I heard the clank of cutlery striking plates and the thrum of conversations as I neared the starch-white dining room.

Helete sat at a corner table, but the woman with her wasn't Mia. My gaze searched for her and my heart raced as time hurtled out of control. Maybe Mia was home right now and wondering where I was. Maybe she was taking a hot bath to soak off this heinous day. Maybe she wanted to explain everything to me first to protect Henry. That's the kind of thing she'd do. Look out for everyone and put herself last.

Keep it together until you find her.

When the fog of panic lifted and my vision cleared, I realized it was my ex-fiancée, McKenzie, sitting opposite Helete in that far corner of the dining room. They were alone and deep in discussion. Seeing their full plates of pasta, I had to assume they'd only just arrived.

Hurrying across the room, I ignored the chatter behind me from security. Shay had caught up with me and I knew he could handle them. I just hoped he'd be able to keep Henry back long enough for me to get through to Helete.

I had caught her attention—she seemed to be expecting me. Her eyes tracked my approach as I weaved around the other tables toward them.

I recognized the blue Louis Vuitton handbag by Helete's feet. It was the same one I'd seen when Galina had taken us into that private office in The Dionysus Club. That office belonged to Helete. A fact I shoved into the part of my brain that was currently focused on not killing her.

"What are you doing here?" Zie smiled in surprise.

I gave the women a dangerous smile. "Why don't you tell her, Helete?"

"This is a woman's club." Zie sounded incredulous.

"I'm aware of that." I glared at Helete. "Where's Mia?"

Zie looked confused.

"I know you removed her from The Manhattan," I said, my tone infused with a warning.

Helete's lips curled with a hint of triumph.

Bravo, Helete, you've struck your revenge directly into my Achilles heel. You've won.

Her smile widened as she read my emotions.

"I'm giving you one opportunity," I told her.

"What's going on?" asked Zie.

Helete feigned a recollection. "I do remember Mia saying something about wanting to train as a submissive with the best of the best."

"You're lying." I held her gaze.

"She knows you're a hard man to keep, Cole. She needed to up her game."

"Helete." I steepled my hands in prayer to draw on my fading patience. "If Mia is in any way harmed—"

She quickly got to her feet. "I've lost my appetite."

A flash of movement rushed from my right. As I regained my balance, Helete leaped back and Zie moved out of the way. Shay and I both grabbed hold of Henry, restraining him.

"Where the fuck is she?" Henry yelled at them.

"Security!" Helete looked furious.

Shay managed to overpower Henry and with the help of a security guard, he struggled to get him to the door. The staff had probably called the police. I faced Helete again.

I had seconds left.

"This will end badly for you." I kept my tone even despite my growing rage. "Unless you tell me the truth."

"What is it that you see in her?" snapped Helete.

"Her innocence," Zie muttered.

Helete looked triumphant. "What happens when Mia follows the same path as Zie?"

"Path?" I knew what she was insinuating. Wherever Mia was, she was in danger. She'd been put in a position where men were free to abuse her. Though unlike Zie's situation, this wouldn't be with consent.

Zie wallowed in depravity. If this was Mia's fate, I would have to live with knowing I was to blame. I'd exposed her to these people.

"You rejected Zie because she was taken by so many men."

Helete's words saturated my senses.

"Keep your voice down," Zie snapped at her.

Terror knifed through me as I tried to fathom how far Helete would go.

"You brought this on yourself," she hissed.

This is what it is to love. I felt like I was being flayed alive while being dragged into the pit of hell. I'd walk through those fires for an eternity if that's what it took to get her back. She was all that mattered.

My fists burned with restraint. "One more chance."

A firm hand wrapped around my upper arm and dragged me backward. Turning sharply, I faced Shay and read his taut expression.

"The police are close," he warned. "We have to go."

I pulled away. "I'm not done."

"If they arrest you…" he said the rest with a glare.

I'd blown it.

Shay led me all the way back to the car with a steel grip.

Back in the SUV, I vaguely listened to him trying to calm Henry down as I replayed my conversation with Helete. Maybe this was an empty threat? A trap to rile me up so I did the unthinkable and burned my reputation with the kind of violence there'd be no coming back from.

"How the hell are you so calm?" Henry grabbed a bottle of water from the cooler and twisted the cap.

I went for the door handle. "I have to go back."

Sirens blasted around us and I realized it was too late.

Shay clutched my sleeve. "It's a trap."

"You didn't hear her threat to Mia?" My heart raced wildly at the thought.

Nothing and no one would change the way I felt about Mia. What Helete couldn't know and would never understand was that Mia had a pure soul, and that's why I'd fallen in love with her. It wasn't about her beauty; her very essence radiated the purest light that would never fade.

Mia was quite simply my everything and I wouldn't rest until she was in my arms again.

Suppressing my panic, I focused on important details. "Zie was surprised to see me. She's not involved."

Shay hung up his phone. "The penthouse is empty. Mia's not there."

"What about Helete's home?" Henry asked. "Maybe Helete believes she's helping by keeping Mia away from all of us?"

I ignored that banal comment which proved Henry had no idea of the danger. I was protecting him from himself, and I sent Shay a look of warning to let him know this was important to me. Henry wasn't fragile, but we'd witnessed one PTSD episode a few months ago and I wasn't sure how much more pressure he could take. He was desperately fond of Mia, which was the only reason I was giving him a pass...though my patience was quickly fading.

"I have a man heading to Helete's place." Shay glanced over at Henry. "We'll drop you off at the penthouse, Henry. Just in case Mia turns up there. Okay?"

Henry looked defeated. "I can't just wait around and do nothing."

"Consider it?" I said.

Henry leaned back and folded his arms.

"Shay, turn the car around," I said. "Take us back."

"How do you propose getting access to Helete's phone? Even if we can get back into that dining room, she's probably left by now." His expression changed as we came to the same conclusion.

"I need access to her private emails," I said, nodding.

"Head over to One East Sixtieth Street," Shay directed the driver. "We're going back to that subterranean parking structure."

We navigated the traffic back to the club, barely making conversation. I blamed myself for not seeing this coming. Henry was a gentleman, old-fashioned just like my father, and anything out of the norm rattled him. Hell, this guy was a staunch conservative and had placed his life in harm's way to defend his beliefs.

All paths of guilt led back to me.

The car slowed as it drove through the underground parking structure of The Dionysus Club. Judging from the flashy cars lined up, they had some of their wealthiest clients visiting.

"Stay here," I warned Henry.

He shook his head. "I'm coming with you."

"I don't need criticism right now," I told him. "I need you to have my back."

He let out an exasperated sigh. "After this is over you're breaking it off with Mia."

My glare held his. "I need to find her to do that, Henry."

Shay went in first and by the time Henry and I stepped out of the elevator, he'd successfully led the receptionist away from her desk. With no idea how long we had, I hurried toward the office that I'd once believed to be Galina's. Now I was fairly certain it was Helete's.

Henry followed me into her office and together we searched the desk for anything that might reveal Mia's whereabouts…a receipt, a phone number, or even a faded message on a post-it note.

I shook the mouse to awaken the iMac's screen and sat down in the leather swivel chair. I threw the back pillow across the room.

Shay was the seasoned tech and without him I might not be able to crack the code to hack the computer. Perhaps it would have been better to have Henry distract the receptionist, but the risk of having him running loose was a worse idea.

He'd burn down the place with us in it.

"It's like a needle in a haystack." Henry exhaled his frustration.

"This is why we need to be focused." I checked beneath the mouse pad in hope of finding Helete's codes there. They weren't.

Henry yanked open the top drawer of a silver cabinet in the corner and rifled through the files. "Who is this Helete?"

"She's married to Lance Merrill. Well, she was. They're divorcing."

"The Senator? Why would a billionaire's wife want to busy herself with running a health spa?"

I sat back and answered with a shrug.

"Well, that makes more sense now." His frown deepened. "If she runs it she calls the shots?"

"Exactly."

"She gets to live out her fantasies anyway she likes." Henry huffed his disapproval and rifled through the folders. "Sounds like she has the resources to hide Mia away anywhere she wants."

My mouth went dry. He was right. Helete had properties all over the world and searching each one would take the kind of time we didn't have.

"Hello there." Henry was looking toward the doorway.

Following his line of sight, I met the gaze of Omani. She was dressed in a long, sleek evening gown that clung to her figure.

"You look nice," I told her, silently cursing Shay for failing to rescue her already.

He'd done a shitty job at getting her out.

"How are you, Nadia?" My gaze flitted to that tattoo on her left wrist—she'd been branded as belonging to a club so it was interesting that she was here now. I wondered just when her name change had come about, and whose idea it was.

I could feel Henry's disapproval. He was probably thinking the same thing I had when I'd first seen her—she was too young for this place.

Omani leaned against the doorjamb. "What are you doing?"

"I'm trying to break in to your boss's computer." I went for honesty.

She came in a little farther and her lips curled with amusement. "Why?"

With that idiosyncratic facial expression, Omani had revealed she likely knew the code to get into this desktop.

I spoke gently. "Because your boss may have done something very bad and I'm trying to save her from herself."

"What kind of something?"

"How long have you been Helete's personal assistant?" I asked.

"How did you know she promoted me?"

"I imagine you gave her your notice?" I said. "She gave you an offer you couldn't refuse." Because Omani was Helete's favorite and she wouldn't want to lose her.

"Have you spoken with her about me?" Omani swapped a wary glance with Henry.

"No. Sure you don't want to work for Cole Tea?" I gave her a warm smile as I leaned back casually.

"We'll double your employer contributions to your 401K," added Henry.

She stood beside the desk. It wasn't enough.

"Get me into this—" I gestured to the computer, "and I'll give you a hundred K." Any higher and she wouldn't believe me.

She narrowed her gaze. "What if Helete finds out?"

"She won't," said Henry. "We promise."

I slid away from the desk so she could get closer to the keyboard. She paused, suspicion in her gaze. This was taking too long. The thought of Mia in distress caused my blood to boil, but if I snapped at Omani to hurry and lost her trust my only way to find Mia could be lost.

"I can't thank you enough," I said softly.

She moved the keyboard closer so she could type. "What is it that's so important on here?"

"Helete has kidnapped my fiancée."

Her flickering eyelashes revealed her surprise at my honesty. "Why?"

"Because Helete does not like me."

"Why are you telling me this?"

I smiled. "Because you may be young, but you're not immune to bullshit."

"I'm not as dumb as people think."

"They probably assume you're naïve. I don't."

"I was once. Before it all happened…"

"It all happened…?" I gestured for her to continue.

"I was happy in France. I had to leave." She used the mouse to enter the password. "This place is not what I thought it was."

"Why don't you go back?" asked Henry.

"Helete offered you money to stay?" I realized.

"Not as much as you. Anyway, where would I go? My old master bored of me."

"Master?" Henry's brows were halfway up his forehead.

Omani stared at him, realizing. "My boyfriend."

"What happened?" I drew her attention back on me.

Pain flashed across her face, but she continued typing. "I got an email telling me not to come home. I was no longer wanted."

"Where were you living?"

"Paris." She stood back and pointed to the screen. "There you go."

France was the country stamped on her passport, I recalled Shay telling me this. So she'd been there before she'd met Helete, perhaps?

"I really appreciate this, Nadia."

"I don't want to do the glory hole thing again. I don't like it. Can you tell her?"

"Sure," I said. "I'll call her."

Henry's eyes narrowed as he tried to work out what that meant, and then his expression turned to horror.

I raised my hand so that he wouldn't respond to her sensitive confession. Omani had just admitted men had fucked her through a hole in the wall, and I wasn't in the mood to ask her if it had happened here or back in Paris.

"I mean," she stuttered out, "I speak five languages. I play the piano. I'm more than they say."

"No one will touch you again...in any way." My stern glare set that as a promise.

She gave me a thin smile. "The day I came into the spa with you and your friend and you walked out on me. You didn't... "

"I remember."

"I'm not used to that."

I gave a nod. "You have my word we'll protect you."

Her expression changed and she looked as though her memories had taken her back to a painful past, to experiences that could not be unlived.

"We have offices in London and Los Angeles." Henry closed the top cabinet drawer. "Helete will never find you."

"Promise you'll leave today," I said. "I can have a car pick you up."

She looked unsure.

"Think about it." I wrote my number on a post-it note and handed it to her.

I grabbed hold of the mouse and opened up Helete's Gmail account, locating her outgoing mail. My gut wrenched when I saw an email titled *blonde*, an exchange between her and Galina. Scanning faster, I read the details of a flight plan for a jet out of New York. The destination was Paris Le Bourget Airport.

The trail of messages swapped between them ended six hours ago with a final email from Helete:

"Present Mia to Master Lucas Chastain directly upon arriving at the house. Tell Chastain's men to have her marked with the society's brand upon arrival. That way she won't forget our gift."

Helete had added a final line of instruction:

"Leave her there. Return. Tell no one."

Hell opened up and swallowed me whole.
They were going to tattoo an "H" on Mia's wrist—like the one on Omani.
I'll kill the man who brands her.
Two weeks ago, I'd bumped into Lucas Chastain at The Ritz Carlton, while having dinner with Mia. I'd had a bad feeling seeing him then. Recalling our interaction, I tried remembering how cordial I'd been.

He was a monster.

Our past included a fight that had left us enemies—him with a broken nose and me with a bruised ego. My say had carried no weight back then. Lucas had turned a fun game, which I had created with Danton for that secret French club, into a reckless pursuit that most of the woman didn't want to take part in. The hunt for our submissives through the woods no longer ended with a master claiming his slave. Now when caught their fate was being brought back to the house and given to the members—*all of them.*

The very reason I'd left.

And Lucas had another grudge to bear. He'd hated what I'd had with Danton. If he even got a hint that Mia and I were together…I drew in a sharp breath and felt my face go pale.

"What is it?" asked Henry.

Shay came in. "How we doing?" He frowned when he saw my expression.

"She sent her to Hillenbrand."

"That's not possible," Shay's voice broke with emotion.

"Where the hell is Hillenbrand?" Henry sounded distant.

"She might not like it," said Omani, proving her knowledge of the place.

My world spun and my flesh went cold.

"What's the address?" I begged Omani with my eyes.

"Don't know." She shook her head, but I could easily tell she was lying.

Because this place was so secret, those who reveled in its existence were threatened with a ruined life if they spoke out.

I broke my gaze from hers and stared at Shay. He nodded to let me know he'd get me on the next plane out of New York.

"I need you to leave." I shot Henry a glare.

"Why?"

"Out you go," snapped Shay.

Henry threw a wary glance at Omani. "I'm staying."

"Go, now!" I wasn't backing down.

"Jesus." He stormed out.

Shay closed the door.

It was time to slice through this delusion. "Omani, obey."

She fell to her knees and peered up at me through heavy lids, slipping into subspace, her breaths short and sharp; those telltale signs of arousal proving she'd been conditioned.

"You like being submissive?" I stepped closer.

"Yes, sir."

"You like being bought nice things?"

"Yes."

"What happened to your master? Did he give you to Helete?"

"No." She glared. "But he no longer wanted me. It was over between us."

"Explain."

"I left the house and went to Paris to shop a little. He'd given me money to spend." She shook her head proving the memory still hurt. "He sent me an email saying not to bother coming home. Not to try to contact him."

"Hillenbrand?" I said softly.

"He didn't want me to come home."

I knelt to better read her face as I realized her master had left her out in the cold.

"Luckily, Helete was in France and she reached out to me. I met her at the Pantheon and she told me she'd help. I had no more money, you see. No job. Nothing. Just the clothes on my back."

"I see."

"I don't know why he stopped loving me. Why he didn't tell me in person. I suppose that is why he sent me away."

I reached for her chin and tipped it up. "You are marked."

From the way she responded I knew she'd been primed by the very best. The greatest tragedy was when a sub lost a master they had a hard time bonding with someone new. And the bastards had left her with a tattoo with no chance of forgetting. She was exquisite, a perfect submissive. It didn't make any sense; Omani would have been a jewel in Hillenbrand's crown.

"Tell me about Hillenbrand?" I asked gently.

Omani dragged her teeth over her lips. "If you fuck me, I'll tell you everything you want to know."

"I made a promise to you," I kept my tone firm.

Her gaze slid over to Shay.

CHAPTER TWENTY-FIVE

MIA

"SIT DOWN," SNAPPED GALINA.

Despite feeling disoriented, I'd shot out of my seat like getting off this plane was possible. For much of the flight, I had slipped back into sleep. That stuff was still in my system.

Despair washed over me.

Galina reached over and yanked me down.

I held back my anger, resisting the urge to yell. I wanted to accuse her of drugging me. My tongue felt wedged to the roof of my mouth. I needed to brush my teeth.

I shouldn't have let Henry persuade me to remove my watch. Hell, I should never have mentioned it to him. I should have packed my things earlier and hurried up to the executive suite and found my new office. The one where I'd have been safe.

"Where are we going?" My wrist stung from the strength of her grip. Foggy thoughts made it impossible to think straight. "Where's Helete?"

"Obviously not here."

She could have been in the cockpit, but something told me she'd distanced herself from whatever was going on here.

We'd have to go through airport security. I'd get my chance then.

"Why is this happening to me?" I asked.

Her eyebrows rose. "As long as you are agreeable, you will be safe."

The time on her watch signaled 1:00 A.M., which meant I'd been out for hours. I couldn't remember getting out of the car.

Cameron would know I was missing by now. He'd be searching for me...using all his resources. I was sure he'd handle this the way he handled every detail in his life, with calm, controlled intensity.

Where was she taking me?

A sudden realization hit me. "How much money did Helete offer you? I'll double it if you turn this plane around and take me back."

She peered out at the view. "We'd need to refuel."

"So...you're open to the offer?"

I need her to see reason.

Her expression changed to unreadable. "Let's discuss it when we land."

Okay, good. Galina was motivated by greed, unless this was her way of keeping me quiet.

Helete and Cameron had clashed when it had been revealed she'd misled her husband, Lance, into believing it had been Cameron who'd threatened his daughter at that private club in L.A. Their rift went deep and now I was being used as collateral to avenge him. Or that's what this felt like.

I considered screaming so loud the pilots would hear and accuse her of kidnapping—though I didn't want either of us to make any impulsive decisions.

Her intelligent eyes flitted to me and then back to the window.

If I was going to survive this ordeal, my attitude would have to change. I had to center myself, think what Cameron would do; he'd be strategic and unpredictable.

I leaped to my feet and hurried toward the front of the plane. What I needed was to rehydrate and caffeinate. I needed to get focused.

Galina caught up with me. "What are you doing?"

"I'm thirsty." I grabbed two cans of Coke. These would be safe to drink.

She stepped to the side and gestured for me to get back to my seat.

I sat down again and chugged the sweet liquid. Bubbles burned my throat as I quenched my thirst.

"If you do that again…" She reached into her Hermes handbag and pulled out a taser. "I will zap you."

Eyeing the taser warily, I assumed it was the same one Helete used on Barret. If it was powerful enough to put a man of his size down…

"I won't be a bother," I said softly, hoping she'd believe the lie.

She tucked the taser back in her handbag. "Do what I say."

I popped the lid open on the second Coke. "Sure."

The plane banked left and, as I peered out the window, I saw lights glinting through the ominous dark clouds. A brightly lit cityscape came into view. "Where are we?"

"Everything you do from now on is very important," she demanded with an even tone. "Should you cause any trouble, I've been instructed to make things very uncomfortable for you." She spoke her threat calmly, fastening her seatbelt before pointing to mine. "We're landing."

The view had become bleak and there were no landmarks to give away our location.

When the wheels touched down we bounced on the runway and then continued toward the lights of an airport. Tears welled up in my eyes. I felt so vulnerable.

This woman knew how to open a plane door. A burst of cold air rushed in. She peered down at the metal steps that were shoved against the plane by some unseen airport employee.

She led me down onto the tarmac. A man in overalls gave a nod of thanks as he accepted a package she shoved at him. I turned to look back at him, but she gripped my arm painfully and pulled me away. It was dark beyond the central lights and I strained to see any clear landmarks that could pin down where we were.

I'd be ready to scream once we entered the terminal.

Only she was leading me directly toward a car. Two burly men exited the vehicle behind it, and closed the gap between us.

I broke away from her grip and bolted toward the terminal, my heels wobbling on the asphalt.

A strong arm wrapped around my waist and dragged me backwards. I elbowed him, striking hard muscle as I struggled to get free.

"Careful with her," Galina yelled.

"Get her in," ordered another voice in the dark.

They shoved me into the backseat of a car and I scrambled over to the other side. Before my hand reached the handle the locks clicked shut.

Through the glass partition that separated the front and back seats, I saw Galina settling in next to the driver. She spoke to him, but I couldn't hear what was said. Not that I'd have understood either of them if I had. Turning in my seat to peer out the back, I saw the two men get in the car behind us.

I was jolted back as we sped off, my panicked gasps echoing around me, my heart pounding fast.

As we approached a highway, I spun around and read a sign. We were leaving Paris Le Bourget Airport.

We weren't even in the States.

They won't find me.

The Russian kept her focus ahead. My eyes stung from the tears I held back. A nagging tiredness scratched at my raw nerves. Rubbing my eyes, I stared out at the dawn landscape, watching as sporadic homes and other buildings whizzed by, along with a few cars and the occasional foreigner.

Where the hell was she taking me?

Up ahead, a middle-aged couple were out walking their dog. I banged on my window to get their attention.

We flew past them.

The partition was lowered.

Galina twisted in her seat and glared at me. "I will put you down if you don't be quiet."

"Why are you doing this?"

"This is all his fault." Her eyes narrowed with rage. "Cameron should never have interfered with our club. He shouldn't have come after her. She belongs to us—" She stopped herself and spun around to face the front.

The glass pane rose once more to divide us.

Who had Cameron come after? Helete?

Her haunting words made no sense: *She belongs to us.*

CHAPTER TWENTY-SIX

CAMERON

I'D BEEN SWEPT UP INTO A NIGHTMARE THAT HAD NO END IN sight. All I could think of was Mia…she was in every deliberation, every intake of breath, every cell of my body burned for her.

Shay and I had spent the entire flight contacting everyone we knew who might have a connection to Hillenbrand. It was virtually impossible to get information, because very few men would admit to any knowledge of the place. Our last hope was Scarlet, but she'd gone to bed and I imagined her phone was on silent.

Outside the oval window of our private jet, grey clouds billowed around us. Now and again the sky lit up with lightning. The European weather greeted us with little regard for our safety.

We were about to pull the same trick Galina had and land with no trace of our arrival in a country with strict immigration laws. This was a diplomatic coup like no other. The flight would be recorded as carrying cargo only. It made me wonder if this was how Galina had smuggled Mia into France.

We'd be mingling with some of the world's most influential men. Entering the house at this point was going to be challenging. We needed strings pulled.

I hated landing in the rain, but this time I was willing to risk lives to get on the ground and be closer to Mia. It had been difficult to sit still for the seven hour flight.

The thought of her being imprisoned within Hillenbrand...*Jesus,* I didn't want to contemplate what they'd do to her.

Would either of us recover? Was I looking at the final deathblow to our relationship because I'd failed to protect her? Would Mia ever forgive me for exposing her to this trauma? These people...*these fucking people.*

Don't think about that now.

I didn't want to believe the gossip I'd heard in the darkest corners of Chrysalis, where whispers had carried from those who'd stayed in Hillenbrand. Stories of the wildest parties that went on for days and the cruelest games at a sub's expense, where pleasure for them was never entered into the equation.

Once, we had shut them down.

We'd managed it remotely so that our names were not involved. Though now, I was about to step into the center of the hive. Hillenbrand had risen from the ashes and membership had become a fiercely guarded secret.

As my fingertips caressed my brow, the realization hit me: Helete probably supplied them with submissives. Maybe that was her connection?

"Let me get you something to eat," Shay offered softly.

I had no interest in food. "You can eat something."

"How about a drink?"

"Water, maybe."

He motioned for the stewardess. "Two waters, please." Then he turned back to me. "Do you regret it?"

I stirred from my melancholy. "What?"

"Omani? Refusing her offer?"

"No."

"What do you think will happen to her?"

I shrugged. "Whatever she wants."

"You surprise me."

"I do?"

"A lot of the time, actually."

"I like to keep things interesting."

"What did you tell Henry?"

"That one of us should remain stateside in case Mia turned up there."

Back at JFK he'd wanted to board with us...

"Listen to me," I held him by the shoulders. "Henry, you can't go where I'm going. That place...those people are dangerous."

"I can't bear to think of her there."

"If anyone can escape, Mia can."

"You should call the FBI."

"If I do that there will be a price on my head from that moment on. The members of this house are more powerful than you can imagine. They'll come after me, and you, and our entire family. I have this, Henry. I'll bring her home."

Leaving Henry behind at the airport had been the only sensible move I'd made these past two weeks. I'd sent him to the penthouse.

"Hey?" Shay stirred me from my daydream. "Mia's strong."

"I know."

He rose and turned to sit beside me. "I'm not landing backwards."

I forced a smile to comfort him. He'd apologized to me through-out the entire flight, beating himself up for letting this happen. He'd refused to let me take the blame. But I took responsibility for it all, wallowing in guilt and self-hatred.

The question I was pondering right now was how I would deal with Helete in the future. She had friends who would protect her. Maybe there'd never be an opportunity for revenge, maybe all we'd have is a life full of memories, having left ourselves vulnerable.

I couldn't see how this would end.

Shay leaned forward. "We still don't have an address, Cole."

He was right. We'd be landing in Paris with no destination.

"Are you sure you don't regret us not...you know, with Omani." He threw his arms up. "She was practically begging for it."

"I promised I'd keep her safe. Keep the bastards at bay." I turned my gaze to those dark clouds.

"I can't believe she refused to tell us the address," he huffed.

Turbulence hit, causing the plane to shudder, but I barely noticed.

"For God's sake, Cole, you're saving that girl from that place. She owes you."

"Omani owes me nothing." I held his stare. "She's scared. And she has every reason to be."

CHAPTER TWENTY-SEVEN

MIA

HE SHOULDN'T HAVE COME AFTER HER.

Those eerie words of Galina's kept running through my mind.

This had to have everything to do with that damn cake and Cameron and Helete playing games with each other. She hadn't liked Cam visiting her club...maybe that was it.

Trying to steel myself against what was to come, I huddled in the backseat of the car and attempted to calm my chaotic thoughts.

We drove for what felt like an hour and though it was useless trying to remember our entire route, I took mental photographs of landmarks like church steeples and quaint stores.

Nausea welled up in me as we swerved along twisty country lanes surrounded by lush green trees and tall hedges on either side that made me feel claustrophobic. Oncoming cars zoomed by way too close.

Finally, to my left, a sweeping field opened up to reveal rows of grapevines stretching all the way to the horizon. The beauty of it wrecked my heart because it reminded me of my father's vineyard in Napa Valley, the place where he had denied he even knew me.

That experience had left me so wounded that I'd been vulnerable to the men of Chrysalis.

No, don't do this...

Cameron and Richard were the only ones who truly understood me, who were kind to me. Despite all their kinkiness they were good men. It was fear that was making me question everything.

Cameron had saved me that day at the vineyard, too. He'd whisked me off to some exclusive hotel with Richard and Lotte and they'd all comforted me, trying to help me forget the nightmare of that disastrous reunion.

My chest hurt from the agony of missing Cameron. His reassuring smile always soothed and his strong arms had made me feel safe. His words of comfort had made things better when my day had gone south.

All those worries felt trivial now.

Helete had powerful friends, because I'd landed in a country without facing a customs officer. This didn't seem possible with the heightened security present at every airport. What if these people were transporting weapons, or drugs, or even women? The thought of human trafficking was too horrifying to ponder.

This kind of favor came from men in power, the kind with access to traffic control towers and private jets. This was the pull of someone in European politics with an interest in a certain lifestyle that meant he had secrets to hide.

Every time a car came toward us I cringed. I'd never get used to driving along such small lanes.

Focusing on what I could control, I memorized our chauffeur. He had a scar on his chin and a boxer's nose that proved he wasn't adverse to a fight. His tweed jacket and corduroy trousers making him look like he'd tried to dress up for the day. He'd wanted to impress the Russian lady.

On a hilltop in the distance rose an intimidating white manor with cathedral spires peeking over a wall. It seemed like we were heading toward it.

I thought of how isolated the place was, and shivered.

Sizable trees arched over a long road and ended at a wide wooden gate that swung open to let us pass through. The car idled outside the front door of the enormous manor. Ivy crawled up the exterior and across the arched windows.

My door was flung open.

"Out," ordered a rugged-looking man.

Galina wrapped her hand around my arm and led me toward the house.

"Do what they say. Understand?"

"I'm not staying." I eyed the men behind us.

"Listen," she snapped. "Tell Cameron I had no choice."

"Fuck off." I tried to pull away and she dug her fingernails into my arm.

"You can't say no to people like this."

My forearms prickled and my chest tightened as I tried to breathe through a haze of denial. I knew how to find this woman again. It would be through Helete. I only hoped Cameron had figured out what had happened to me by now. I hoped he would be able to find me here.

"Don't mention Cameron's name." She gave me a thin smile.

"Why?"

"That's me being kind, Mia."

"Kind?" I repeated bitterly.

"If you try to run they'll torture you." She grabbed the iron handle shaped like a bear.

My focus shot to what lay ahead.

Peering through the open doorway, I saw dark wooden floorboards, soft lighting, and antique furniture. Just by the sweeping staircase stood three men, all of them dressed smartly in suits. They looked wealthy and this meant they had the kind of authority that could keep me here indefinitely.

They stopped talking with each other and turned to stare at us as we entered the foyer. Galina's grip burned my arm.

More faces to memorize—they were menacing, despite their striking features. Their sharp eyes roamed over me, assessing, deliberating, as though they'd been expecting us.

It was late here, maybe 2:00 A.M.

The idea of not mentioning Cameron to these people brought on a fresh wave of panic. Surely he was the kind of person who would wield power or have some influence here. Doubt crept in and I wasn't sure if anything this woman told me could be trusted.

Back in New York, Cameron had followed my movements everywhere; the danger was ever present.

Scouring the vast foyer, I considered making a break for it as I breathed in the scent of expensive cologne mixed with the aroma of rosemary and garlic. The sound of plates and pans clanking to my left drew my attention, and I peered through a door into an old-fashioned kitchen. A long table sat in the center with benches along each side. I could see dishes and glasses had been left over from a meal. More men were in there, around twenty maybe, and their cheery conversation contradicted the sinister mood out here.

"Is Lucas here?" asked Galina.

I tried to recall where I'd heard that name.

She addressed the men. "Let him know we're here."

"You're not settling her in?" asked the man with a crew cut.

"I have to catch a plane." She glanced my way. "Remember what I told you. Do not defy them."

"Good advice!" The loud voice came from above.

We stared up at the man walking along the balcony. When he reached the stairs he paused for a moment. A Doberman appeared by his side.

Galina visibly trembled.

The tall figure began his descent toward us. Just a few days ago he'd approached Cameron in The Ritz, after we'd had dinner there. Cameron had sent me to the car so we hadn't been formally introduced. Later, when I'd finally gotten Cameron to open up about who this man was, he'd shared why he'd wanted me out of there.

He was the reason.

"Where am I?" My voice shook…because I knew.

Don't scream…don't scream.

Two of the men manhandled me toward the foot of the staircase. I refused to look at the dog that had followed him down.

My gaze rose to meet his grey eyes and then roamed over his familiar, distinguished features, and that salt and pepper hair. He was Lucas Chastain…the man who moved in dangerous circles.

Galina had brought me into the most dangerous place our society knew. I remembered that warning from Cameron spoken in the back of the car…

"Add a touch of sinister and throw in a dash of nefarious and congratulations, your cocktail is laced with the potency that is Hillenbrand."

"I want to go home," I stuttered.

"Is she legal?" asked Lucas, and then his expression changed to recognition. "Where do I know you from?"

I swallowed hard, unsure whether to tell him.

Lucas's cold glare found Galina. "Explain."

"She's a gift from Helete." Galina stepped back. "I have to go."

Those emotionless grey eyes fell on me again. "Does her master know?"

Galina looked confused. "You are her master."

"Are you trying my patience?" His voice was deep and refined. His accent was South African, maybe?

"I do not know what you mean." She looked terrified.

Galina wouldn't know this man had seen me with Cameron. He'd know I was connected to him and some minor research on his part would confirm our relationship.

Lucas's heavy-lidded gaze swept up and down my body. "No one touches her."

"Sir?" asked one of the men. "House rules."

"She belongs to all of you," added Galina. "House rules."

Lucas moved swiftly, gripping Galina by the throat. She flinched in pain, eyes bulging, but she didn't move.

Lucas's voice rose. "Do not tell me how to run my house." He released her.

Galina's lips trembled. "I do not know what I was thinking. Forgive me, Master Chastain. I am your humble servant."

"It will please me if you stay awhile. Entertain us."

"Helete ordered me straight home."

He turned to the men. "Film it. So I can enjoy it later."

Galina was escorted away. When I looked back she was gone.

The men holding me gripped my wrists tighter and I cried out. "There's been a mistake. I'm not meant to be here."

"Well, you're here now," he said. "It is no small feat getting in."

"I was kidnapped," I burst out. "Brought here against my will. You must let me go."

I'd exposed Galina for the wretched women she was, but I could see no other choice.

Lucas's eyes closed for a moment, as though my panic gave him pleasure. "Is that so?"

I gave a wary nod.

He scratched the back of his head. "We should let you go then. Help you get home."

"Thank you."

He rolled his eyes. "Bathe her. Then bring her to my room." He tucked his hands into his pockets. "If you'll excuse me."

"You need to let me go!"

He tilted his head as he stared at his men. "Why are you still here?"

I was dragged up the staircase and into a spacious bedroom. My legs weakened when I saw bars on the windows.

One of the men, the one with a crew cut, remained in the bathroom with me. "Take off your clothes and get in." He pointed to the shower.

"Get out first," I snapped.

"Don't make this harder on yourself."

"I'm not meant to be here." I watched him lock the door. "Please, can you help me? I need to get a message to my family. They'll be worried."

"Didn't you see Lucas's anger when Galina defied him?" his tone was even. "Now, if you don't want the same fate, get in."

Blinking in confusion, I couldn't move, couldn't think, and couldn't fathom how anyone would let this place exist.

He raised his arms in frustration. "You are dead to the world. You no longer exist. You belong to Hillenbrand."

"If you lay one finger on me…" I pointed at him.

"If I return you to him like this—" He gestured his disgust. "Lucas will kill us both."

"Why are there bars on the windows?"

"Why do you think?"

"Danton?" I realized.

"I don't know who he is. No one gets in or out now without Lucas's permission."

I hugged myself and turned my back on him, ready to kick him if he came any closer. My mind splintered and I tried to wrestle with the overwhelming feeling of hopelessness.

After my shower, I was told to dress in a black lace bra and panties that had been placed on the bed. I was ordered to style my hair so it fell over my shoulders. My dress was taken away; that beautiful Elie Tahari was the last piece of my old life.

"How's it going?" Cameron sought me out in a Bloomingdales fitting room.

"I thought you were in the Disney Store?"

His gaze swept over the Elie Tahari I was trying on. "I love that on you. I'm buying it."

"How did you find me?"

"Spidy senses." He winked.

"What were you doing in the Disney Store?"

He beamed at me. "You know, checking it out for future visits with our kids."

I ran into his arms, laughing.

All I wanted was to pull him close to me.

They took my boots away, too, and I was made to walk barefoot. If they thought this would prevent me from running they were dead wrong.

When Crew Cut seemed happy enough with my new appearance, he led me out toward the staircase and I fixed my gaze on the front door as we descended.

"The last sub who tried to escape had her pinky finger cut off," he said flatly.

I tried to read the expression on his face. "Where are you taking me?"

"To the boss." He led me down a hallway.

I was shoved into an office and he left me there with instructions not to touch anything. My gaze roamed around the room, taking in all that dark wood and fancy furniture. The antique furnishings would fit just as well in an old church; though there was nothing spiritual here.

Chastain strolled in. "How did Philip treat you?"

"Why do you care?"

His brows narrowed as he considered me.

"I don't want to be watched in the shower."

He walked with a grace that contradicted his menacing presence, turning to lean back against the table with his hands shoved into his pants pockets. "Okay."

"Thank you."

"Of course."

"Are you going to hurt me?"

"I'm undecided."

I tried to hide my fear. "This is all a misunderstanding. I'm sorry for any confusion."

"Apology accepted."

"When can I leave?"

He looked thoughtful. "You were having dinner with Cameron Cole? At the Ritz?"

I gave a wary nod.

"Your connection?"

Turning around so he didn't read my expression, I strolled briskly toward the bookcase and reached for an old tome. I flicked through the pages, looking at photos of Africa.

"You like elephants?" He peered over my shoulder.

"Doesn't everyone?"

"Some men like to hunt them."

"They're evil." I stared up at him realizing he might be a hunter.

"I own a safari park. Its main purpose is conservation."

I exhaled. "That makes you a hero."

"Or just an animal lover."

"What's your dog's name?"

"Pascal."

"I love dogs, too."

He reached for an envelope on the desk and peered down at it. "I have your contract."

I shook my head. "I'm not signing anything."

"Why?"

"I'm Cameron Cole's fiancée." I held his stare to make sure he believed me.

Ignoring Galina's warning could be a mistake, but she had no idea Chastain had already seen me with him. It was a risk I had to take. "Helete kidnapped me. She doesn't like Cameron, and I think that's why I'm here."

His head tilted thoughtfully. "She needs to get in line."

Oh, no... "Why would anyone hate him?"

"Cole believes he is morally superior to us."

"Is this Hillenbrand?"

He smiled.

"Once, a long time ago, Danton Belfort rescued a submissive from here. Can you rescue me?"

His expression shifted to one of recognition. "Danton?"

Lucas strolled back to the bookcase. He dragged a leather-bound book off the shelf and opened it, turning the pages until he found what he was looking for. He stared down at the page, affection softening his features.

"This man?"

Hurrying over, I looked at a photo of three men. One of them was Cameron, looking so young and handsome in a pinstriped suit. He was standing beside a shockingly beautiful tall man with dark hair and piercing eyes. I'd seen Danton in a photo Scarlet kept in her home. I could see why she'd fallen in love with him.

It was heartbreaking to think a brain tumor had taken him too soon. Cameron and Scarlet had been there when he'd died. Their bond was still strong from that experience. Chastain was also in the photo and he, too, was strikingly handsome back then.

Resting my fingertip on the photo I said, "Danton played the cello."

"He played for me sometimes."

"Scarlet still has his cello."

Chastain held my gaze. "I didn't know that."

I hoped I'd not just given away her secret. "She loved him very much."

"I miss him, too."

"I'm sorry for your loss."

"I was young and jealous." He closed his eyes for a beat. "So, now you are here and I have an opportunity to settle a disagreement."

"What do you mean?"

"Come on. There are house rules that we must abide by."

"I don't want to go."

"It can't be done in here."

"What are you going to do?"

My heart pounded and my palms felt wet. I stayed close beside him thinking that if I could just push away my fear and find some common ground he might take pity on me.

When the scent of bleach hit me, I froze. Chastain pulled me into a room that looked like a doctor's office—with a gynecological chair.

I didn't have time to run, and I was no match for his strength or speed.

He picked me up like a ragdoll and flung me into the chair, strapping me into it. My legs were spread and my ankles strapped into each foot pedal.

"Don't scream," he warned.

I struggled. "I'm begging you. Don't do this."

"Relax, Mia. It'll be easier on you."

"I don't deserve this. I haven't done anything wrong!"

He blinked at me as though considering this. "Just breathe, okay. This can't be helped."

In horror, I watched him reach for what looked like a staple gun and then he grabbed a thin bracelet from the countertop. I jerked when he bolted it to my ankle. He'd not broken my skin but it felt like it. That ankle bracelet looked like it needed a saw to hack through it.

"See, no pain," he soothed.

"Danton wouldn't want you to hurt me," I stuttered out.

His expression turned to grief. "If you're going to use his name make sure you do so with respect."

"Danton was friends with Cameron, so there must be some saving grace about him?"

"Cole revels in perfection." He arched a brow. "That right there is a flaw."

"He's a good man."

Lucas gestured to his nose. "He did this."

It was still regal despite being crooked. "You're still handsome."

He laughed. "You're divine."

But not brave enough to ask why Cameron had punched him.

"No!" I flinched when I saw him pulling on surgical gloves.

"I suppose you don't trust me?"

"No!"

"I wouldn't either." He sat on a small stool between my thighs and rolled closer to my body, his gloved hand trailing up my leg until it reached my thong. "Scream."

"Don't you dare!"

"Mia, scream."

"Don't!"

His hand gripped my thigh and he pinched so hard a scream tore from me as pain seared my flesh.

The door burst open and Crew Cut appeared. "Everything okay?"

Chastain removed a glove. "She's a virgin. We'll save her for the hunt."

"They sent you a virgin?"

He forced a smile. Crew Cut left, closing the door behind him.

Chastain turned to me. "I've bought you some time."

Tears filled my eyes and spilled over. Maybe I was getting through to him because he hadn't examined me—just made it look like he had. "Bought me time?"

"For Cameron to find you."

My head crashed back with relief. "Will you tell him?"

"I won't have to. He'll work it out."

"I'm not sure he will."

"He's on a plane heading for Paris."

"How do you know?"

He gave me a wry smile. "Trust me."

"Thank you."

"Don't thank me, Mia." He rose to his feet and ripped off the other glove. "As soon as Cole gets here I'll make his life hell."

"Why?"

"He stole Danton from me." He came closer and gripped my throat. "And now I have you."

CHAPTER TWENTY-EIGHT

CAMERON

MY BACK JOLTED WHEN THE PLANE TOUCHED DOWN ON THE runway, braking hard on the wet tarmac. There was too much rain hitting the window to see out.

Shay and I dragged our suitcases down the metal staircase as the downpour hit us. We'd packed enough clothing to suggest we had planned a decent stay—tuxedos, casual clothes, and the kind of items that wouldn't arouse suspicion when searched. The kind of items you could leave behind.

Getting out of Europe without a stamp in our passports was going to be interesting.

We rolled our cases behind us through the rain toward the blue Alpha Romeo—the only car here.

Scarlet had come through and found us Hillenbrand's address. They'd even sent a car. We weren't told the name of her contact.

As we climbed in the back I ran through the plan. Get in. Rescue Mia. Get the hell out.

I'd memorized the passphrase, "Belle journée pour un mariage blanc."

The driver threw back a customary greeting as we left the airport.

"Welcome to Paris." Those would be the only words he spoke for the entire journey.

Shay and I remained silent sharing nothing but the occasional glance.

For all our driver knew, the most sinful activity that went on at Hillenbrand was the drinking of exorbitant wines and the lighting of illegal cigars, along with the occasional prostitute to entertain and make it a pleasant stay.

Hillenbrand had been described as a chateau on a hill, not a small manor surrounded by farmland.

So wherever the driver was taking us wasn't right…

The car cruised up the lengthy driveway and pulled up to a country estate. Our driver opened the trunk and removed our luggage. He dragged them toward the front door. I took a few seconds to steel myself before entering, bringing my suitcase with me.

Inside, the place looked like a hunting lodge—with that private club feel. Trophies in the way of beheaded animals hung from the walls and one of them, a deer, stared down at us with an accusatory glare.

"Don't look at me," I said to amuse myself. "Not guilty."

A door opened and a voluptuous thirty-something strolled toward us dressed in a severe high-necked silk blouse and short black skirt; her spiked heels would double as a weapon. Her brown hair was pulled up in a chignon. She was carrying a bottle of Krug Clos du Mesnil in one hand and two glasses in another. She placed it all on a nearby table and proceeded to uncork the bottle, pouring two glasses of champagne.

Two forms also lay on the table. They looked a lot like contracts. There was a fountain pen beside them.

"Welcome, gentleman," said the woman. "I'm Mistress Delma." Her accent was pure German.

"It's an honor," said Shay, accepting the glass.

"The phrase you gave the driver?" She raised her chin. "It is outdated."

My jaw tensed with that inconvenient revelation. Scarlet had done her best, but no doubt they changed it frequently.

"We've come a long way," I said, sitting my suitcase down.

She handed the other glass to me. "We've arranged an appetizer."

There is still a way out of this without violence.

We were being tested with the kind of verification that wouldn't be passable if we were the law.

Shay strolled toward the table to read the forms and then signed his name at the bottom. His signature was wide and sweeping, nothing like his usual autograph. He handed the pen to me.

I took it from him and signed with an uncharacteristic swirl. "You're wasting my time."

"Excuse my friend," Shay interjected. "He's impatient. You want to test us. Let's get this over with."

"Americans." She thinned her lips.

"We didn't come all this way to talk," I snapped.

She spun on her heel and strolled back toward the door. When she opened it, she held out her hand, making a gesture of an offering.

The tall vision of a masked beauty appeared, taking elegant strides toward us. All she had on was a delicate black thong. Her breasts were pert and her waist small. Blonde curls cascaded down her back. She reminded me of a Vegas showgirl; the kind with a perfect body and the ability to walk effortlessly. When she reached Shay, she knelt at his feet and raised her masked face to hold his gaze.

He peered down at her with interest.

Delma snapped her fingers. "On the table."

She rose with grace and moved over to the table, then spun around to sit on the edge, her eyes flitting between Shay and me. I tried to read her, tried to rule out collusion. She looked like she'd done this before. She acted like she wanted it.

Delma waved a hand in her direction. "This is our show of faith."

And she wanted to see ours.

Shay set his glass down on a side table and then walked over to the masked woman. "You like this?"

"Lay back, Annalisa," Delma ordered. "Show our guests how welcome they are."

Shay glanced over at me without doubt showing in his eyes.

He went with the moment, reaching out and parting Annalisa's thighs, then stepping between them. He rested his palm on her chest and nudged her back. She raised her hands above her head in a submissive pose, barely missing that bottle of champagne.

"Take off your mask," I told her.

Delma glared. "She must keep it on."

A flicker of doubt shown in Delma's eyes, and our gatekeeper looked like she was close to escorting us out. Still, we had to be sure this was legal.

I strolled over to Annalisa and reached for her mask, sliding it up to reveal a striking beauty, a woman of at least twenty. From her heavy-lidded gaze, I could tell this was as much to fulfill her fantasy as it was for the clients who enjoyed her.

A moment passed between Shay and me, and then he returned his focus to her, snapping off her thong. He bent low and pressed his mouth to her sex, kissing, lapping, and flicking her with his tongue as she arched her back.

Her languid gaze met mine as I gripped her wrists and held her down.

I looked away, wanting no part of any emotional connection in an erotic scene that didn't include Mia. "Obey."

She let out a long groan of pure want.

My alpha equal was on fire for her. Shay suckled furiously between her thighs. His greediness could be seen in the way he devoured her, ravaging every crevice until her moans became louder and she writhed furiously, thighs trembling. Her nipples hardened to beads as she came violently, drawing in precious gulps of air as another orgasm owned her.

Shay stood straight and wiped his face with his sleeve. "Did you like that?"

She nodded.

He reached for her hand and lifted her up to face him. "What a beautiful whore."

"Are you a whore, Annalisa?" I purred the question.

She nodded again, her gaze reflecting an insatiable need.

"Present yourself to us at the house." I grabbed a fistful of her hair and yanked her head back. "When we actually get there." I flashed a warning look at Delma. "Are we done?"

"The car will take your friend to the house. However, if you want to join him—" Her cold stare slid over to Annalisa.

I closed the gap between myself and Delma and grabbed her by the back of the neck, guiding her firmly to Annalisa. A smile formed on Delma's lips at my flash of anger, or pride, maybe? A dark amusement? In any other place I'd be hailed a monster and thrown out, banned even, and yet here this behavior was celebrated.

"I like to watch," I bit out. "So let me."

Excitement flashed over Delma's face. I shoved her all the way into Annalisa's pussy and held her there until she was lapping at the beauty's cunt, expertly flicking her clit with her tongue. She was so absorbed in her submissive's sex, it proved to me this activity was familiar, something desired between them. Annalisa's moans and the way she grabbed her mistress's hair to hold her there confirmed she wanted this.

Shay walked up behind Delma, who was still bent over and feasting, and he hoisted her skirt over her hips revealing her stocking tops. He slid aside Delma's panties and began finger-fucking her. She ground against his hand, moans filling the air.

I watched the lustful scene unfolding, cursing our delay.

Delma broke away and tugged down her skirt, her lips shiny and wet.

"Was that nice?" I asked darkly.

Her tongue ran along her lower lip. "Satisfactory for our needs today."

Shay gave a nod. "We approve."

"Gentlemen, your car awaits." That soft blush on Delma's neck was yet to dissipate.

She gave Annalisa a nod of permission. The submissive slid off the table and strolled out with the same grace she'd exhibited upon entering.

We left Delma and exited the farmhouse, remembering to bring along our luggage. I didn't make eye contact with Shay until we were once again ensconced in the back of the Alpha Romeo.

When Mia was in my arms again, I'd refuse to let her go. My possessiveness before would pale to how I'd protect her now.

Shay uncorked a bottle of Veuve Clicquot and then poured the champagne into two crystal flutes. We were two rich American rogues with money to burn, on the hunt for the kind of adventures only a place like Hillenbrand could provide. We clinked glasses and faked a toast that we'd made it.

We were heading in.

None of this fazed Shay. In fact, he was in his element. I wondered if he had any real idea of what he was stepping into.

"How much do you think that Krug Clos du Mesnil cost?" he muttered.

"I'm sure it won't go to waste."

"After experiencing you," he countered. "They'll need a drink."

I turned my attention to the passing scenery. I had a very strong feeling that Chastain knew we were here.

CHAPTER TWENTY-NINE

MIA

CHORAL MUSIC POURED OUT OF HIDDEN SPEAKERS FROM somewhere in the kitchen.

Sitting on the floor next to Lucas's chair, I glanced up at him wearily. He'd taken his position at the head of the long wooden table and was lording over the men who were enjoying a meal together. Occasionally, Chastain reached out and petted me.

I resisted the urge to bite his hand. He was lying. Danton and Cameron had never been like that. He was a cruel man running a cruel place.

I was ravenous. Yet at the same time this nausea wouldn't ease. Chastain's threat against Cameron had sent me reeling. I wanted to curl up in a ball and hide my face, shamed by this humiliation. The rising rage inside me felt like dynamite ready to ignite.

I knew many submissives enjoyed this kind of thing…craved it even. They yearned for an erotic degradation—and from what I'd seen Hillenbrand was for the highly trained. I wasn't ready for this.

"Here." A piece of meat skewered on a fork was pressed to my lips.

I shook my head, refusing it from Chastain.

"If I offer you food…" he scolded.

The room had fallen silent and all eyes were upon us. Opening my mouth, I accepted the morsel and my mouth watered at the salty deliciousness. He offered me another chunk of meat from his plate. This was Chastain's revenge for what Cameron had done all those years ago. I was the pawn in a game that was as deranged as this awful place.

Holding Chastain's gaze, I begged him not to do this and he reached out and played with a strand of my hair.

I was so close to biting him.

A tall glass of wine was offered to me and I accepted it—needing something to drown my shame and sorrow. The crisp white wine I gulped tasted like chardonnay.

From the way the men deferred to Chastain, he had to carry all the authority, so I remained quiet and didn't complain. I tried to remain invisible as much as possible. Chastain was the man keeping me safe at least for a while.

After dinner, he carried me upstairs in his arms, and the scent of food and voices faded behind us. He kicked open a door and lay me on a sumptuous four-poster bed.

He settled in beside me and rested his head in his palm. "You didn't eat enough," he said softly.

"Why are you being nice to me?"

"You remind me of someone."

"Who?"

He shook his head as though reluctant to discuss it.

"Your submissive?"

His smile revealed a fond memory. "She was everything to me."

"Why aren't you still together?"

He hesitated, but then said, "She left."

"I'm sorry."

"You're similar. She was very sweet. Very caring."

"Tell me about her?"

He rolled onto his back and reached for the TV remote, flicking through the channels.

I closed my eyes and dozed off.

When I woke it was to the sound of the door opening—Chastain was carrying in a tray. "I brought you something."

I slid off the bed and padded out to the bathroom. When I came back he'd rested the tray on a corner table.

"Beef Bourguignon." He pulled a chair out for me.

I joined him at the table and ate.

"Have some bread." He pointed to it. "Dip it in the sauce."

"Did you really chop off someone's finger?"

"That's hardly dinner conversation."

Jesus, he had. "Why?"

"She deserved it."

The bite of bread I'd just eaten swelled in my throat and I swallowed hard. "Is Cameron here?"

He shook his head. "Not yet."

I dabbed my mouth with the napkin. "What's the hunt?"

He held my stare. "We can talk about it later."

I watched his expression. "What did you do to Galina?"

Chastain reached for my arm, pulling my wrist toward him. His forefinger swept over my wrist forming an "H." His pale eyes held mine. "You will be worshipped, Mia. If you stay."

"Is Galina still here?"

"She's leaving."

"Can I speak with her…before she goes?"

"Why?"

"I want to make sure I'm doing everything right to please you."

He gave a nod of approval. "Come on."

We walked down the longest hallway and I turned to see the Doberman following us. Pascal's gaze was fixed on his master.

"She's in here." Chastain knocked on the door.

I waited for him to open it.

"Return to your room afterward."

"I promise."

His tap on my nose was affectionate and he snapped his fingers for Pascal to follow him.

Galina was sitting in a corner chair. She was reading something in a beige folder. She wore a fur coat and looked ready to leave. Her make-up was flawless and her hair was styled to perfection.

She looked up. "What do you want? Where's Chastain?"

I raised my head with pride.

Her stare flitted to the door. "Be quick. I'm leaving."

"I was worried about you."

Her gaze narrowed and she pushed herself out of her seat, moving slowly toward me. "You want to wallow in how much I suffered at Chastain's hands?"

"No."

"Yes, you did."

"I'm a better person than you."

"Is that so?"

"Why is Helete angry with Cameron?"

She gave me a smug smile. "He wants our premiere submissive."

"Why?"

"Why do you think?" She threw the folder onto the bed. "He's tired of you."

You're lying.

My throat tightened, but I forced out the question. "Who is she?"

"Someone very beautiful. And very special. She is your opposite. She speaks five languages. Plays the piano. She is only eighteen and has already mastered chess. She is the greatest fuck. So well trained. She once thrived here…unlike you."

"How do you mean?" My voice wavered.

"She is perfect for a man like Cole."

Bile rose into my throat and I struggled to swallow it.

"He wants what he can't have," she said.

"Why did she leave here then? If it's so wonderful?"

Galina's glare snapped over to the door and she looked worried.

As though she'd said too much.

"I don't believe a word you've said."

"We're done here, Mia."

"Cameron will kill you for what you've done to me."

"Do you know why Helete sent you here?"

My heart pounded in my chest.

"After Zie had her fun at Chrysalis, Cameron no longer wanted her. She was tainted as far as he was concerned."

"What does that have to do with me?"

"You'll share her fate, Mia."

Fear clutched at my heart. "Chastain has promised no one will touch me."

"Until tomorrow night."

The hunt?

"You're going to be part of one of Hillenbrand's most prestigious games."

"I'll refuse to play."

"That would make it very easy for them to catch you."

"They won't let you leave either."

Her head fell back in a laugh. "Chastain honored me last night." She eased up her left sleeve to show me the tattooed "H" on her wrist, overshadowed with inflammation.

I caressed my wrist as though feeling the sting of the brand I was being threatened with. "Chastain promised."

She reached for her handbag. "I'll give your regards to Zie."

I followed her along the hallway until she reached the top of the stairs. A young man wearing a tuxedo was standing at the bottom of the steps staring up at us. "Go back to your room, Mia."

I ignored him. "Please, tell Cameron I'm here, Galina. I'm begging you."

She drew in a deep breath. "I'm not quite sure what I was expecting here."

"Mia," shouted the man. "Do you want me to come up there?"

"Galina?" I pleaded.

She'd made it halfway down when she stopped, turning to taunt me with a smirk.

"I forgive you," I called out.

Her frown deepened and a rash of conflicted emotions flashed over her face.

"Mia!" the man yelled.

Turning sharply, I headed back to my room.

I didn't know why I'd said that, maybe hoping she'd find it in her heart to tell Cameron I was here.

In a daze, I walked into the bedroom and crumpled on the bed.

Had Cameron found someone new?

No, don't doubt him.

With these thoughts burning in my brain, I tossed and turned late into the night.

I awoke in a sweat-drenched panic.

Not caring about my skimpy attire, I climbed off the bed and pushed open my door. Tiptoeing toward the staircase, I felt a draft blow over my skin, giving me gooseflesh.

Oh, no...

Pascal was sleeping in the foyer.

I moved slowly down the steps.

When I reached the bottom of the stairs, he raised his head. I carefully turned and walked in the opposite direction toward the kitchen.

The pots and pans and dirty plates were now gone. Everything from last night had been cleaned away...everything except the memory.

A flash of inspiration hit me and I hurried over to the refrigerator. In the back on the lowest shelf was a stack of beef labeled as Kobe. This shit was expensive. Like hundreds of dollars a pound expensive.

Pascal was about to be spoiled.

With my bribe carried in its paper wrapping, having just pulled it apart into several bite size pieces, I checked to make sure the way was clear and then headed into the foyer.

"Pascal," I whispered, throwing a chunk down.

He had the look in his eyes of an animal that knew it was about to get duped, but was too interested in the scent of delicious meat to make a good decision.

"Come on, boy." I threw down another chunk.

He sniffed and then wolfed it down, wanting more. I broke off another piece and threw it. In less than a minute, I had my hand on the door knob.

It was unlocked.

I lay the rest of the meat down, then slipped outside and closed the door behind me. Barefoot, I sprinted toward the gate. At the front of the house were several potted trees. I dug around the base of one and ripped out the small trunk, spilling the soil, and then laid it on its side. With a shove, I had the pot rolling toward the gate. With another heave I had it upside down. Standing on it, I was able to reach for the top of the gate and hoist myself up and over, dangling.

I stared down at the ground, wrestling with fear. If I fell wrong, I could break a leg. My arms felt the strain of my weight, my fingers burned.

Pascal barked.

I slid down and landed badly, pain wracking me from feet to shins as I rolled on the ground. I lay there for a minute, catching my breath.

I forced myself up, gritting my teeth in agony while staring at a road that could lead to freedom. When the feeling of agony lifted enough for me to begin hobbling, I headed down the tree-lined road. Trying to shake off the lingering terror, I sped up until I was sprinting.

A motorbike came to life and the wooden gate opened.

My feet carried me faster along the asphalt, but I knew I'd make it if I could just reach the bend ahead and then bolt into the woodland. With heavy gasps and aching limbs, I fought the urge to glance back.

The bike roared by in a gust of wind and skidded to a stop ten feet in front of me—cutting me off.

Another bike zoomed by in a flash, almost knocking me over. It skidded to a stop farther down. Both helmet-wearing men were looking in my direction. They dismounted their bikes.

I was so close. All I had to do was get by them…

I bolted left and went for it, but one of the men leaped right and grabbed me from behind. I struggled in his ironclad grasp, kicking my legs and wriggling to get free.

A flash of bright headlights shone our way and I shielded my eyes from the glare, my chest so tight it hurt to breathe. A silver sports car pulled up and idled a few feet away.

Chastain climbed out of the driver's seat and strolled around to the passenger door, opening it wide.

"I want to go home!" I burst out.

"You are."

The men dragged me toward him.

"You've made a terrible mistake, Mia," he said.

"You can't do this to me!"

"When we get back, put her in the dungeon," he ordered coldly.

My thoughts fractured as I was shoved into the car. When we pulled up to the chateau I was dragged out, kicking and screaming.

A slap across my face silenced me.

They manhandled me through long, cold hallways and down a winding staircase.

I was shoved into a musty cell that smelled of fear. I saw a bed sparsely covered with sheets. I heard the clanging of the door as it was slammed shut.

Then blackness enveloped me.

After a while, my vision adjusted to the darkness and I gripped the bars, screaming into the echoing chamber until my voice gave out.

Hours went by. I paced like a caged animal. Eventually, I flopped onto the bed and felt the assault of the springs beneath my spine.

Eventually I heard a noise and raised my head off the lumpy pillow.

The silhouette of a man loomed before me as he entered the cell and locked the gate behind him. He closed the gap between us.

The shadows fell away from Chastain's face. "Have you learned your lesson?"

"Fuck you."

He was carrying an iPad. "Time to see your fate if you mess up again."

Dread shot up my spine as I watch him move closer.

No, I don't want to see it.

I didn't want to watch what they did to that girl's hand.

Tears streamed down my cheeks.

He sat beside me on the bed and it dipped beneath his weight. His finger swiped over the screen. The scent of his expensive cologne wafted over me. I feared I'd never get the smell of it out of my head.

Chastain held the iPad in front of my face. I stared at the image of a dungeon, recognizing the woman who sat on the end of a bed. She didn't look afraid, but she did look wary. The camera pulled out to reveal five men standing before her.

"Galina?" I whispered.

"So it is," Chastain said darkly.

"She showed me her tattoo." It was easier to look at him than the screen.

"You're about to see how she earned it."

My gaze was on Galina and his was on mine as I watched the recording.

Galina pushed herself up and the men moved toward her, helping her undress. My hand slapped to my mouth when I realized…

She sank to her knees and the scene unfolded like an erotic painting that had stirred to life, a visceral vision of a dominatrix being outnumbered. Her fate was set as she accepted their cocks offered one by one, suckling and pleasuring the men as a prelude to what was about to unfold…a fusion of alpha power and a vixen's submission.

"Why doesn't she try to run?" I whispered.

"She chose them." His eyes crinkled into a smile. "Am I not merciful?"

"I won't try to escape again."

"Eyes on the screen, Mia."

Chapter Thirty

Cameron

THE TREE-LINED LANE OPENED UP TO REVEAL A WHITE GOTHIC hilltop chateau. Within minutes our car was idling before a massive wooden gate. When it opened, we drove through and I noticed the walls surrounding us. The place was like a fortress.

We left the car and entered through the unlocked door. We were being watched from somewhere, I knew, with a suffocating focus that carried a threat. A valet unloaded our suitcases and carried them up the staircase.

I took in the country décor and breathed in the scent of male domination. My gaze snapped to three naked female submissives who hurried through the foyer. Mia wasn't one of them. They followed their master, who walked several steps ahead of them. When he turned and berated one of them for lagging behind, I knew we'd arrived at the correct destination.

We were greeted by a young, smiling male submissive, wearing leather pants and a tight leather collar. He escorted us in an easterly direction. We ended up in a swanky office that smelled of lemon furniture polish. The décor was all antique pieces with a gothic flair.

We were instructed to wait.

Noting the subject matter of the books scattered along the shelves, whoever this room belonged to loved to travel. I suspected it was Chastain, since many of the volumes were about Africa. Resting on the seat of a leather chair was a paddle and a discarded ball gag. The thought that either of these had been used on Mia caused my back to stiffen.

My adrenaline scorched my veins. As the jetlag lifted, it would give me the strength to search every room. I'd tear this place apart until I found her.

"Do you think there'll be another test?" Shay whispered.

There came a knock on the door.

The master of the house had again sent in one of his finest to welcome us—this time in the guise of a handsome twenty-something male with designer stubble. The tailored suit he wore fit his physique well, but something in the way he walked revealed he preferred more casual clothes.

"Hey, there," he greeted us with a warm smile and a sharp British accent. "How was your flight?"

"Great." I reached out and shook his hand, then he turned and held Shay's gaze for a beat too long.

He pulled the door shut behind him. "I'm Alton."

If he wanted our names he wasn't getting them. I assumed the guests paid well for the privilege of privacy.

Alton shoved his hands into his pockets. "We have a brief initiation."

I gave Shay a reassuring glance. "Whatever you need."

He nodded and then asked, "Would you like to freshen up?"

Shay leaned back against the desk. "We showered on the plane."

Alton rounded the desk and reached for two brochures with the Hillenbrand logo stamped on the front. "Let the concierge know if you want anything not offered on the lists," he said, handing them to us. "We'll make it happen." He paused and then added, "I think you'll find that most proclivities are covered."

I flicked through the brochure that was a catalogue of the specialties offered, and all of it made the porn industry seem tame—exactly what Hillenbrand was famous for.

And then I saw it. "You still have the hunt?"

"Yes, we have one tonight," he said. "VIPs only. You won't be able to participate, but you will be able to enjoy the scene afterward."

My fists curled, longing to rearrange his face.

"Looks fantastic," said Shay. "How does one become a VIP?"

"Through our Grand Master." Alton gave a nod. "He selects members. These events are carefully managed as they're outside. Still on the property, but the risk of an escape is real. We tag them so if anything goes wrong we can get them back."

"Do they try to escape often?" asked Shay.

He gave a thin smile and held my gaze. "We had one last night who tried to bolt. An American."

"What happened to her?" My throat tightened.

"We've locked her in a dungeon."

My blood turned ice-cold.

"You like dungeon play?" asked Alton. "We can set you up down there if you like?"

"Dungeons it is." I glanced at Shay.

Alton gestured for us to follow. "We suspected you'd be into the dungeons so we have a scene ready for you."

If Mia was in the room he was about to lead us to, I'd tear every last man apart in her vicinity.

The route we took had us walking through a maze of rooms. We had no choice but to follow Alton down the winding staircase.

We stopped in a cavernous dungeon and its main focal point was a four-poster bed in the center. Sitting on it were three naked female submissives wearing diamond collars. Their curious gazes flitted to Shay and then back to me. They didn't look scared…yet.

A long table to the left was strewn with the kind of torture instruments meant for a museum.

Alton motioned toward the bed. "They've been selected for you."

I held Alton's gaze to see if the fucker knew who we were. He was hard to read.

My gaze slid over to the right wall and a large rectangle of two-way glass—whatever was about to happen could be watched from the other side. Shay threw me a wary glance when he read my conflicted emotions.

"Enjoy our delicacies," said Alton as he walked to the door. "Remember, to refuse our gift would be considered rude."

"What would happen if we declined?" Shay risked the question.

Alton looked surprised. "You'd be escorted from the house, gentlemen." He smiled. "Don't worry, they're all well-trained. Afterward, you'll be free to explore." He turned to the women. "Serve the house."

"Yes, sir," they replied in unison.

I stared at the two-way glass, wondering if Chastain was standing behind it.

"I'm ready," whispered Shay.

CHAPTER THIRTY-ONE

MIA

I LEANED AGAINST THE TWO-WAY GLASS WITH MY TREMBLING hands splayed against it, staring through at Cameron and Shay.

They were here. They'd come for me.

Cameron's hair was disheveled, and with his five o'clock shadow he actually looked dangerous. Shay matched his ruggedness and was looking at him with concern.

I could see why.

Upon that four-poster bed sat three pretty naked subs, waiting patiently for these two alphas.

No, please no...

Don't betray me.

My elation was fast disappearing. I dared to look back at Master Chastain. His eyes were filled with amusement as he tapped a leather whip against his palm. "You're about to see what kind of man you were going to marry."

"I'm still going to marry him." I turned to face the window.

They were just one room away. If I ran out the door and through the next one...

Chastain walked over to a control panel and turned a switch. The sound came on in the room. We'd hear every word they spoke. Every noise.

Everything...

Cameron and Shay's whispers carried; they were huddled in the corner talking privately.

"Hey!" I shouted.

"They can't hear you," warned Chastain. "If you bang on the glass again, I'll whip you. If you try to escape, I'll whip you. If you fail to watch, I'll fuck you."

"Why are you doing this?"

"It pleases me."

I turned around and hurried toward him. "Whatever disagreement you have with Cam, it was a long time ago. You were cordial in the restaurant. You looked like you were friends."

He peered over my shoulder. "You're missing it."

"We have money. We'll give you whatever you want. I'm begging you."

The tip of Chastain's whip lifted my chin. "I will be checking to see how wet you are afterward."

"You're a monster."

"You flatter me, Mia." He spun me around and flung me over the back of a velvet chair. "Just to prove I always mean what I say—"

He grabbed a handful of my hair as his whip struck my ass with a snap. I yelped from the intense pain, unable to escape his grasp. My fingers curled into the velvet as I rode out the agony of each strike, my heart aching for Cameron, who was so close and yet so far away.

"Would you like to watch?" Chastain yanked my head back.

"If it pleases you," I bit out.

"Go have fun." He released me and pointed to the window.

I rose and moved away, wanting to spew out words to express my hatred and disgust for him. I wanted to tell Chastain what a sick and ruined human being he was, but the stinging of my butt was a strong deterrent.

I stumbled back toward the window and pressed my hands to it again, wishing that Cameron could sense my presence. I wanted to run into his arms. I wanted him to sweep me up and carry me out of here. I needed him more than the air I breathed.

He would find me. I had to believe that. He'd come this far.

So close.

"No playing with yourself," he snapped.

"Fuck you," I spat at him.

"One more word and I'll fuck you as you watch."

"You promised no one would touch me."

"I didn't mean me." He came closer, peering through. "Well, I didn't expect this."

Cameron was dominating the scene as only he could, and I realized he was turning this into the session Shay had once begged for. Right now, he was ignoring those wide-eyed submissives. Somehow, some way, I'd forgive Cameron if he fucked Shay.

But them?

Cameron removed Shay's jacket and then unbuttoned his shirt, helping him out of it. When he tugged down Shay's pants and underwear, his enormous erection bounced free. Cameron gave it a slap. Which only made Shay harder. Shay was completely naked now.

Cam peeled off his own shirt and threw it over the same corner chest where he'd laid Shay's clothes. He kept his trousers on, but took off his shoes and socks.

Bare-chested and barefoot, Cameron emanated the presence of an alpha, all toned muscles and six-pack abs, his extraordinary physique exposed. From the way the submissives studied him hungrily, they all wanted a taste of him.

He was mine.

Cameron walked Shay over to the foot of the bed and positioned him to pose with his feet slightly apart. Then he knelt at his feet to secure the ankle chains, wrapping the other end around each post at floor-level. When Cameron rose to face him, Shay obediently held out his arms so the metal handcuffs could be attached to his wrists before being pulled tight, securing Shay's taut outstretched arms to the bed posts.

Shay focused on his master's every move with anticipation. Perspiration spotted his brow, electricity crackling between them. Though I knew they were trying to act like seasoned guests, and this was probably how they'd gotten in. This had to be their way of maintaining their cover.

Still, everything about this scene was erotic and dangerous and forbidden.

So very Hillenbrand.

The pretty submissives resting on the bed couldn't take their eyes off the sculpted back of the spectacular man bound before them. Their eager expressions hinted they wanted to become part of the scene. I, too, had once stared upon Cameron in awe, never once believing a man of his stature and male beauty could be mine.

He carried himself with a graceful authority, ruling the room like a king, knowing he carried all the power. Cameron found the wall panel controlling the light effects. He turned a dial and the lighting dimmed to a deep red hue.

I tried to read him, but his expressionless façade made it impossible, which was so like Cole when he was under pressure. He strolled from one end of the room to the other to find the music panel, where he took a few seconds to choose the very piece I'd requested for our last session: *Heroin* by Maya Beiser.

Perhaps this was his way of paying homage to Danton, who had introduced him to this life, because I suddenly heard the strings of a cello rising up to flood the chamber, transforming the mood like a menacing fugue.

Perhaps he'd never stopped loving Danton.

My thoughts were so addled I couldn't grasp what I was watching. It felt like glimpsing a private moment I had no right to see.

From the many accoutrements hanging neatly along the left wall, Cameron chose a six foot braided leather flogger and carried it back. The men held each other's stares as they took a moment to prepare.

Cameron seemed to be mulling over whether he was really going through with this, and at the same time testing Shay's resolve.

A nod of consent came from his naked captive, so subtle he could have missed it if he'd turned away. Before him stood a proud man with a hefty erection that throbbed with anticipation, a bead of pre-cum glistening on the tip of his shaft, as he flexed his muscles preparing to be mastered entirely. Permission was given with an adoration that couldn't be faked.

Cameron flicked the flogger and it snapped Shay's cock, causing him to wince but not shy away. He merely gritted his teeth and accepted this extraordinary gift of a continued assault at a steady pace. Cam struck Shay's chest and then moved slowly to his biceps before expertly moving down to meet his trembling thighs, deliberately missing Shay's pulsing cock. Those figure eight movements continued in a hypnotic rhythm that caused Shay to slip into subspace. He greeted each hit by leaning forward with his arms pulled back as he sank further into a delicious trance.

With Shay finally lulled, Cameron threw the flogger down and attached spiked clamps to his sub's nipples. Shay gave him a look of defiance, but after a moment or so his heavy-lidded expression morphed into pleasure.

Watching as though I were alone, I followed Cameron's movements, his calm stroll across the room, his focus as he rifled through the toys until he'd found the one he was looking for—a red bejeweled butt plug.

When it was held to his mouth, Shay suckled the tip of the plug to wet it, and then he braced himself as Cameron placed his right knee on the bed so he could reach behind Shay, opening his butt cheeks so he could insert the plug. Shay winced with the strain and then surrendered to the bliss of the pressure he felt inside.

Cameron seemed to be waiting for those sensations to settle as he cupped Shay's balls and whispered to him, giving him a few moments to recover.

I knew all too well how he read what a sub needed. Soothe when doubt seeped in. Calm when the sting burned too harshly. Correct and punish when disobedience was detected.

With a nod of approval, Cameron reached for the wooden paddle and again leaned on the bed to reach Shay's buttocks, striking so hard he had to be hitting that plug too, as wails of want and frustration filled the room; the violence unfolding in an exquisite way.

Shay's expression reflected agony that morphed into one of exhilaration as he rose higher and higher with each strike, his jaw tight, eyes squeezed shut, body trembling, cock rigid as he yelled through his rising climax.

"Not until I permit," warned Cameron.

I knew this game, this cruel tease that was virtually impossible to comply to. Only a seasoned sub trained in edge play could obey and not release. Only a sub with a strong will could tolerate this level, because at times it felt like the body itself would rebel against the mind and plunge itself into an orgasm; only a seasoned master could pull him back.

"My cock feels amazing." Shay's arms trembled against the strain.

"Silence," ordered Cameron.

For one of them, the pretty brunette, it was all too much and she reached between her thighs and began strumming her clit.

Cameron grabbed her by the throat to make her stop and she complied. His show of power stunned them all. They rose up on their knees and brought their hands behind their backs in a pose of submission—all three pussies glistening.

Cameron turned his attention back to Shay.

Within a minute, he had slid a gold-colored cock ring onto Shay's mighty erection and worked it all the way down with nimble fingers to slide over his balls until they were captured within. The ring dug into his flesh, making his thighs tremble. Fascinated, Shay peered down and then his gaze met Cameron's in total awe—this contraption would contain him and bring stabs of delicious pain into his groin. Shay seemed to yearn for more, his hips pumping as though chasing after the burn; I imagined his body had released endorphins to carry his consciousness to a state of bliss.

"Fuck you," Shay challenged him.

A fierce slap across his face made him moan.

From the cock ring, Cameron attached a fine chain that led all the way to Shay's nipples. With gentle tugs, he sent ripples of pleasure through Shay, who begged with his eyes for his master to stop, or to never cease, his expression one of tortured bliss as the veins bulged along his shaft.

The tension between them continued to crackle as Cameron grabbed the shaft of Shay's cock and slid off the ring and then removed the nipple claps. He wrapped his palm around Shay's length to taunt and squeeze it with a slow gliding motion that would have caused a lesser man to come.

"Forgive me," said Shay.

"This is what you begged for," seethed Cameron. "So how is it?'

Shay glared at him. "Everything."

"It better be."

"It's…"

"Don't come," warned Cameron. "Under any circumstances."

"Mercy, please, Master."

"Too much?" asked Cameron.

"Yes." Shay bit down on his lip as though that might help.

Cameron whispered something to him and Shay's head snapped back in surprise. Whatever words had been spoken had seemingly had a profound effect. Shay looked around the room as though searching for answers, his posture shifting.

The scene unfolded as Cameron pinched and slapped him and then used some of the unusual instruments of torture on Shay, going back to the table each time to find a new device to inflict pain—spiked accessories, scissors that he dragged across reddened flesh, and when he threatened Shay's cock with a spiked glove, I closed my eyes.

Shay's yells filled the room and I dared not watch.

Yet when I finally braved a look, Shay was in a trance-like state of martyrdom, his gaze turned skyward, seemingly having reached nirvana.

"Come before I permit you and I will destroy you." The warning came with a snap of Cole's fingers to get the blonde's attention.

She leaped off the bed and followed his order to kneel before Shay. Her mouth opened as the tip of his cock was brought between her lips with precision.

"Just his tip," Cameron instructed her. "Suckle."

Shay's moan echoed throughout the dungeon.

Cameron walked away to grab a chair and drag it back across the room. He sat in it, crossing one long leg over the other, leaning back to watch.

"Jesus Christ," hissed Shay.

"As I've told you," Cameron said defiantly, "I like to watch."

"I'm gonna come." Shay pulled on his chains, but they were too fixed to move and he couldn't pull his groin away from the blinding pleasure.

This was the cruelest tease. The sub merely held his tip just inside her mouth, still and obedient, posed on her knees with her hands behind her back and saliva trickling.

"Steady your breathing," Cameron instructed him. "Center yourself and relax."

Shay breathed through the rising pressure and his expression changed to pure focus as he followed the order, striving to tolerate the cruelest pleasure.

"She's flicking her tongue around my head," Shay complained.

"That's fine." Cameron looked amused. "What I need is for *you* to obey me."

"For God's sake." Shay shuddered violently.

"Show me how well you adhere to your master's rules."

"I can do this." He panted through his struggle. "I'll do it for you."

"Good." The way Cole's hands were held together in a contemplative arch, the way time fell away at his command, it seemed both magical and majestic. "You know me well, Shay. I'm giving you the session you deserve."

I wondered if Shay regretted his request. His face was scrunched in concentration, his body bound and owned from the building pressure of his nearing climax, his breaths short and sharp as tears formed at the corner of his eyes. "I'm in love with you."

"So you told me."

And I had known this all along. This wasn't a revelation. Though now, I wondered if Cameron loved him as deeply.

"I can't..."

"Prove your words. Obey."

Shay barely nodded, his body drenched in sweat as he forced himself to hold on longer. Cameron pushed himself to his feet and snapped his fingers, indicating the submissive should let Shay go.

Within seconds, Shay's bindings were loosened and he was sitting on the edge of the bed with his thighs trembling. His expression fraught as he watched another of the young submissive's scramble over to sit on his lap. As directed by Cole, the redhead faced forwards and slid down onto him until his cock was buried deep inside her and her legs rested on either side of his with her toes off the ground. She gave Cameron a Mona Lisa smile.

"You've all been very good girls." Cameron smirked his approval. "Time to reward you."

The blonde was still kneeling before Shay, only this time her mouth was clamped on the redhead's pussy. The sounds of her lapping filled the room. As they rose toward orgasms, their groans mingled with the hypnotic notes of a cello.

Again, Cameron stood back to admire his finely orchestrated erotica, his face showing compassion for the man before him.

To prove Cameron was indeed a master of the dark arts, he ordered each woman to take a turn riding Shay. They circulated obediently as the other knelt before them and performed cunnilingus to the one riding Shay. Each taking turns, rotating until Shay was dripping in sweat and begging for release.

Cameron sat down once more to watch the vision unfold as the women found their rhythm and continued to share.

Shay begged Cameron with his eyes as a submissive writhed and squirmed with his cock buried deep inside her, bouncing and squealing her joy as the woman between her thighs ravaged her clit, bringing her friend over in a fit of screams.

Cameron rose and moved near them.

He leaned past the girl riding Shay, grabbing either side of his face with what looked like an ironclad hold.

Shay licked his mouth. "I'm gonna pass out."

"You may come." Cameron held his stare. "Look at me when you do."

Shay surrendered, jerking his seed into the woman riding him, his jaw slack, finally yielding after enduring what seemed like an eternity of ecstasy. The session ended, leaving heat-soaked bodies and spent submissives who tumbled onto the bed behind them.

Shay sat on the edge, a panting, trembling mess, his torso glistening, a look of adoration on his face for the one who'd orchestrated the play.

"Out." The submissives were ordered to leave by Cameron.

They slid off the bed and with big smiles hurried toward the exit. Somehow, some way, Cameron had managed to leave everyone sated without touching them intimately.

He glared at Shay. "There's your session."

A look of confusion flashed over Shay's face. Cameron saw it and reached up to run his hand through his friend's hair, ruffling it with affection to bring him down, perhaps as a prelude to the aftercare.

His captive was freed from his chains and allowed to climb onto the bed behind him. As he rolled onto his side, Cameron covered him with a fur throw.

Then he sat beside him, watching and waiting, perhaps for any sign he might need something more.

Cole finally rose from the bed and walked over to face the glass window; his chest glistening with perspiration, his breathing measured, his dark glare staring through with a deadly precision that both terrified and exhilarated me. I became aware of the dampness between my thighs; I was aroused.

My passion for Cameron was as fierce as ever. After all, this had been the kind of play that had excited me when I'd had a glimpse behind the veil at Chrysalis.

And then I realized…

Cameron was staring at his own reflection in the glass, his face taut with confusion.

CHAPTER THIRTY-TWO

CAMERON

I STUDIED MY REFLECTION AND REALIZED THAT I NO LONGER knew the man staring back.

The gentleman who had once desired his sex with a grand measure of dark was gone. The master who had taken pleasure in ruling a room and owning each crescendo, reveling in every moment, every strike, every flash of pain, every rise.

All I want now is Mia.

Guilt seeped out of my pores over this delay.

I snapped my gaze to Shay, asleep on the bed. I knew all too well how easy it would be to fall prey to this sort of dangerous erotic spell.

I hoped I'd healed him…even here.

Making my way to the door, I tried the knob, hoping to do what I'd come here for and locate Mia. I wasn't surprised to find that someone had locked us in right after the subs had left. Dreadful thoughts of what might be happening to Mia were almost more than I could bear. I forced myself to sit in the corner, watching Shay sleep.

It wasn't much longer before they came for us.

We were escorted to our rooms and told that after we freshened up and changed into our tuxedos, we'd be invited to tour the house. No room, no dungeon, no area was inaccessible to us now and no pleasures would be denied. Should we see a submissive we liked, she would be ours in any way we wanted and for as long as we pleased.

We entered the kitchen and shared a look of relief when the waiters left carrying trays of food with them. Shay rummaged around in the fridge and pulled out two bottles of water, handing me one. I watched him shove hors d'oeuvres into his face, which he'd lifted from a tray. I refused to eat until Mia was back in my arms, but I gulped the water.

"Wanna talk about it?" I asked, moving closer to him. "I need to know you're okay before we step out there."

He reached for a salmon-topped appetizer. "You gave me what I asked for."

"Did I push you too far?"

"You know the answer to that."

"I need to hear it from you, Shay."

He looked amused. "My balls are still throbbing."

"It can never happen again."

He rested his palm on his chest. "How did you know?"

Shay was referring to what I'd whispered to him during his session, the truth that had lain dormant all these years and yet I had known it from the moment we met.

How had I known his father had beaten him? Because that's what he'd looked for in me. A guardian. And that's why his desire for a session would never be quenched until I'd delivered him over to the other side. He was free to continue exploring his penchant for a Dom. His body had released all that tension and he'd fallen...finally surrendering.

"It will get easier from here on," I assured him. "To submit."

"I never told anyone," he whispered.

"How do you feel now?"

"I'm glad you know. Makes me feel accepted, like you understand why I am the way I am."

"I was waiting for you to open up." I motioned for him to finish his water.

He drained the bottle. "Let's go get your girl."

We roamed the chateau freely, searching each room for Mia.

As we moved into the ballroom, joining a thriving cocktail party that was in full swing, we examined the many faces around us. The room was filled with fifty or so submissives and they were all dressed in costume, and all of them were collared. We saw leather-clad kittens, white-tailed bunnies, and angels with outstretched wings strapped to their backs. They mingled politely, some serving drinks, others kneeling beside their masters' feet, some fucking each other.

I moved slowly about the room, my stiff collar and overly starched shirt making it hard to breathe. Finally, I trapped an angel in a corner and as she stepped back, her feathers bent, making her look like a wanton nymph.

I ran my palm over the edge of her left wing, ruffling her feathers. "What's your name?"

"Reni." She was French.

"I need your discretion, Reni," I said softly.

She peered up at me with the look of an angel who yearned for danger. From the "H" branded on her left wrist, I knew she had to be a member.

"Have you seen a young, blonde American woman?" I glanced around to make sure we weren't overheard.

She took my hand and led me across the room to a tall, very pretty submissive whose wings were black. If this symbolized seniority and she had any loyalty to Chastain, we'd be screwed.

"He wants an American," Reni whispered to the other angel.

The black-winged cherub raised her hand to gesture for drinks to be brought over. "What do you want her for?" Her voice carried a tone of protectiveness.

"I have a gift for her." I thought that sounded reasonable.

She narrowed her gaze. "An American is with Master Chastain. You have to go through him if you want her."

My mouth went dry with the revelation. He'd seen me with her. He'd know how jealous this would make me. The thought of his hands on her...

Don't think of this. Don't allow these poisonous thoughts to ruin your focus.

With champagne flutes in hand, we were led out into the garden. The dark angel glanced back at me with a nod to indicate Mia was this way. I looked around for Chastain, my fists curling. I had to remind myself that violence wasn't an option here.

My heart beat faster as I searched every face, falling on each alpha with a woman at his feet, scanning the guests until my gaze fell on an empty cage at the end of the garden. Just beyond it flowed the River Seine.

The cage was big enough to hold a human, but it was empty. I'd dabbled in cage play myself, but the idea of Mia being trapped in one stirred my rage.

"They've left." The dark angel pointed across the water. "She was selected."

"Where did they go?" Even as I spoke the words I knew...

Mia had been plucked out from amongst these submissives to take part in the hunt. As my horrified gaze swept out over the river, I sensed it had already begun.

Across the water, the five small yachts tethered to the other side had been used to transport Mia and the men who would chase her. Beyond the bank stretched a dense forest and I could see thirty or so men heading into it.

It was a cruel irony that the game Danton and I had created all those years ago continued today, a chase so dark I cringed when I thought of it. The submissive wouldn't make it far.

My submissive.

The rules had since changed. After Mia was caught she'd be brought back here, and what followed would be witnessed by everyone.

I stared up at the angry sky, threatening rain.

Yes, please wash this day away.

Across the water, a smaller crowd straggled behind the others. They, too, were about to disappear into the trees.

Mia.

She turned to look back at the house and her gaze found mine. I saw relief flash over her face and she began struggling, trying to break free. The two men on either side of her quickly overpowered her.

"Cameron!" she screamed.

Ripping off my jacket, I sprinted toward the edge of the river. A strong hand yanked me back.

"It'll look suspicious," snapped Shay.

"She's right there." I pulled my arm out of his grip.

"There's a strong current."

"Don't care."

"They won't let you leave with her," he added. "It's too dangerous."

I sprang up onto the wall and dove into the river. With strong breaststrokes, I swam toward the other side, fighting the drag of the water. "Mia!"

I'd lost sight of her.

The sound of yelling came from behind me, and I heard men diving into the river. Ignoring them, I kept my gaze set on the line of trees where Mia had disappeared.

Violent hands suddenly grabbed me, forcing me under the water.

CHAPTER THIRTY-THREE

MIA

I TRIED TO WALK LIGHT-FOOTED ON THE FOREST FLOOR. EVERY step threatened to give me away, every branch crunching underfoot, every breathless gasp I made when there was a noise. The tracker wouldn't come off.

Alone now, my heart pounding, I turned around and around trying to remember which direction I'd run from, finally admitting to myself I was lost—though far away I could still hear voices and music.

I wasn't leaving without Cameron.

Gritting my teeth in the cold night air, feeling completely chilled in this skimpy corset and thong, I hated every second. I was never coming back to Europe. Never leaving Cole's side.

He doesn't want you. He wants her...that girl with a flair for music and a gift for submission.

I had to find the riverbank.

I couldn't waste any time. Seeing Cameron was safe was more important than my own life. He'd looked like he'd wanted to dive into the water after he saw me.

I slapped my hand to my mouth when I heard my name called,

followed by a string of foreign words.

The men were closing in.

Kneeling, I tugged at the tracker on my ankle, trying once more to rip it off. My hate for Chastain would never fade. The next time I saw him I'd kick him in the shins and scratch his eyes out.

The other women at Hillenbrand acted like they wanted to be here. Though I'd been kept apart from them for most of the time.

The screams that had carried down the dungeon hallway had sounded real. I'd glimpsed their flushed faces when we'd moved from room to room. Had they been kept here against their will this would have been a nightmare for them, too.

I breathed in a steadying breath and hurried toward the river, following the twinkling lights of the chateau through the trees. The sound of dogs barking sent a jolt of fear through me as I scrambled toward one of the tethered yachts. It was smaller than Cameron's back in L.A., so I hoped it would be easier to control.

After clambering in, I unwound the rope that anchored it to the shore and soon felt the boat begin to drift with the current. I scanned the control panel and quickly found the ignition switch. When I turned it, the boat roared to life.

Glancing back, I saw a man burst out of the trees and sprint toward me.

I steered the boat in the direction of the house, the air chilling my bones as I picked up speed. Lights flickered from the other side of the river and music blared down on the fancy partygoers mingling in the garden. I estimated there were over one hundred privileged men in attendance, all of them wearing tuxedos. The women were dressed in skimpy costumes.

A blast of cold air froze my hands and I blew on them to ease the stiffness.

In a moment of panic, I questioned whether I should turn the wheel and let the current carry me down the river...carry me away from this torment.

CHAPTER THIRTY-FOUR

CAMERON

MY HEAD WAS POUNDING.

At some point it had exploded and someone had been kind enough to put it back together—that's exactly how it felt. My damp clothes clung to me like failure.

I lay on a bed in a darkened room with no idea how much time had passed. "Mia?"

"Steady." A light shone in my right eye and moved to my left.

When my vision cleared from the blinding flashlight, I made out a man in a white coat. I pushed myself up. "Am I still in Hillenbrand?"

"Take a breath."

I tried to climb off the bed, but a wave of dizziness washed over me and I fell back onto a pillow.

"You have concussion."

"How?"

"You were hit with the butt of a pistol."

"I have to get out of here." *Have to get to Mia.*

"You're not going anywhere."

I slapped his hand away and dragged my feet over the side of the bed. "What time is it?"

"Will you listen?"

I was so close to her.

"How's the patient?" The familiarity of Lucas Chastain's South African accent made me look his way.

Carried in my glare was a tsunami's worth of hate.

"I was impressed with your session in the dungeon," he said. "Quite the spectacle."

"Where's Mia?"

Chastain glanced at his watch. "The hunt is on. Pity you'll miss it. I was considering inviting you to take part in it, but that performance in the garden ruled out any chance of that. You must follow the rules, Cole."

If I could just get over this vertigo.

I was hit with an onslaught of emotions…feral panic and an escalating fury. I knew the cruel futility would overwhelm me if I didn't guard against it.

"She's quite the treasure." Chastain walked toward me and then turned his gaze on the doctor. "Will he live?"

"As long as he doesn't make any sudden movements. He's concussed."

"I'm fine," I snapped.

"You were out for an hour."

Jesus Christ. This kind of injury ended footballers' careers, shortened lives and ruined relationships. It messed with minds.

And I was already fucked-up so we were all in for a real treat. "Where's Shay?"

Chastain stepped closer. "You boys are quite entertaining."

"If you hurt him—"

"He's not opposed to a little pain, apparently. But you know this."

My fists curled into balls as I readied to fight.

"Your submissive is quite the pet." Chastain gestured to the doctor. "Leave us."

The man reached for his medical kit and headed out. "You don't pay me enough."

Chastain's gaze found mine. "He's a vet."

My jaw dropped. "As in veterinary surgeon?"

"He takes great care of my Doberman."

"And I didn't think things could get any worse."

"Oh, they can."

My lips tightened. "What did you do to her?"

"She is divine in every conceivable way."

"If you laid one hand on her—"

"I can see the obsession." He inhaled a sharp breath. "She's complex and yet not high maintenance. Beautiful, but not vain. Feisty, but compliant."

I tried to think of the best way to reason with him. "How much?"

"To buy her back?"

"Yes?"

"I don't think any amount would be worth more than watching her being taken by our eager guests." He shoved his hands into his pockets. "I've been looking forward to it."

He removed a hand from his pocket and opened his palm to show me a tracking device. "Just in case."

I leaped off the bed and sprinted toward him, throwing a punch.

He ducked and twisted with an expert move and hit me in the stomach.

I doubled over, gasping for air.

Chastain went for me again, smashing his fist against my jaw and snapping my head back. When he tried another strike to my abdomen, I blocked him and landed a kick to his groin.

With him stunned and writhing on the floor, I rummaged in his pocket for the GPS tracker.

But he recovered faster than I expected, shoving me backwards, knocking the tracker out of my hand. He straddled my body and wrapped his hands around my throat.

I fought him furiously, managing to loosen his hold on my neck. "Why?"

He eased up. "What?"

"Tell me…why?"

"She was given to me."

I shook my head. "Galina kidnapped her. This is Helete's doing."

"A gift I happily accepted." He glared down.

"You're a psychopath."

"Flattery won't work."

"Is this because of Danton?" I snapped.

"You betrayed me."

"It was Danton's decision."

"Mia belongs to me now."

"Did you hurt her?"

"Why? Do you love her?"

I gritted my teeth. "Yes."

"I had a submissive like her once. She was everything to me. I found her. I trained her." He broke my gaze. "I hadn't loved anyone else like I loved Danton. Not until her…"

I sensed his grief and I understood it. If anything happened to Mia, I'd become as messed up as him. "What was her name?" I whispered.

"Does it matter?"

I gripped his hands and held them to the side. He didn't resist.

"Mia reminds me of her," he muttered to himself. "Not in the way she looks, of course, but in her sweetness, her purity, her trust."

"Did you break it?" I snarled. "Her trust?"

"Mia requires careful handling."

Feeling nauseated, I tried to push away thoughts of what he might have done to her. "I can see why your sub left you."

He sat back, pulling his hands free. "I treated her well."

"Sure."

"My *dabacsanaan*." It was barely a whisper.

"What the fuck does that mean?" I had a spark of intuition. "What language is that? Somali?"

He looked ready to finish me, and I knew my hunch was correct.

"What was Helete's relationship to your submissive?"

"This conversation is over."

"You're talking about Omani?"

He got off me, kneeling nearby. "You knew her?"

"I think I've met her. I may know where she is."

"How?"

Then I realized…Chastain had been in New York looking for Omani.

"Helete lied to you," I seethed. "What is even more interesting is that you believed her."

Lucas stared at me. "Why should I believe you?"

"Call The Dionysus Club in New York. Omani was told you didn't want her anymore. She thought the email was from you."

"I will end you if you're lying."

"Make the call."

Dragging myself up, I climbed onto the bed and lay still, feeling dazed. *Her* face flashed into my consciousness.

Mia.

Chastain had his phone pressed to his ear as he stormed out and slammed the door behind him.

I slid off the bed and staggered toward the door, but my legs failed me. I slumped to my knees and fell forward, crashing to the floor.

I fought another wave of dizziness. When my vision cleared I lifted my head and saw the tracker underneath the bed, where it had skidded during my fight with Chastain.

I would use it to find Mia.

Taking a deep breath, I willed my body to obey and attempted to rise up.

A shoe suddenly stomped on my hand, causing me to cry out in agony.

Chastain loomed above me with the phone still pressed to his ear. "Did you fuck her?"

"No!"

He knelt and extracted the tracker from my palm, and then blackness filled the space around me.

Eventually I became aware of fingers gently stroking my hair. The sound of a familiar female voice carried like a lost prayer. "Oh, dear God, what did he do?"

"We're here now, Cam." That sounded a lot like Richard Booth. "Can you sit up?"

I opened my eyes, trying hard to focus and figure out if my friends were really here.

"We came right away," said Scarlet.

I shoved myself up, taking in Scarlet's pretty features, her silk dress and her wavy brunette hair.

Richard's blond locks were ruffled to match his debonair style, and he wore a tuxedo like he'd been invited to enjoy himself. There was a bloodstain on his cuff. I assumed it was mine.

"Come on, buddy." Richard helped me to the edge of the bed. "Get him some water, Scarlet."

My tongue stuck to the roof of my mouth. "Shay?"

"He's in the ballroom looking for her."

"I have to help him."

"You need to rest for a bit," said Richard. "You're bleeding."

I felt for the dampness on my scalp. When I examined my hand I saw the blood. "Can you find me another tuxedo? I need shoes, too."

Scarlet held a glass to my lips. "Let us handle this."

I pushed the water away and tried to stand up.

Eventually, after I'd growled one too many times at them, they gave me what I asked for. From somewhere, Richard stole a black tuxedo that fit well enough, despite it being for a slightly bigger man. He also found a pair of shoes I could wear. At least I'd not draw unwanted attention.

Back at the party, with Scarlet and Richard by my side, I looked around for Chastain, worried that he would set his men on us. Still, the place was packed with mingling guests who had spilled out into the garden.

Standing on the short wall, I stared across the mist-covered water toward the woodlands, remembering how I'd failed to reach Mia. As soon as they brought her back, I'd grab her and I'd kill any man who tried to stop me.

I turned to Richard and Scarlet. "Thank you for being here."

"As soon as Shay called to say Mia was missing," said Richard, "we jumped on the corporate jet. Scarlet had our flight diverted here."

"I have to help her," I said.

Richard was staring at the river, his face contorted in horror.

Scarlet tugged on my jacket. "That boat's coming in way too fast."

I let out a shaky breath. "It's headed right for us."

CHAPTER THIRTY-FIVE

MIA

"**S**LOW IT DOWN!" SHOUTED SOMEONE.

I cut the power but the boat still shot toward the wall.

"Hard left!" a man yelled.

I yanked the wheel left, turning the boat sharply, but was still too close to stop in time. People jumped out of the way. The right side of the boat scraped along the wall, causing sparks to fly. The floor of the boat shuddered as shards of wood flew around me. I fell onto my hands and knees to cope with the quaking as the boat threatened to break apart.

Behind me came the thud of someone boarding, and then footfalls closed in fast. I braced for an assault.

A hand rested on the back of my head. "Remind me never to let you drive my Bugatti."

"Cameron?" My eyes sprang open. I turned to face him and flung my arms around his neck. "I came back for you." I gasped at the sight of his split lip and dark bruises.

He beamed at me as his hand cupped my cheek and moved over my jaw. I realized he was checking me for injuries.

"I'm fine." I kissed the palm of his hand.

Cameron glanced to his left. "We have to go. Can you stand?" He helped me to my feet and I saw Shay at the helm of another yacht pulling up to our left. He gestured for us to hurry.

Scarlet and Richard were on there, too, and they helped us climb aboard.

We flung ourselves onto the leather seats at the back as Shay revved the throttle. We sped away from the chateau, and I didn't dare look back to see if anyone was following. I couldn't bear the thought of Chastain catching us.

Richard knelt at my feet, examining my ankle bracelet. "We have to get this off."

"Check for a toolkit," Shay called back.

Nuzzling against Cameron for warmth, I couldn't imagine ever being away from him again. He removed his black tuxedo jacket and wrapped it around my shoulders. The scent of cigars wafted over me and I realized it wasn't his.

"Thank you." I cupped his face with my hands, hardly believing this was really happening. I was out of there...I was finally out.

He reached for my hand and kissed my wrist, his expression fraught.

Richard found a wire cutter and used it to slice through the tracking device on my ankle. He threw it overboard into the river.

I turned my gaze to Scarlet and Richard—too overwhelmed to find the words I needed to express my gratitude. They'd risked so much.

The yacht cruised quickly up the Seine, and we stared at the sparkling lights coming from all of the modern and historic landmarks.

We left the yacht tethered to a dock and grabbed a taxi to Charles de Gaulle Airport, where a private jet was waiting.

It was only when the plane's wheels lifted off the ground that I allowed myself to relax a little. I lay down on the bed in the private cabin, feeling the distance growing between myself and Hillenbrand.

Richard opened the door. "Hey, how are you?"

Staring past him, I looked for Cameron. "I'm okay."

"I brought you a nightcap." He carried in a tumbler of golden liquor.

"Cameron's idea?"

"Maybe." He handed it to me. "Hungry?"

"No, thank you." I'd missed Richard and that bad boy sweetness.

He sat beside me and patted the mattress. "Looks like you get all the perks."

"You can sleep here, too, if you like."

"I'm joking."

I let my head crash back on the pillow. "I've missed you so much."

"Missed you too, pumpkin."

That made me smile. "So much has happened. I'm working in marketing—"

"I heard you're doing great."

"Cameron thinks it's safer for me to be near him..." My eyes filled with tears.

"Mia." He took my hand in his.

I sprang up and rested my cheek on his shoulder, trying to hold back the tears. "You're getting married?"

"Yes."

"I'm happy for you."

"Me too."

"When?"

"December. Andrea loves Christmas trees so she wants that as the setting. You and Cam are invited, of course."

"Everyone's settling down."

"Just as it should be."

I pulled back to look at him. "I shouldn't have gotten in Helete's car."

"Don't. Everything is fine now."

"I'll never forgive myself." My gaze roamed toward the door. "I never asked you how Winston is doing."

"Silly mutt still misses you."

"No, he doesn't."

"He does. He's always sniffing around the garden looking for the treats you used to hide for him."

"It was a good time between us wasn't it?"

"The best, Mia."

"I'll always care for you, Richard."

"Mia—" He looked sincere. "You saved my life. You know that, don't you? You came to me at a time when all felt lost. I'll always be grateful for that. Now it's my turn to look out for you."

"I'll always be here for you and Andrea."

He looked at me as though I were fragile. "No matter what happened to you…no matter what was done, Cameron will always love you to the end of the world and back."

"You want to know if Chastain raped me?" My voice sounded faint.

"Did he?" he asked softly.

My gaze shot to Cameron in the doorway, pain reflected in his gaze.

Richard rose and gave Cameron a look of sympathy. He left us alone at last.

Cameron came in and shut the door behind him. "Are you tired?"

"A little."

He looked concerned as he came closer. "I'm going to have a forensic team waiting when we land. So it's best I don't touch you."

"Richard touched me."

He gestured to the drink. "Take a sip."

I reached for the glass and swallowed some of the liquor. It burned my throat, but warmed my body and soothed my mind.

"Mia, do you feel up to talking?"

I nodded.

"I love you. I love you like I've never loved anyone."

"He didn't touch me, Cameron."

"It makes no difference to me."

"How's Henry?"

"Devastated."

"Don't blame him."

"I'm so sorry this happened." He flinched as he said it. "I vowed to keep you safe."

"I can look after myself."

"I'm proud of you, but still..."

"Can I ask you something?"

"Of course you can."

I mulled over how to say it. "You and Danton...?"

The look on his face revealed the truth.

I sat up straighter. "Were you...?"

"Yes."

"Why didn't you tell me?"

"It was a long time ago."

"Who else knows?"

He shrugged. "Scarlet. Richard."

"Shay?"

He gave me a wary nod.

I wiped away a tear. "But...you didn't tell me."

"His death was...I don't talk about it because it's...painful."

"Because you were with him when he died?"

His smile was sad. "I've never been with any other man."

"Other than Shay?"

"Were you on the other side of that glass, Mia?"

I swallowed hard. "You love him, too?"

"What happened in that dungeon was a ruse. Turns out it was used against us. It's you I love, not Shay." He stepped closer. "Let me hold you."

"No one will touch me again. Cancel the forensic team. I don't want them near me."

"Mia—"

"I mean it."

Ask him…ask him about her.

I studied his face, trying to read him and work through the fog of uncertainty and mistruths.

"Can I ask you something else?"

"Anything."

"When you were at The Dionysus Club, did you meet a submissive there?"

He perked up. "Yes. You know about her?"

I forced myself to swallow the lump in my throat.

"I tried to do the right thing." He shook his head. "That club was one big mistake."

"Even that girl?"

"I wanted to help her."

"Like you helped me?"

He fixed his gaze on me. "Nothing happened between us, Mia. You believe me, right?"

Yet he'd set me up with a new career at Marcella's.

Galina had filled in the last piece of the puzzle. Cameron had been at The Dionysus Club to be with *her*, his new passion.

I wanted off this plane and away from all this agony. "I'm going to sleep now."

He stepped forward as though coming to hug me.

I lay down again. "I need to sleep."

"Right. You need to rest."

My chest ached as though my heart had fractured.

It's time to let him go.

"I think it's for the best, Cameron…"

"Say it. Anything, Mia, and I'll make it happen."

"I don't want to marry you."

"We can wait."

"No." I pulled the blanket up over me. "I think we should break up."

"Mia?"

"You know more than anyone the importance of giving a person space after something like this."

"Of course."

"And respecting their wishes. Not making their recovery harder."

"Don't end us, Mia," he whispered. "Not like this."

I turned my back to him and pretended to fall asleep.

CHAPTER THIRTY-SIX

CAMERON

SEEING MIA SO SHAKEN AND FULL OF PAIN WAS AN AGONY I couldn't bear. As I closed the door to her cabin, it took all my willpower not to go back in there. Doing so would have been the single most selfish act I'd ever committed.

Henry was right…I didn't deserve her.

I returned to my seat and rejoined Richard, Scarlet, and Shay, who had cracked open a bottle of Nicolas Potel.

I finally allowed myself to eat, though I merely picked at my steak—the hollandaise sauce was too rich and my guilt too full to manage much else. My body ached from head to toe from the fight with Chastain, but my pride was hurt worse. I'd lost the most important person in my life, who I'd risked everything to save.

Scarlet and Richard did their best to comfort me. We talked into the night. I'd missed them and this was a strange reunion. The fact that they'd interrupted their lives and sprang into action to fly to France and enter Hillenbrand proved our friendship was enduring.

Mia will come round…

And what then? The danger for her would never be over as long as she was associated with me. I chose to stare out the oval window, wondering how the hell I was going to find the strength to do what was right for everyone.

It was mid-morning when we landed at JFK. A car was waiting for us on the runway.

I insisted that Scarlet and Richard return to L.A., and arranged for the jet to be refueled and for a fresh pilot to be commissioned to get them home. Our goodbye was an emotional one because I owed them the kind of debt that could never be repaid.

Shay, Mia, and I were all too jetlagged to make much conversation in the SUV as we drove through the streets of New York. Mia rested her head on my shoulder, dozing off. I eased my arm around her and stroked her hair, savoring this closeness that I knew would soon end.

We arrived at the penthouse just after midday and Henry was at the front door ready to greet us.

Mia ran into his arms and hugged him. He wore the expression of a man who didn't believe he deserved her affection. As we moved into the living room, Mia seemed more concerned for him than herself.

When she excused herself to go catch up on some much needed sleep, Shay, Henry, and I sat quietly in the living room, wallowing in our guilt and going over what we could have done differently.

"Can I come stay with you?" I broke the silence, holding Henry's stare.

"Of course." He swapped a wary glance with Shay. "We need someone to stay here, though."

Leaning back on the couch, I felt a twinge of jealousy as the obviousness of this statement rippled through me. "Maybe one of your staff?" I looked at Shay.

"I'll stay," he said, then realized his mistake and offered an alternative. "I'll have a female officer stay."

I pushed myself up. "I'm gonna hit the sack. I'll head in to work tomorrow."

I stopped halfway down the hall, debating whether sleeping with

Mia was a good idea. Of course I knew it was futile, but the thought of sleeping in our guestroom left me feeling bitter.

Henry followed me. "Are you gonna to tell me what happened?" He gestured at my bruised face.

Caressing my jaw, I mulled over what was safe to share. "I walked into a wall."

"You're an annoying bastard."

"Lately, you've leaned toward being an asshole yourself."

He sighed. "How's Mia?"

"Shaken, understandably. She needs to talk it through with a specialist. I'll set up an appointment."

"What did they do to her?" he whispered.

I led him farther down the hallway and into the bedroom that I would be using now. Up until this point it had been reserved for our guests, and Mia had enjoyed decorating it so those who stayed would feel welcome. The soft colors she'd chosen made it feel cozy. Everything in here reminded me of her.

"It doesn't appear that anyone assaulted her." I said, letting out a relieved breath.

"Did she talk much?"

"Briefly."

"Maybe she's holding back?"

"Can we talk about this tomorrow?"

"Maybe we should take her to the hospital? Get her examined and have forensic specialists take—"

"She refused."

"Are you going to prosecute?" He gave me a hard look. "Cameron, this was a kidnapping."

"Shay is going to take it from here." I shrugged. "Talk to him."

"I'm talking to you."

Looking past him, I saw Mia standing in the doorway.

I gave her a comforting smile. "Hey, you okay? Can I get you something?"

She stepped inside. "I'm fine. To me, it seemed like the women wanted to be there. I recognized some of them…politicians and other VIPs. I think it best if we put this behind us."

I reached out to her.

Mia raised her hand to keep some distance between us. "I'm going to stay in the marketing department."

"We'll talk about it tomorrow, sweetheart," I said.

"No need." She returned to our bedroom and shut the door.

No, it's not ours anymore.

My world shifted off its axis.

"What happened in Hillenbrand?" asked Henry.

"Look, I'm tired, can't this wait?"

"You had to fight to get her out?" He rested a hand on my shoulder. "I want to know where this Hillenbrand is located."

It was not going to happen. The last thing we needed was for Henry to go in there with guns blazing because he was on some superhero kick.

"Sorry to interrupt." Shay's cautious gaze danced from Henry to me. "I need a word. Like now."

Raising my gaze to the ceiling, I began counting to ten. I really was done with this day, and this week could go back to the hell it had crawled out of.

I followed Shay into the kitchen.

He glanced cautiously over my shoulder. "The doorman just called up. Helete's in the lobby."

"Why?"

"Shall I send her away?"

I stayed silent, trying to figure out my next move from an inferno of choices.

"What's going on?" asked Henry.

I turned to face him. "I'm dealing with a situation. If you want to be let in on it you must promise you'll let me handle it."

"More fucking drama?"

"Yes, Henry," I said, "shit just got real. Since you left Mia in The Manhattan with one of your thugs, plenty of drama has unfolded. And now there's a woman in our foyer who is desperate to stay alive and the chances of her doing so are slim."

Chastain had come for Omani.

I stared at Henry. "Can you be reasonable?"

"Invite the bitch up."

I gave the command and Helete rode the elevator to our floor. We met her in the hallway, just outside the penthouse. We didn't want Mia to overhear the commotion if Henry decided to go rogue.

Helete hurried toward us clouded in expensive perfume and an equal measure of fear.

Her face looked flushed and she stared at us wide-eyed. "Cameron, you've got to help me."

"You're brave," snapped Shay. "Showing up here."

"I have to talk with you," she stuttered.

I gestured to Shay. *I want to handle this.*

"I'm sorry," she burst out.

"Save it for Mia," I snapped. "For everything you put her through."

She seemed close to crumbling. "Forgive me. I was…"

"I want this behind us," I said through clenched teeth.

She gave a wary nod. "I can't find Nadia. I think Chastain has found out the truth."

"You can try apologizing to him too." I kept my tone even.

Her lips trembled. "I admit I stole Nadia away from him."

"You mean Omani?"

"You told him I had her, didn't you?"

"He figured it out." I shrugged. "Why'd you lie to him? Why'd you make it look like she didn't want to go back to him?"

"I was waiting for the right time." She glanced past me. "He films everything. He uses it as leverage. I was going to tell him where she was as long as he agreed to give me the footage of what happened at Hillenbrand. All those things I did…"

I'd suspected they were filming Shay and I during our session in the red-walled dungeon, and now I knew for sure. No doubt Chastain believed he owned me.

Henry folded his arms across his chest. "Mrs. Merrill, maybe you should hide out at The Manhattan. I've heard it's pretty safe there."

She ignored him and gave me a pleading look. "Can you help me?"

"I'll call him," I said reluctantly, doubting it would do any good.

She hurried away toward the elevator.

On the one hand, I wanted to reassure Helete that her life wasn't in danger. On the other, I didn't want to give her false hope.

"Cam," Shay called to me.

I spun around.

He grinned. "Sucks to be her."

"Not funny."

"It's hilarious." He ushered me into the penthouse.

I left Shay and Henry talking in the kitchen and went in search of Mia. She was still in bed, snuggled under the covers. I wasn't sure if she was asleep.

Quietly, and very gently, I sat beside her on the edge of the bed and ran my fingers through her long, golden locks. I wanted her to know I loved her so much, I was willing to give her what she'd asked of me and let her go.

CHAPTER THIRTY-SEVEN

MIA

I HEADED INTO THE KITCHEN JUST IN TIME TO CATCH CAMERON pulling off his T-shirt and giving me an eyeful of his rock hard abs. He looked surprised to see me too, and froze near the central island. From the perspiration covering his chest, I could tell he'd gone for his morning run.

He threw his damp shirt over a barstool. I was tempted to scoop it up and bury my nose in it, breathe in the scent of him like I used to do.

Then I remembered last night…I'd felt his fingers trailing through my hair while I'd drifted off to sleep and it had felt like he was saying goodbye.

Cameron's gaze wondered over my Armani two-piece pantsuit, the one that would give me the courage to return to work. Maybe my colleagues would assume I'd already moved upstairs. Maybe that transition had bought me time.

Staring at the most beautiful man alive who was still smiling back at me, I tried to pretend I was actually doing well. I had managed to get out of bed and walk fifteen steps into the kitchen.

"Why are you dressed like that?" He shifted uncomfortably.

"For work?"

"You're going in?"

I strolled over to the coffeemaker and inhaled the java's delicious aroma.

Hairs prickled on the back of my neck. Cameron was right behind me.

"You don't think it's a good idea," he hesitated, and then added, "to take a few days off?"

"Why?" I spun around and looked up at him.

"Decompress from all you've been through?"

"Are you going in?"

"I have a billion dollar business to run."

"And I have a small cubicle in which to run my own empire." Which sounded kind of silly but I held my head up anyway.

He looked so damn gorgeous with his hair spiked and his chest glistening from his recent exertion. If he came any closer I'd be forced to place my hands on his chest and push him away.

Or dig my nails into his chest and pull him closer.

I turned my back on him and grabbed two Cole mugs, pouring us both some coffee. "I'll make my own way in."

Being trapped in the back of a car with him would be the end to my resistance.

We were over, and this was us pretending to be civilized because we were still living under the same roof. Until he moved out. Or I did...which would probably be better. Then I wouldn't be surrounded by memories of *him*.

"I put your watch over there—" He pointed at the Rolex on the central island. "I think it's a good idea for now."

I let out a frustrated sigh.

"Do you want to talk with someone?" he said gently. "I can arrange it."

"I'm fine. Maybe you need a therapist?"

"Maybe."

"Are you okay?" I reached up to cup his cheek and then drew my hand back.

"Mia?" He leaned in as if to kiss me, his lips lingering close to mine, his fingers moving through my hair as he pulled me toward him. "Is this what you want?"

"Yes." *Oh, yes.*

He let go and turned with a resigned nod, scooping up his T-shirt and heading out of the kitchen. "I'll have a car take you in."

I watched him walk away. "Cameron?"

He turned his head slightly, but he didn't look at me. "I'm going to stay with Henry."

Staring out the kitchen window, I could see rain was imminent. It would make my commute particularly slow, so I'd be wise to leave soon. My body was shuddering with regret for not saying what my heart was screaming...I loved him and I didn't care if he'd fallen for someone else.

Remember to breathe.

I relented and slipped on my Rolex; this way a part of him would always be with me.

With a shaking hand, I picked up my coffee mug and hurried back to my bedroom...*our bedroom.* I couldn't fight off the memories that surrounded me here...the long nights we'd made love...those mornings when I'd lain in bed and watched Cameron get dressed for work.

How many times had I made him late?

I finished getting ready and made my way down to the waiting car.

It was like nothing had changed. Everyone worked diligently in their cubicles and I was pretty much ignored as I settled back into my little space.

"How are you feeling?" Kelly leaned over my cubicle. "I heard you had the flu?"

I smiled. "Actually, I was whisked off to France where I was kidnapped by a sex demigod and held captive." I waggled my eyebrows.

"I missed you so much." She came around and rested her palm on my forehead. "You still feel hot."

I was grateful to have her as a friend. "How's it been here?"

"They had the semi-finals for the Cole Tea design and my entry made it."

"That's fantastic."

"How did you do?"

"I ended up not entering." I gave her a warm smile. "I'm happy for you."

"Can I get you anything? Some hot tea?"

My gaze drifted toward the coffee room. "I'm fine, thank you."

She glanced around to check no one was listening and then lowered her voice. "Mr. Cole, the CEO, was looking for you after you left. He was searching your desk. I thought you should know."

Cameron would have been frantic looking for clues. We'd not talked about it.

"Maybe they were looking for my design." It sounded credible.

"I hope you don't mind," she said. "I've asked to move over here when you go upstairs. I love your view."

I blinked at her. "That move isn't happening now."

"You best tell Mr. Cole's assistant. Sue was down here ten minutes ago, all ready to help you carry your stuff up."

I rose out of my chair. "I'll be right back."

Hurrying toward the elevator, I counted the seconds until the doors slid open so I could step inside and rally myself. I felt relieved no one else was in here with me. The pressure in my chest verged on crippling.

Stepping onto the executive floor, I saw Sue sitting behind her desk typing away.

She stopped when she noticed me. "I was just looking for you."

I heard raised voices behind Cameron's closed office door. It sounded like a heated conversation.

"I'm just going to have a quick chat." I headed straight for his door.

"You can't go in there!"

I turned the knob and burst on in, stopping suddenly when I saw Cameron's dad sitting on the leather couch with Henry beside him. They looked equally surprised to see me.

Sue hurried in behind me and gave the men an apologetic look. "I'm so sorry."

Henry got up and came toward me. "Mia, are you okay?"

"She just barged in, Mr. Cole," said Sue.

"That's okay, Susan. You can leave us now." He waited for her to shut the door and then asked, "How are you, Mia?"

I felt myself blushing. "I'm looking for Cameron."

"Come over here," said Raif, his kind eyes reminding me of his youngest son.

"I didn't mean to interrupt," I said, moving closer.

Henry shoved his hands into his pockets. "Cam's not at work."

A jolt of uncertainty hit me because he'd told me he was coming in.

"Mia." Raif gestured to a small box on the table. "Thank you for this. I love it."

Resting there was a mock-up of my design for Cole Tea's new brand. It had Raif Cole's signature swirled along the side, a dark blue oblong creation that reflected a timeless elegance.

Raif beamed at me. "Henry just showed me what he and Cameron put together. Apparently you helped make this happen? And here I thought I'd been forgotten."

"It was all Mia's design, Dad," said Henry.

The hairs prickled on my forearms as I realized my design would be in every store around the world and that Cameron had chosen it after all. "I'm so glad you like it." Then guilt washed over me. "My friend Kelly has a great design, too. She works in marketing with me."

Henry smiled. "We've still got that competition running. Your design will be for the new brand we're rolling out for the holidays. It has a nostalgic feel and we'll utilize the concept in our campaign."

"Thank you." I was almost trembling with excitement. I wanted to rush into Cameron's arms and thank him for this chance. Seeing how happy it was making his dad filled me with pride.

"Want a cup of tea?" asked Raif.

I was going to have to tell him the wedding was off, but now wasn't the time. "I should get back."

I said my goodbyes and left Cameron's office with my head bowed as I strolled past the reception desk.

"Sorry for any confusion," Susan called after me.

"You were just protecting the boss." I threw her a smile, but it faded when I saw Shay.

He looked liked he'd been waiting for me.

"We have a meeting." He threw a nod of thanks toward Sue and then gently took hold of my arm and led me to the elevator.

"I'm not sure about this," I said softly.

"Not with Cole."

My anxiety increased. "He's really not here?"

"He came in briefly. He's decided to take a leave of absence."

Now I understood why Henry was in Cam's office.

I was vaguely aware of stepping into the elevator.

We shot past my floor and kept descending. I watched Shay warily, wondering if he was going to escort me from the building. We stopped on the ground floor and I felt Shay's fingers intertwine with mine. He led me into the foyer and we took a sharp left toward the Cole Tea Shop.

"What's going on?" And then I saw him…

Chastain was sitting in the corner sipping a drink. His grey gaze rose slowly to meet mine.

"No." I refused to take another step.

"Please, Mia, this is important." Shay faced me. "Chastain has something for Cameron and he'll only give it to you."

"What is it?" I braved a glance in his direction, and noticed the strikingly beautiful woman beside him. She was bewitching.

"I won't leave your side for one second." Shay gave me a squeeze of reassurance. "Please, do this for Cole."

"Does Cameron know he's here?" I glared at him.

"Not exactly."

The only reason I'd face Chastain again would be to help Cole. I raised my chin high and strolled toward them. Chastain pushed to his feet ready to greet me and so did his friend. I approached their table warily.

"Omani, this is Mia," he said, "and of course you know Mr. Gardner."

The woman looked at Shay fondly.

Chastain gestured to a seat. "Join us."

I hesitated. "What do you want?"

"Please." Omani came around the table and rested her hand on my shoulder. "We wanted to thank you."

My gaze fell on the brown envelope on the table. "What's in there?"

Shay pulled out a chair for me and we both sat close to each other.

"First," Chastain swapped a wary glance with Shay, "I came to see how you are?"

"How do you think I am?" My tone sounded as bitter as I felt.

"Of course," he said, sliding the envelope toward me. "I understand."

I peeled open the seal and peeked in. It was a non-disclosure agreement. "I'm not signing this."

He shook his head. "I signed it. It's for Mr. Gardner and Mr. Cole. It states that all footage was destroyed and it will never be used against either of you."

"I appreciate it," said Shay.

"And you believe him?" I asked curtly.

Shay tapped the envelope. "That's why we have this."

"What do you want in exchange?" I asked.

"Nothing." He looked lovingly at his beautiful companion, taking her hand in his. "He gave me Omani back."

She flashed us a smile. "Mr. Cole told Lucas where he could find me."

I pushed my chair back and stood. "Can I have a private word with you, Omani?"

She looked at Chastain for permission. When he gave it she followed me out.

I walked her away from the Cole Tea Shop and across the foyer to a secluded corner. "Do you really know this man?"

She smiled. "Yes, I was his submissive for a year."

"At Hillenbrand?"

"Yes."

"You're too young for him."

"I love him. He's good to me. When I lost him I hated life. All I could think of was him."

"So you know he chopped someone's finger off, right?"

Her laughter echoed around us. "No, that was an accident."

"That was no accident."

"A submissive cut the tip of her finger off while cooking and he took her to get it sutured. Afterward, he scared everyone with a story of how he'd done it. He likes to play the bad guy."

I shook my head. "Are you sure?"

"Yes." She raised her index finger to show me the scarred tip. "It was my mine."

A realization hit me. "You were working at The Dionysus Club?"

"Yes, and then Mr. Cole offered me a job here." She looked around at the people coming and going. "I would have liked it."

"You didn't accept his offer?"

"No, I'm going back to France with Lucas."

"Do you speak five languages?"

"Yes, why?"

I glanced back at the Cole Tea Shop. "I thought you ran away from him?"

"No, Helete made me believe Lucas no longer wanted me."

"Why?"

"Because she wanted to blackmail him. He had footage of her at Hillenbrand. She was with a politician and Lucas filmed it. It's how he protects the club. Helete didn't want her husband to know. She thought if she had me, she had collateral."

"So you and Cameron were never intimate?"

She looked amused. "He's a gentleman. He saved me from The Dionysus Club. He promised to get me out. And he did."

My hand slapped to my mouth. I'd been wrong, so terribly wrong. Cameron had been a hero and I'd misconstrued everything.

"We should go back." She linked her arm through mine.

I'd lost my one true love. He'd never forgive me for believing anyone but him.

We returned to the table. Shay, who hadn't taken his gaze off me the entire time, pulled me into a protective hug.

I turned to Chastain. "Don't hurt Helete."

He gave a shrug.

"We all deserve peace of mind," I added, needing it more than ever.

He rose to his feet. "She won't come near you again. You have my word."

Shay and I watched the couple stroll off toward the front door.

"They're kind of cute together," muttered Shay.

"I'm not so sure about that."

"She's in love with him, Mia. Something tells me he'll take good care of her."

I grabbed Shay's wrist. "He's coming back."

Chastain had left Omani standing by the exit and was making a beeline for us.

"Ms. Lauren," he addressed me formally.

I straightened, standing my ground. "Yes."

He came closer and whispered, "Do you want to know why you remained untouched at Hillenbrand?"

My chest tightened at the memories, as that feeling of helplessness rushed back.

There was gentleness in the way he looked at me. "Danton was looking after you while you were there. I sensed his presence around you. It appears he approves of you." With a curt nod he spun on his heel and made his way back to Omani.

As they disappeared from view, I pressed my hand to my chest, trying to process his words.

I heard my name called and turned to see Henry hurrying toward us.

"Are you okay?" I reached for his hand.

Henry beamed at me. "So it appears you've been summoned, Ms. Lauren."

"By who?"

"My brother. Cole has a jet fueled at JFK. Looks like you're flying to Los Angeles."

"Is Cameron on the flight?"

"No." Henry exchanged a knowing glance with Shay. "He's gone on ahead."

CHAPTER THIRTY-EIGHT

CAMERON

CHRYSALIS HADN'T CHANGED ONE DAMN BIT AND IT FELT LIKE I'd never left.

Bel Air's grandest mansion still served as an international beacon for the elite. As I stood in the foyer staring up at the enormous crystal chandelier, fond memories swirled around me, taking me back to the time when I ruled this dominion.

Many years ago, I'd discovered this property with my senior dominatrix Scarlet Winters, and together we'd turned this place into a decadent haven.

I was home.

My beloved Chrysalis was a sacred part of my soul.

I turned to face the pretty submissive heading quickly toward me, and gave her a warm smile. "Hey, there."

Her gold-braided bodice and thong looked like something Richard would have had a hand in designing. Or maybe Andrea, his fiancée, had felt inspired to implement this baroque style.

"Do you have an appointment?" she asked.

Her question amused me. But this was how Richard and I had

planned it…any memory of me being wiped as with a forgotten season.

She was looking at the very man who had often made the staff tremble. "Is Booth here?"

"You'll need an appointment. May I take your name, sir?"

"I know the way." If Richard had kept the same office…and by the way she glanced in that familiar direction, I knew that he had.

"Is he expecting you?" Her eyes widened with concern.

"No."

"Then you can't come in."

"Cole!" Richard's yell reached me in the foyer.

I saw him hurrying toward me, beaming with happiness. He pulled me into a hug.

"Didn't expect to see you again so soon."

The submissive fell to her knees. "Master Cameron Cole?"

So the myth had survived. My bruised ego felt soothed.

God, it was good to see Booth.

Richard waved her off. "Go call Scarlet and Penny and make sure you put a call into Lotte, too."

I loved that idea. "You look well."

"I'm fine. Fantastic, actually. How long are you in town?" He looked past me. "Is Mia here?"

"Back in New York."

"How is she?" He gestured for me to follow him down the hallway. "After Hillenbrand we were all worried about her."

"Surprisingly well." I followed him into my old office.

I didn't want to taint our reunion with tales of how my life had gone off the rails.

The room been elegantly decorated to match Richard's taste and passions. Black and white prints hung on the walls, evidence of his adventures from around the world. The gorgeous painting hanging mid-center was of Andrea Buckingham—not her face, but that body was unmistakable. The starlet had swept Richard up into a whirlwind of self-discovery. She was the woman who'd stolen his heart.

I nodded at the painting. "When does her film come out?"

"Next year." He grinned. Richard had been the Dom who'd trained Andrea in the art of BDSM and given her an authentic edge to pull off the role. "I'm going to the Cannes Film Festival with her."

"Good for you. Should be fun."

"Bring Mia, she'd love it."

"That's generous of you."

"So, why are you in town?" He raised a finger, wanting me to hold that thought, and pressed a button on his desk phone. "Hey, Pilar?" he called out. "Please bring us two cups of Cole Earl Grey."

"Right away, sir," came Pilar's reply from the kitchen.

"She's going to freak out." He rolled his eyes and mimicked her accent, "Mr. Cole never did it like that."

"Still, her pot cookies were something else."

"True." He arched a brow. "She was forced to make them by a wayward submissive."

"She wasn't forced to eat them though."

We laughed at the fond memory of a high Pilar, and strolled over to the leather couch, the same one I'd once sat in all those months ago when I'd held meetings here. A slice of the past that brought nostalgia. Even the submissive support frame hanging from the ceiling made me reminisce. I recalled capturing Mia upside down in it and fucking her deliciously.

I miss her.

"You were about to tell me why you're here?"

"The construction on the new building downtown is almost complete."

"Hmm…and the real reason?"

I smiled. It was impossible to get much past this man. He was super sharp and we'd known each other long enough to see through the bullshit. "I'm here to ask a favor."

"Anything for you."

"First, how have things been here?" I asked. "Anything new?"

Richard updated me on the transition. It was good to hear

everything had gone smoothly.

There came a bang at the door and Richard leaped to his feet and hurried over to open it. He beamed at Pilar. She had kicked the door because her hands were full carrying a tray. So very her.

Richard took the tray from her. "Look who's here."

Pilar's gaze found me and she shrieked, "Dr. Cole! I should have known when Mr. Booth ordered Earl Grey."

I got up and greeted her with a big hug. "How are you?"

She waved that off. "Always good."

"How's the boy?"

"He graduates soon," she said proudly.

I swapped a glance with Richard. "Which university does he want to go to?"

She looked dumbfounded. "He'll be getting a job."

"Richard and I want to put him through Uni. I think Berkeley would be a good fit for his nature."

Richard sat back down. "I agree."

"It's on us." I smiled to reassure her.

Pilar blinked. "You make it sound like you're paying for lunch, Dr. Cole. This is too much. You've done too much."

"I'll be the judge of that." I joined Richard on the couch. "Tell him to get good grades so he makes our job easier."

Her face lit up with joy. "Do you want a cookie?"

"No!" we answered in unison, laughing.

Pilar left us to catch up. It was fantastic seeing Richard happy and managing this place with confidence. We sipped our tea and recalled our happiest memories. This man was the reason my family's company had survived a potential hostile takeover and I owed him. His wizardry on the stock market had saved an empire.

"Love agrees with you," I said fondly.

"Wish I could say the same. You look like shit. Are you sleeping?"

"Remind me...what is sleep, again?"

"You and I need a chat."

"Sounds like a plan."

"Come on." He pushed himself up. "I want to show you our new dining room. I think you'll approve."

We headed out and the scent of vanilla wafted around us. Passing the Harrington Suite, I marveled that this room no longer filled me with dread. The last time I'd been in there I'd taken Mia passionately, and those new emotions of euphoria had replaced the old ones.

"How's Shay?" asked Richard.

"Good." I let out a long sigh. "I'm thinking of introducing him to De Sade."

"Seriously? You think he's ready for him?"

"I do."

"He's five years older than him and he hasn't changed since Harvard."

"Shay's ready."

"De Sade is here, actually. You can talk to him if you like?" Richard opened the door to the dining room.

I followed him in. "I'd like to see him in action."

"We can do that." He watched my reaction. "What do you think?"

The décor was pure French. I admired the sophisticated paintings scattered on the walls, and as I looked around at the leather seating and white table cloths, I recognized the influence of my senior dominatrix. Her touch was everywhere.

"I thought Scarlet was leaving?" I turned to Richard.

"This was her going away present to us."

I closed my eyes. "She doesn't want to be forgotten, either."

Richard slapped my back. "You will always be part of this place."

"I like it." Even though it didn't really match my taste, the thought of Scarlet leaving behind a piece of herself felt right.

"De Sade has a client in the dungeon. Wanna take a peek?"

"Thought you'd never ask." I grinned.

"What's going on with you?"

"Later."

"You've got me worried."

"Me?"

"Yes, Cole, you."

"How are the peacocks?"

"Still pea-cocking. Think they own the place." He laughed. "Let's get some fresh air."

A burst of heat hit us when we stepped outside, and I had the urge to leap into the crystal blue swimming pool. So many mornings I'd dived in there and swam laps to start my day. My gaze turned up toward the window of the room where Mia had stayed when I'd kept her here during her training.

Tearing my gaze away, I felt another stab of doubt. I wondered if Mia would ever forgive me.

Off in the distance, a female peacock crested the hill. It really was as though I'd never left this place.

"Funny how it's reversed with them," said Richard. "The males have the flashy plumage."

I turned to face him. "Remember that time when you told me you were giving up BDSM?"

"Yes."

My expression changed, telling him what I couldn't say. This lifestyle had always been a big part of who I was; it had defined me, and yet something within had altered.

"Does Mia want to go vanilla?" There was sympathy in his tone.

"No."

"Just a suggestion, because it's what you'd say to me—"

"My testosterone levels are fine."

"You can't blame me for being shocked. You're Cameron Cole."

"I can't, Richard. Can't do it. I can spank her. Tie her up. Fuck her hard. Just can't..." I turned to face the horizon. "Pain has no appeal anymore."

Had she changed me or had this been inevitable?

"So you're leaving us?"

"Hell, no, I still like to watch." I arched my brows playfully. "Just can't inflict pain on Mia. I want to make her laugh. I want to make her constantly delirious with happiness." I wanted to make her toes curl in pleasure for hours.

This sounded wrong because so many couples had great relationships and it never affected them like this. They could separate the play. Their sadism was a thing of beauty and nothing to pull back from.

"Let me see if we can change your mind?" Richard elbowed me.

We walked back into Chrysalis and a blast of air conditioning chilled my flesh.

"De Sade?" I warmed to the idea.

"This will be fun."

I used the handrail as we descended into the lowest chambers. "Booth, you've gone quiet?"

"I'm trying to work out where your head is."

"I may have lost Mia."

He stopped suddenly and stared up at me from the lowest step. "What makes you say that?"

"Since Hillenbrand…"

"What happened to her?"

"She says nothing. But the experience was traumatic. Still, Chastain didn't touch her, apparently."

"You believe her?"

"Yes."

"You have to talk with her." He tilted his head to get me to follow him. "What the hell are you doing here?"

We strolled down the darkened hallway that led off to numerous dungeons. I heard the snap of a whip, telling me that a session was underway.

"How can you not miss this place?" asked Richard, as he turned the knob of a deep burgundy door.

"New York has my full attention."

"You're always welcome here."

I strolled into the lavish seating area that faced a long wall of glass. It wasn't unlike the two-way window back at Hillenbrand.

The luxury viewing booth allowed for an excellent angle to observe the BDSM session that was being led by Master De Sade, the ex-NFL player who had been knocked out of his profession when he'd sustained a neck injury. He'd come out of rehab with a renewed sense of life and penchant for pain.

"He teaches football to college students now." Richard approached the glass window.

"That's interesting."

"Apparently he's great at it."

He'd earned himself a reputation during our Harvard days for pushing subs too far. That jock attitude had gone to his head.

Watching De Sade, the way he stroked his sub's cock with panache, the way he spoke softly to him to ease him into the play, it was hard to imagine him ever turning violent, and yet this was what his clients yearned for.

The sub's thighs were shaking as he squeezed his eyes shut to focus on not coming in De Sade's hand, his squirming hinting he was close.

Back in the day, De Sade had helped me wrangle Scarlet to get her to France so I could match-make her with Danton. But after he'd left a scar on her thigh, I'd refused to talk to him.

"De Sade is single," said Richard.

"If Shay falls for him, I want there to be an emotional connection."

"You've changed your tune."

"If I can change, so can De Sade. Everyone deserves a second chance."

De Sade had his submissive crawling around on his hands and knees. Then his focus lifted off the man at his feet and his gaze rose to the window. He studied his reflection intently—and for a second it looked like he was holding my stare.

In a smooth and yet aggressive manner, De Sade pulled the sub up and positioned him to lie on his back upon a table. He stood between his legs and thrust his cock deep inside the man's ass, at the same time owning that man's erection with long, sleek glides. His hips edged him on like a savage piston. It was a visually spectacular, erotic showpiece to prove this master owned his sub. De Sade's captive groaned, writhing in bliss, soaring closer. His heavy-lidded gaze turned our way and again came that uncanny feeling.

"He needs to slow it down," I said firmly.

"Let's hope they can't read lips." Richard threw me a warning glance.

"They can't see us."

"Yes, they can. We switched the glass out so they can watch the guests watching them."

My jaw dropped. "What if I had pulled my dick out?"

"It would make their day."

A laugh rumbled behind my lips, and I snapped my attention back to see the sub looking at his master now with pure adoration.

"Don't you dare laugh," muttered Richard, as he held his laughter in check, too.

Head down, with my fist pressed to my lips, I burst out of there. Richard followed me and as soon as we cleared the room, we slid down the wall, holding our bellies as we slipped into hysterical laughter that made my stomach ache. I had missed these moments when we were more than brothers, when spontaneity was ours, and our lives belonged to us. Two rogues living it up in the club.

Richard was howling.

"I think he's perfect for Shay," I said, taking a breath. "He's a reprobate."

"Hilarious."

"I needed that." More than I realized.

"Are you gonna tell me why you're really here?"

"I need your help pulling off a coup. And it has to be here."

"I can do that." He pushed himself up. "Come on. Let's go back in for the grand finale."

"You always were a pervert, Richard Booth Sheppard."

"I learned everything I know from the best." He winked at me. "I'm glad you're not tired of kink."

"It's who I am."

"You're also that man who fell in love with a girl you'd do anything for. Fight for her, Cole."

"I must do what's right for Mia, Richard." I leaned against the wall, willing myself not to falter on that conviction.

CHAPTER THIRTY-NINE

MIA

CAMERON'S MOUTH CRUSHED MINE, DOMINANT AND LOVING. *I yielded to his kiss, opening my mouth to accept his tongue, letting it tangle with mine as I swooned against him, so grateful that we were together again. I melted into his comforting embrace, my lips tingling.*

Stirring awake, I blinked at the towering mansion ahead and then turned my sleepy eyes on the chauffeur who was driving the limo toward it.

Even in my dreams I'd been drawn back to *him,* the man who had captured my heart from the first moment he'd kissed me in Enthrall's dungeon. No, that was a lie…it was the moment he'd first strolled into Enthrall's coffee room with his "out of my league" attitude wearing that tailored suit, with his raven hair just so and those chestnut eyes that saw into my soul.

And later, he'd saved me from the kind of memories that could ruin a life. He was my savior, my lover, my reason to live. I'd always be grateful to him.

I'd ruined everything and I suspected I was here in L.A. so he could ease my life back to what it had once been—an ordinary existence. No longer would I experience the complications that resulted from living with the eccentric and brilliant Cameron Cole…a man who had transformed a working-class girl into a woman fit for high society.

His experiment was complete and I suspected this was where my journey would end—I was to be set free like the butterfly this place prided itself on cocooning.

This was Chrysalis.

But the spectacular manor on this Bel Air hill no longer intimidated me.

The car door was opened for me. I gave the chauffeur a nod of thanks and approached the entrance. A wave of old emotions hit me, the excitement I'd once felt fueled by an intrigue that had taken my life to an entirely new level…

He's here.

Cameron stood beneath the foyer's crystal chandelier. Two long red ribbons tumbled down behind him. Shards of light reflected off his face, and I wondered if he truly knew the profound effect his presence had on me. His face wore that familiar unreadable expression.

"How was your flight?" He shoved his hands into his pockets.

I ignored the question. "It seems I've been summoned."

"Ah."

"I refuse to talk about the weather, if that's your next question."

"How about the traffic?"

Cam always knew how to make me smile. He was being kind, but I wanted this over with. "Where is everyone?"

"We're alone."

"You still have influence, then?"

"Apparently." He lowered his gaze. "I wanted us to be able to talk freely."

"I'm sorry, Cameron." I was sorry for everything…misunderstanding him, doubting him, and especially for not trusting him enough to believe we'd been perfect for each other.

"No apology needed." He rested his palm on his chest. "Except from me." He raised his hand in protest. "Please, listen."

I braced myself for what he had to say.

"I wanted to bring you back to where it all started."

"It started at Enthrall."

"For me, it started here." He gestured in the direction of his old office. "This was where Tara showed me your photograph."

"Very dramatic."

"What I have to say deserves this." He gave me an endearing smile and pointed a finger at the chandelier above.

Opulent lights sparkled down upon him.

"Danton taught me how precious life is," he began. "And yet my affection for him pales next to what I feel for you. Mia, I chose you for Richard because you were beautiful and loving and, most of all, forgiving." He shook his head. "I didn't believe I was the one for you because I'd given up on love for me. Then you came into our lives and I fell hard.

"My love for you has never been in question. My devotion to Richard meant that I had to give you up to him. When you finally became mine I had to grapple with the fact it was now my job to keep you safe." He gestured with open palms. "I failed."

"No, Cameron."

"Please." He held up a hand to quiet me. "I created Chrysalis because I believed this house could help people. Save them even. I, in turn, used pain to leverage out my past. Each crack of the whip, each strike by my hand, each prolonged agony soothed my soul, just as I saw it doing for others." He took a step forward. "But men change. Sometimes they have no other choice but to evolve. What I am or what I am not can't be defined by those around me...only by me alone. Ask me what changed in my life and I will say you, Mia. It was you.

"I no longer need pain to forget my past. Neither do you. We are whole. Complete because we found each other. Moving forward we must no longer suppress our pain but use it as a catalyst to do profound good in this world.

"I have a plan. Henry will take over as CEO. It's what he wants and what he deserves. This was his destiny and I won't deny it to him.

"I will champion the philanthropic endeavors of Cole Tea. I'll bring more water to Africa, more hospitals to India, I'll go to the most dangerous regions of the world because I refuse to live in fear. That's what I learned from Hillenbrand, that you and I have what it takes to survive. No matter what we endure.

"There's only one more question in all of this." He held out his hand to me. "Do you want to be by my side, Mia? Will you share a future with me, no matter what it brings?"

I hurried to close the gap between us, reaching for his hand. "I've grown so much since I met you. Because of you, I have the kind of friends who love me enough to come rescue me when things go bad. You were willing to risk your own reputation and Cole Tea itself. I look back at my time here and at Enthrall, and even the months we spent in New York, with no regrets…only pride."

Cameron pulled me close and pressed his lips to mine, hard and passionate, our tongues lashing furiously. Then the mood changed and we kissed gently, slowly, savoring each other, feeling the trust between us, him leading me in this final dance of persuasion.

We pulled apart, finally, and I brought his hand to my lips and kissed his fingers. His other palm rested tenderly against my cheek.

"Mia, are you sure you want to join me on this spectacular adventure?" He brought me in for another hug. "No pressure, but the right answer is—"

"Yes." I squished my face against his firm chest.

Chapter Forty

Cameron

Drawing the two long strands of red ribbon toward Mia, I wound them around her body, securing her to the enormous crystal chandelier above. I'd stripped her naked and she stood with her arms raised above her head and her feet barely touching the ground, balancing on her tiptoes.

One with the chandelier.

I stepped back to admire my handiwork and my stunning lover. She emanated tranquility, her inquisitive gaze focused on my every move.

I stripped off my clothes, thinking it felt right to be so exposed within Chrysalis. With no secrets between us and nothing to hold us back.

Stepping forward, I lifted her chin and kissed her tenderly, her mouth soft and yielding as it opened to mine.

Bowing my head, I sucked on her left nipple and it beaded between my lips, a soft moan escaping her. I moved to the other and her areola tightened as I drew it into my mouth lovingly. I caressed her breasts, lavishing her with affection until her body trembled.

Kneeling at her feet, I ran my thumbs along her sex to ease her apart, licking and kissing her clit, worshiping her with the tantalizing tip of my tongue until her soft groaning echoed around us…her scent bewitching.

After she'd trembled through an orgasm, I rose to my feet and wrapped my hands around her waist, lifting her up. With a gentle shove, I buried my cock inside her and slowly moved deeper until we were perfectly one.

Rocking into her leisurely, below the grand chandelier's prism of light, I spoke the words my heart yearned to say.

"Mia Lauren," I whispered, "I take you to be my lawfully wedded wife, to have and to hold, from this day forward, for better, for worse, for richer, for poorer, in sickness and in health, until death do us part." I pressed my lips to her throat and held the kiss.

"I want to be your wife," she said softly. "I love you so much, Cameron."

"I will cherish you, protect you, love you, worship you and make you the happiest woman in the universe," I promised, grinning at her.

She moaned and it sounded like a plea.

We climaxed together, me pumping into her hard with her legs trembling around me, her muscles clenching possessively, our groans echoing around us.

Eventually, I untied her and carried her to the spa.

We took a shower together and got dressed, ready for an afternoon of fun.

Leaving Chrysalis in the late afternoon in my convertible Bugatti, I drove us to The Sunset in Malibu for a late lunch. We enjoyed a view of the ocean from our table. Her hand stayed in mine, and we were constantly glancing at each other with affection. From our vantage point, we watched the yachts drift by as we sipped iced tea and shared a warm chocolate tortino, our spoons playfully clashing for the last bite, our hysterical laughter threatening to disrupt the other guests.

I took Mia to one of my favorite places in the city, Amoeba Music, and we strolled around rifling through the massive collection of vinyl records, searching out those rare finds.

We ended up in Santa Monica, where we left the car parked for the night and rented two bicycles. Mia and I cycled alongside the ocean all the way to Venice Beach. Sitting next to each other on the sand, we sat looking out at the sea with no words needed between us.

When the weather turned chilly, we gave up the bikes and walked the short distance to my beachfront property. I'd had it prepared for our stay.

The two-story house was filled with flowers, and Mia ran from room to room in awe of the beauty surrounding us.

"I wanted to make it special for you," I told her.

"Everything always is with you," she said breathlessly.

We made our way upstairs and tumbled onto the king-sized bed, our limbs entwined.

"Happy birthday, Mia." I pressed my lips to her forehead.

When she looked up at me questioningly, I added, "I put this house in your name. It's yours now. You'll always have a safe place to come home to. And it just happens to be my all time favorite."

She snuggled against me. "You're my home, Cameron, and you always will be."

I let out a sigh of happiness.

She was in my arms again…Mia, my one true love.

EPILOGUE

Two Years Later

MIA

MARCELLA'S FALL COLLECTION WAS ABOUT TO GRACE THE runway any second now. Backstage, the models were scurrying around having the final touches done to their hair and make-up, and some last tweaks to Marcella's glamorous gowns as they prepared to step out.

This promised to be her best show yet.

With Scarlet squeezing my left hand on one side, and Henry holding the other, we sat close to the stage, eager for the show to get underway. There was a tangible excitement in the air, with guests taking their seats, and friends greeting each other warmly. I recognized a few seasoned journalists who'd want to corner Marcella afterward, no doubt for an exclusive interview.

The buzz caused by New York's Fashion Week crackled in the air and all of the butterflies in my stomach refused to settle down. This was probably the most exciting day of my life. I'd been invited to showcase one of my own designs in Marcella's line-up.

No, on second thought, my most exciting day had been when I'd met Cameron—though it had been equally as wonderful as our wedding day. I'd worn my gorgeous Vera Wang gown and felt every part the stunning bride. I'd fallen in love with it, and Cameron had insisted that no one should ever derail what made us happy. The memory of seeing his face light up when I had walked down the aisle would stay with me forever. His expression had been one of pure happiness.

We had somehow persuaded Cam's mom to let us downsize to an intimate affair in the Hamptons, low key and very *us*.

Everyone we cared most about had made it to New York for our big day. We'd managed to elude the press and keep them from capturing a photo of Andrea Buckingham with Richard Booth—and also Cameron Cole and his new bride.

I'd designed the elegant, deep blue bridesmaid dresses, and Scarlet, Lotte, Penny, Bailey and Tara had looked lovely in them.

Both Richard and Shay had escorted me down the aisle and had given me away just as they'd promised to do. Henry had enjoyed being Cameron's best man, and everyone agreed he'd given one of the most heartfelt toasts ever delivered.

Our wedding cake had tasted divine. It was a rich chocolate sponge because, well, what else could it have been if not Cam's favorite flavor?

I loved visiting New York. We'd arrived a week ago and were staying with Henry, who was now living in our old penthouse. When we weren't traveling, we were living between our beach home in Venice and Cole's big old mansion in Beverly Hills. That way Cameron could get his surfing in and I could sketch on the patio with a view of the ocean.

One day I'd have a collection like this of my own. My heart soared with the possibilities.

Right now, Shay and his boyfriend, De Sade, were house-sitting in Beverly Hills, and Cameron had joked we'd have a hard time getting them out when we returned. It was good to see Shay in love, and De Sade looked happy, too. They were so damn hot together...though I kept that saucy thought to myself.

"I wish Cameron could be here," whispered Scarlet. "He would have loved this."

I let out a sigh. "Our babysitter couldn't make it. So he stepped up."

Henry shook his head. "Still can't believe my brother is a stay-at-home dad."

Though that was true, Cameron had perfectly balanced working from home on our philanthropic pursuits with the duties of fatherhood.

"You have got to be kidding me," said Scarlet, staring off into the crowd. "Is that the great Cameron Cole?"

I blinked in surprise.

Cameron had our baby strapped into a sling. My cute little guy, Raif, who was only six months old, had his adorable head peeking out in front of daddy's chest. He took everything in with those large chestnut eyes; the same eyes his daddy had. Cameron threw us a wave, and Raif's toothless grin made us laugh.

"This feels like an alternate universe," joked Henry, who surrendered his seat to his brother and moved over one.

"I'm not missing this," said Cameron. "This is Mia's day."

"Apparently you're great in the diaper department," laughed Scarlet.

Cameron grinned at me. "I have ninja skills when it comes to wrangling this one." He pressed his lips to Raif's forehead. "We couldn't miss this, right buddy?" He looked at me. "It was this little guy's idea, Mia. I was all for having a quiet afternoon at home."

I laughed and popped Raif's pacifier into his mouth. "Is he hungry?"

"He's okay."

Leaning into Raif, I breathed in his sweet scent and smiled contentedly. Now, we could tell him he was at Mommy's first show.

"This is so much fun." Scarlet beamed at us.

Exquisite notes rose from hidden speakers and a minute later the first model stepped out onto the runway, her stride graceful and serene. Her gown was elegantly embroidered gold tulle, with a deep V-neck illusion and a full A-line skirt. It was embedded with delicate crystals that reflected the light as the material flowed and shimmied around her.

Scarlet gasped. "Is that yours, Mia?'

"I'd recognize her taste anywhere." Cameron winked at me. "You are talented, Mrs. Cole."

I was hardly listening. Seeing my gown in a fashion show had left me awestruck. As the other models trailed out behind her, I was filled with pride that my design was worthy to be showcased alongside Marcella's work.

Reaching for Cameron's hand, I mouthed, "Thank you. Thank you for all of it."

He tilted his head toward Raif. "Same to you."

"I'm going to buy it," Scarlet piped up. "What's the name of your dress?"

"I drew inspiration from Chrysalis," I whispered.

The twinkling lights of chandeliers, the truest freedom, and the beauty of it all. The sacredness of light.

"It's a Mia Cole," said Cameron proudly. "And I love it."

I beamed his way. "I called the gown Enthrall."

A beautiful beginning…

ACKNOWLEDGMENTS

Writing the ENTHRALL SESSIONS has been an incredible experience, and I am grateful these wonderful characters came into my life. I have also loved hearing how real they feel to you, and I feel the same way. Many of you have embraced the world of ENTHRALL and its inhabitants and some of you have told me you drew strength from them. This is incredibly moving.

A big thank you to my wonderful literary agent Kimberly Whalen. Your unwavering strength, wisdom, and exceptional knowledge reminds me every day how lucky I am to be with The Whalen Agency.

I'm so grateful for my wonderful editor, Debbie Kuhn; thank you for your time. I always hand off my work to you knowing it's in the most capable hands.

Another big thank you to Lauren Luman for your keen eye and endless enthusiasm. Your generous spirit and passion for our genre is felt by us all.

Thank you to Hazel Godwin. Your continued support of my writing is deeply appreciated, and I love hearing from you. SueBee, your kindness to readers and passion for making Goodreads a happy place is inspiring.

A big thank you to Stacey Blake at *Champagne Book Design* for making this book look so pretty. To my *gals* in the Diamond Romance Lounge, a big hug to you all for keeping me calm during the book release week. Endless gratitude to E. L. James whose passion and talent inspired me to take the leap from paranormal author over to romance and this literally changed my life forever and all for the good. Again, thank you for all you do for the romance community. Louise Bay, I owe you oodles of tea and crumpets for always being there. You rock as an author and inspire me daily.

Heather Pollock, Louise Sandford, Kathi Goldwyn, Maureen Goodman, Lydia Rella, and the incredible Pam Stack over at Authors on the Air, thank you so much for your kindness and support! Your messages and warmth are never taken for granted. Hugs to Laird Sapir who makes my website look so damn gorgeous!

To Debra Presley and Drue Hoffman over at Buoni Amici Press PR, thank you for all you do to promote and share my books with the world! You make a book release look easy, but we all know it takes patience, precision, and passion. I'm honored you are part of my team. Your advice is everything! Your knowledge is exceptional. Thank you for being part of my journey.

Thank you to all my readers far and wide, including my wonderful fans in France!

Thank you to everyone on social media who reaches out to me. I absolutely love hearing from my readers and if you want to ask a question about my work, I'm usually on Facebook most days or hanging out in the Diamond Romance Lounge.

Endless love to my wonderful husband Brad who supports all I do and cheers me on. ;)

I could write books in the ENTHRALL SESSIONS forever, but I feel ending here with ENTRHALL CLIMAX delivers their well deserved *happy ever after.*

I will forever cherish them in my heart.

ALSO BY VANESSA FEWINGS

THE ENTHRALL SESSIONS
ENTHRALL
ENTHRALL HER
ENTHRALL HIM
CAMERON'S CONTROL
CAMERON'S CONTRACT
RICHARD'S REIGN
ENTHRALL SECRETS
ENTHRALL CLIMAX

THE ICON TRILOGY

From Harlequin

THE CHASE
THE GAME
THE PRIZE

Vanessa is on Instagram, twitter, Facebook, BookBub, and Pinterest
@vanessafewings

For those wanting to chat more with Vanessa, visit the *Diamond Romance Lounge* on Facebook

ABOUT THE AUTHOR

Vanessa Fewings is the USA TODAY bestselling author of the ENTHRALL SESSIONS.

THE CHASE is the first in her sizzling new romantic trilogy from HQN Books followed by THE GAME. The third book THE PRIZE will be released in June 2018.

Prior to publishing, Vanessa worked as a registered nurse and midwife. She holds a Masters Degree in Psychology. She has traveled extensively throughout the world and has lived in Great Britain, Germany, Hong Kong, Cyprus and the USA. Born and raised in England, Vanessa now proudly calls herself an American and resides in California with her husband.

Made in the USA
Middletown, DE
17 June 2020